Praise for *The Intrusion*

Kristin Detrow has succeeded in writing a novel with substance. *The Intrusion* lifts the veil of deception, shame, and anguish that lies hidden within the fight for life and gives the reader a glimpse into the spiritual battle that wages for the lives of people, especially the unborn. Not only is this book difficult to put down, but it also serves to challenge the idea that abortion, or any sin for that matter, is an easy, pain-free decision. It demonstrates the forgiveness and redemption only offered in Jesus Christ. *The Intrusion* will be more than just another fictional story in your hands; it will spread your arms wide open to people who are carrying the painful burdens of past decisions.

—David Vance, Lead Pastor of Faith Christian Fellowship; Chairman of the Hagerstown Area Pregnancy Center

The Intrusion gripped me with its gut-wrenching transparency. I have experienced post-abortion issues myself and help others work through their issues by the grace of God. The characters in this story reveal the inner turmoil that takes place in the lives of those impacted by abortion. *The Intrusion* has all the intrigue and mystery of Randy Alcorn. Yet this book displays a sincere emotional depth laced with humor, the inner struggle of humanity to matter to someone, and the heart's intimate search for God. It breaks my heart to remember all that God has saved me from and inspires me to reach out in His love to others who are still in pain. This is a story of His amazing grace and His mighty strength that sets us free and heals our wounds. This book is also an honest revelation into the "back-door" operations of the abortion industry and how we must be educated and on guard against such devious works.

—Jaime Haines, Founder of New Creation Refuge

The Intrusion

Written by
Kristin Detrow

Publishing

Published by
Innovo Publishing, LLC
www.innovopublishing.com
1-888-546-2111

Providing Full-Service Publishing Services for
Christian Organizations & Authors: Hardbacks, Paperbacks,
eBooks, Audio Books, & iPhone/iPad Books

THE INTRUSION
Copyright © 2010 by Kristin Detrow
All rights reserved.

Biblical quotes are from the Holy Bible, New Living Translation,
Copyright ©1996 by Tyndale House Publishers, Inc.

ISBN 13: 978-1-936076-30-7
ISBN 10: 1-936076-30-6

Cover Design & Interior Layout: Innovo Publishing, LLC

Printed in the United States of America
U.S. Printing History

Second Edition: August 2010

Acknowledgments

I am blessed to have the most awesome group of girlfriends, AKA "mafia chicks". Beth, Dawn, Jaime, Heather, Becky, Maggie, Taylor, my Wednesday night prayer buddies and game night friends- Thank you for the prayers, encouragement, and the laughter so intense my abs ache for days after an evening with you. Rachel- not only are you a miracle worker, you are a miracle. Alicia- I enjoyed our late night editing sessions giggling like schoolgirls. You are an amazing person and I indeed love you like a sister. Nicole, I could never thank you enough for all your help. I am also grateful for my parents, husband and kids that allow me to dream and give me room to grow. Let's all remember to live each day as if it were our last and give the glory to God!

Author's Note

As I developed the characters in *The Intrusion*, I believed it was vital for this novel to send a strong pro-life message. You see, for me, an infertile woman who is incapable of conceiving without the aid of a doctor and a slew of other modern medical miracles, it was a cinch to be pro-life. It was truly a no-brainer. Of course, ending a pregnancy snuffs out a life. I mourned and lamented the loss of those innocent babies often as I struggled to conceive a child of my own. Endless invitations to baby showers heightened the sorrow. Month after month passed without conception. A much anticipated treatment cycle would fail. Hopelessness crept in and proceeded to transform itself, ever so slowly, into bitterness. Condemnation. Hard-hearted judgment.

It never really occurred to me that this spiritual cancer had taken root in my heart. When the subject came up, I freely gave my opinion, not only from a political and spiritual standpoint, but at times I would proceed to freely assassinate the character of any woman who would choose such a thing. I finally did conceive (twins!) and endured an incredibly difficult pregnancy. Terbutaline pumps, bed rest, at-home fetal monitoring, and even the mention of therapeutic abortion were a daily reality. Spiritually, I dug my self-righteous heels in deeper still. Just look what torment I was willing to endure for the lives battling to survive inside of me. If I was prepared to go to such lengths, what kind of woman would choose to end the life of her own child?

Do any of you have mental snapshots of yourselves from the past that simply make you cringe? I am afraid that I have more than my fair share. God does use those moments to humble us and, if we allow him, to teach us to reflect and learn from our past behavior. When my twins were around two, I attended a Bible study that met in the homes of some women I did not know well. Each week I showed up, Bible in hand. My big, black Bible. The one that was completely covered with stickers screaming slogans such as Abortion is Homicide. Did I mention that it was big?

Several weeks into the study, it was time for a lovely woman named Jaime to speak. By lovely, I mean that she was actually employed as a professional Cinderella. Not only was she fairy-tale stunning, she was warm, kind, and quite a character. Of all the women who attended the study, she was the one I was most drawn to and enjoyed conversing with.

Notebook in hand, I happily anticipated the wisdom that Jaime had to impart. I was not prepared when she dropped the bomb that not only had she had an abortion, but also a second.

Something broke in me that night as Jaime spoke. Besides the fact that had she been desperate enough to have an abortion, I was forced to put a face to the act that I had spoken about with such flippancy. When I found out that she not only attended church at the time but taught Sunday School, I was floored. Tearfully, she explained that she was more afraid of being found out and judged by her fellow church members than she was of ending her pregnancy. I was filled with shame. How convenient it was for me to hone in on the one sin that I was pretty much assured of never committing. It was quite easy to sit on my spiritual high horse and claim that I would never do such a thing. Instantly, my mind was flooded with scenes from my own past, both before I had yielded my heart to Christ, and after. Drunkenness, drug abuse, lies and rebellion, promiscuity, gossip, and slander made the short list. It occurred to me that perhaps infertility had been God's grace for me, or I also might have made a decision to enter a clinic as Jaime and countless others had done. The fact is that on our own we are all wretched sinners, desperately in need of the grace of God.

Am I still pro-life? Absolutely. Is abortion murder? I believe that it is. However, now I am not only concerned for the pregnant mothers who enter abortion mills every day. I care deeply for the broken women who walk back out those doors and live with that decision for the rest of their lives. I no longer pontificate about the evils of this sin or that, or focus on the ugliness of any particular vice. Instead, I focus on the grace of God and marvel that God came to seek and to save us.

If you want to contact me for any reason, please visit my web site at www.theintrusionbook.com. I would love to hear from you.

Kris

Chapter One

J ake and Arin Welsh's anxiety levels mounted with each hollow tick of the clock and wooden advance of the second hand. Beads of sweat formed on Jake's forehead despite the cool recycled air that poured on them from above. The office of Dr. Halter, Chief Psychologist for the Paramount Fertility Clinic, oozed self-importance. Rich mahogany shelves were stuffed with volumes of psychobabble and diagnostic manuals. The bottom row was devoted solely to exotic tribal figurines.

Arin, infamous for her inability to remain still for any stretch of time, rooted through her purse, willing gum to appear. Her mouth was parched and her hands were slippery with sweat. It certainly seemed that they had been waiting much longer than the few moments promised by Dr. Halter's ditzy secretary.

"Forget the gum. You chew like a cow," Jake whispered, his broad shoulders squared and back ramrod straight. "We're trying to make a good impression, remember?" Arin's eyes narrowed to slits and she jabbed his ribs with her elbow. After a moment of consideration she decided against the gum. Begrudgingly, she conceded that her chew was similar to that of a farm animal.

"I still don't understand why they're forcing us to go through this," Jake grumbled for the hundredth time, pulling at the blue paisley tie encircling his muscular neck as if it were cutting off his flow of oxygen. It was the only tie that Jake Welsh owned, acquired several hours ago for this very occasion. "Seriously, what are they going to do if their shrink decides we're unstable? You think they'll refund our money and send us home, maybe recommend we start with a plant and perhaps work up to a fish or a Labrador?"

Arin opened her mouth, prepared to explain for the hundredth time that it was the policy of Paramount Fertility Clinic to perform a comprehensive psychological evaluation of all of their potential clients. Instead she shrugged, snapped her jaw shut and gnawed on her bottom lip. It was an exercise in futility to attempt explaining the process to Jake, one, because she knew he was not listening, and two, because she agreed, it was a complete waste of time. Arin had a hunch that even if they admitted to being ax-murdering schizophrenics, the clinic would most likely look the other way as long as they were paying cash.

A large portion of their anxiety was due to the fact that their less than stellar pasts would soon be open for discussion. It also didn't help that neither of them cared to be evaluated by doctors of any kind. The same unspoken fear nagged them both; they would be denied their chance to become parents, their *only* chance. Infertility was an unfair creature. It infuriated Arin to no end when she considered that when John and Jane Q. Public decided to have a child, they simply jumped in and gave it a try. In no time, Jane appeared to have swallowed a watermelon seed, as the old folks liked to say. They weren't first subjected to psychological profiles and probing intimate questions. No pasty-faced clinic worker picked through their pasts, scrutinizing each dreadful decision to determine if a baby would be appropriate. If not for their frantic longing to have a child, Arin and Jake would have called it quits long ago. This evaluation was the last hoop to jump through before they would finally be given the green light to begin treatment. Adding insult to injury, these hoops had been extremely costly and time consuming. Fueled by desperation, Jake and Arin resisted their strong non-conformist tendencies and had sailed through the hoops like trained seals chasing the scent of fish.

Restlessness, curiosity, and boredom ultimately got the better of Arin. She rose from her chair and snuck across the sizeable office to peruse the leather bound volumes and peek at the pewter-framed photos on the impressive desk. Before she had even made it halfway across the room the door swung open. With her usual lack of grace, she flung herself back into the chair, painfully clipping her shin on the edge of a magazine rack. Momentarily incapacitated by the pain, she doubled over and swore under her breath, rubbing her injured shin. Jake, completely mortified by Arin's behavior, quickly recovered and rose to shake Dr. Halter's extended hand. A few intense moments passed before the cloud of agony lifted. Arin stood to offer a limp hand to Dr. Halter, a man of medium height and build who looked astonishingly similar to Kenny Rogers. The resemblance was uncanny.

"Has anyone ever told you that you look exactly like-"

"Kenny Rogers. Yes, yes, Mrs. Welsh. I've actually been told that a number of times over the years," Dr. Halter replied rather curtly. Apparently he was not a big fan of Mr. Rogers.

"Let's have a seat and get started, shall we?" The Welsh's sank into their leather chairs and took a moment to find a comfortable position. Arin leaned back, arms folded across her chest. Concerned that her stance may appear closed, she uncrossed her arms and scooted forward in the chair, her clammy hands neatly folded in her lap, hoping that she didn't appear childlike. Jake was a slab of granite beside her, hands on his knees, back straight.

"Thank you for coming, Mr. and Mrs. Welsh, this is a formality, really, but an important step nonetheless." Dr. Halter then proceeded to drone on and on concerning the challenges of raising children, especially multiples, which were often a factor with IVF conceptions. He pontificated on the pain of infertility. Arin doubted his ability to educate them on the subject. They practiced their active listening skills, obediently nodding in agreement and inserting comments when appropriate. Dr. Halter finally concluded his obviously well rehearsed monologue and turned his attention to an ominous red folder placed in the center of his desk. Arin strained to see the contents, but unfortunately, the massive desk did not permit peeking.

"You have been married for about five years," he read, not looking up. "Mr. Welsh, you work as a mechanic."

"Actually," Jake corrected, "I'm part owner of D&J's Automotive Technology Center." Dr. Halter scribbled, unimpressed.

"And Mrs. Welsh, you work as a freelance sign language interpreter?" He must have found this remotely interesting, because he looked up from the precious red folder.

"Yes."

He continued to peer at her over his glasses. What did he expect, a demonstration, or perhaps a quick tutorial in American Sign Language?

"Your parents were deaf, is that correct?"

"Foster parents, actually." Arin drew in a sharp breath, steeling her resolve to remain calm and unemotional. Dr. Halter made a note and looked up, his face a question. She waited, courteously holding his gaze.

"And your birth parents?" he finally asked, obviously more than a little annoyed about having to drag it out of her. Well, Arin thought, she was annoyed to have to discuss her life story with a Kenny Rogers look-alike with an attitude. Who was she trying to fool pretending that she was a cookie-cutter suburbanite mommy wanna-be? Immediately, she dropped the act and shot from the hip.

"My birth father is dead and my birth mother is drunk," she blurted, her voice flat and void of emotion. It felt good to not put on airs. Jake sank down a little lower in his chair. So much for making a great impression.

"I'm sorry..." Dr. Halter looked lost. Arin almost pitied him. Almost.

"Oh, thank you, but it's okay, really. I'm completely over it now." Arin was amazed that her voice was virtually free of sarcasm.

"What I mean, Mrs. Welsh," Dr. Halter sighed dramatically, " is that I'm going to need a little more information."

Arin shrugged and offered the cliff notes version of her childhood. Born to a family she did not remember, her father died of some form of cancer when she was barely two. It was then that her mother emerged from the closet as a full-fledged alcoholic, somehow managing to drink Arin into foster care by the time she was three. After several months of shuffling from shelters and foster homes, she was finally placed with Paul and Donna Duvall, a childless deaf couple. The first few years with the Duvall family were silent and confusing to Arin, who had no prior exposure to the deaf.

"Were your foster parents abusive in any way?" Dr. Halter asked, his pen poised to record any horrific acts of abuse she may have suffered.

"No, not unless you consider terrible meatloaf three nights in a row abusive," Her attempt at humor fell flat. She cleared her throat and continued. "The Duvall's were good to me, especially by foster care standards. I had my own room, I was assigned chores but wasn't a slave. They did their best to include me in their family. In no time at all I was picking up American Sign Language."

"Normally, foster children don't spend more than a few months at a home unless they are actively being considered for adoption. For some reason, my mother refused to sign the paperwork that would have released me for adoption. Nevertheless, the Duvall's came to depend on me to interpret for medical appointments and such. They begged my caseworker to allow me to stay and he did, going against regulation. I like to think of it as his good deed for the decade. Maybe it helped him sleep at night." Arin threw up her hands and abruptly concluded her monologue. "Any questions?" she asked, after what seemed like a full minute of nothing but a roomful of crickets.

Following yet another uneasy silence, Dr. Halter posed the question that Arin had anticipated, yet rage welled inside her when the words were spoken aloud. "Have you considered using an egg donor?"

Lucky for Kenny Rogers, Jake decided to field this one. "We are fully aware of the risks of alcoholism, and know that certain cancers run along family lines. We're willing to accept those risks." How eloquently put. Arin may have asked Dr. Halter if he had considered where he could put that pretty red folder of his, although that would probably not have been the most productive response.

"Mr. Welsh, could you tell me a little about your upbringing? Your file states that you are estranged from your family?" Dr. Halter had all the dirt. What had the clinic done, hired a PI to stake them out? Arin made a mental note to search for plain cars parked on her street with newspaper-reading tough guys stationed in them.

Jake drew a deep breath, disgusted that the clinic thought this was necessary to determine what sort of parent he would be. "My parents are Lutheran above all else, and consider it more important that you be a tithing attendee of the Lutheran church than a member of the human race. I was never the son they wanted, and despite their best efforts, somehow I failed to be molded into a proper Lutheran. They were less than thrilled when Arin and I married. For the sake of all involved, we just send a card at Christmas and leave it at that." Despite Jakes best efforts not to project bitterness, there was an uncharacteristic edge to his voice. Dr. Halter scribbled up another storm. Arin put her hand on Jake's knee and squeezed, hoping the bell would soon ding and they would be finished with this round of "This Was Your Life."

"Can you tell me how you met and how long you dated?" Dr. Halter addressed the question to either of them, and for a few moments there was more silence and fidgeting. This was not one of the questions that they had anticipated and rehearsed an acceptable answer to. Arin's mind scrambled for some believable tale. Perhaps they had reached for the same pack of ground beef at the Piggly Wiggly, or were stuck in an elevator and spent twelve hours clinging to each other until they were daringly rescued. Just as she was putting the finishing touches on the latter, Jake tactlessly blurted the truth.

"We met in a cult."

"Oh," Dr. Halter managed weakly, rubbing his temples and sighing deeply. This session was apparently not going as planned. "May I ask about your involvement with this cult?" Arin covered her mouth with her hand to stifle a wave of nervous laughter. She was sure he had mental pictures of them dancing naked in chicken blood, or following a Charles Manson type through the night with flaming torches singing "Helter Skelter." Perhaps he even imagined them chanting at the airport with shaved heads and tambourines. The truth was much more vanilla.

"We were introduced in The Covenant Family," Arin explained, speaking in a voice that she normally reserved for third graders. "We were both at vulnerable places in our lives, and the group seemed like the answer. We needed to escape, they specialized in escape. For a few years it was great. Our lives consisted of communal living, campfires, eating lots of sprouts, and daily indoctrination by the shepherd of the group. Jake and I were married by the leader less than a month after we met."

"It was the tradition of the group to quickly marry members off in hopes of repopulating with little cult babies as soon as possible." Arin looked at Jake and then back to Dr. Halter, who by this time had dropped the pen. His mouth was slightly agape, which was not an intelligent look for him or Kenny Rogers. "We did not, however, have a litter of little cult babies, despite our most sincere efforts. That is what brings us here, Dr. Halter. Do you think you can help us?" It took him a few long seconds to collect his thoughts and form an intelligent sentence.

"You are no longer affiliated with this group?" he asked with what Arin felt was an accusatory tone that she did not appreciate. This guy must have a thing against former foster children and ex-cult members.

"The cult disbanded when the shepherd and several of the members in leadership were arrested for fraud, theft, and kidnapping of underage members, among other things. We decided to make our marriage legal and did so the next day. We have been madly in love ever since." Arin tacked on that last part in an attempt to salvage the interview by wrapping their crazy past up in a pretty bow. She failed to mention that they were married in their cut-offs and flip-flops, and for their honeymoon they visited a payphone and called Cousin Dave collect for a bail out. Somehow, she did not think divulging all the facts would provide the sense of stability that they needed to convey.

Dr. Halter sat back in his huge leather chair and made some notes, rubbing his short white beard. He took his time studying their medical forms and other assorted paperwork in the mysterious red folder that held a halting and incomplete version of their journey. At last he stood and half-heartedly offered his hand to Jake and then to Arin, stating that all was in order.

His official findings were that Jake and Arin Welsh would no doubt make model parents and that they were emotionally stable enough to begin the grueling process of in vitro fertilization. Money doesn't talk, it screams. On the way out, they were to meet with their nurse to schedule the first cycle, which they prayed would be their last. Arin shot out of the stuffy office and squealed in delight, skipping towards the nurse's station, oblivious of the show she was putting on for the receptionist. This was one woman who seriously wanted a baby. It was all Jake could do to keep from skipping after her.

***

For five long years, Jake and Arin had tried unsuccessfully to have a baby. During that time, Arin had painted herself a rosy mental picture of pregnancy. Boldly, she declared that no amount of discomfort would ever be enough to cause her to complain. She was going to treasure every second of the nine months that her baby grew inside her. After countless injections, blood tests, sonograms, and procedures designed to do what nature stubbornly refused to, they received the call. Breathlessly they waited, their eyes boring holes into the speaker phone. Even Cooper, their goofy brindle Boxer, stared at the phone anticipating the news. At last, the nurse gave congratulations instead of dreaded condolences. Jake and Arin embraced and hooted, their tears of joy washing away the previous ones of longing. Even Cooper let out a howl and ran around in circles. At last they were going to be a family.

The first thing Arin did was to go directly to the Motherhood outlet in town and buy a white maternity shirt with a red arrow pointing to "Baby". She insisted on wearing it immediately, despite her slim build and the hugeness of the shirt. Jake attempted to keep his snickering to a minimum. After all, it was silly things such as this that particularly endeared his wife to him.

After the initial blood test and heartfelt congratulations, they were abruptly fired by the fertility clinic, left alone to select someone from the vast sea of obstetricians. There was no doubt in Arin's mind which doctor would monitor the life growing inside her and ultimately deliver her baby. One benefit of being an interpreter was having firsthand knowledge of every doctor in a fifty mile radius. She would accept none other than Dr. Chen.

Dr. Chen's grumpy receptionist, on the other hand, had a different plan. She snipped that she was very sorry; Dr. Chen was not accepting any new patients. Arin hung up, deflated but not defeated. Several minutes later she called back and Snippy answered again, this time Arin was ready for her. She had a plan.

"Yes, I need to make an appointment with Dr. Chen, as soon as possible please."

"Have you been here before?" the snippy one quipped, itching for another chance to blow someone off.

"Oh yes, many times," Arin stated confidently, wincing a bit. Technically this was true. She could not count the number of interpreting jobs she had taken with Dr. Chen's patients, that's how she knew that he was the best.

"Last name and date of birth please." Snippy seemed resigned to the fate of having to actually do her job.

"Welsh, October 29, 1975." This was where things were going to get a bit dicey. After spelling her name four times, offering her social security number, address and phone number, Snippy announced that there was no Arin Welsh in their system, hence she was not a patient of Dr. Chen's.

"I guess I'll need to speak to a manager," Arin bluffed indignantly. "I've been visiting Dr. Chen for the last five years. This is ridiculous." Her eyes were squeezed shut and fingers tightly crossed for luck. She was placed on hold, and who of all people but Kenny Rogers serenaded her through the next few moments. She was just beginning to hum along when Snippy interrupted.

"Mrs. Welsh, you are going to have to fill out all new paperwork as if you are a new patient, and that will take some time."

"Mail it please. I'll bring everything back with me." For credibility she added, "I'm familiar with your paperwork from my past visits. There's a ton if it." Snippy promised to send everything out that day, squeezed her in the following Tuesday, and apologized profusely for the mix up. Arin was very gracious and forgiving. After all, everyone made mistakes.

***

Arin rolled out of bed Sunday morning ever so gently, concentrating on riding out the current wave of nausea. If she moved slowly enough or held her head just so, maybe it would roll on by. Or maybe not. She cupped her hand over her mouth and sprinted for the bathroom, tripping over a slumbering Cooper. She barely made it. She'd convinced herself that pregnancy would be an enchanted time, nine months of maternal bonding between her and the life growing within her. Instead, she felt green and spent most of her time hugging toilet bowls. Good thing she was a meticulous bathroom cleaner, she mused, as she tried to avoid puking in her hair.

She felt Jake's hand on her back, circling reassuringly. "Is there was anything I can do?" he whispered. Arin knew that this was an act of pure sacrificial love on her dear husband's part. Jake could hardly stand to be within a square mile of someone vomiting. One time in the cult a little girl was vomiting way at the other end of the bus. He had immediately turned green and tossed his cookies as well. Feeling merciful and more like being alone, Arin waved him away. Grateful, he took off, closing the door behind him. She was left alone with Cooper and Mr. Tidy Bowl. She really could have used someone to hold back her hair, she thought, feeling a bit sorry for herself.

"Can I get you some crackers?" Jake offered through the security of the closed door. Arin flushed, got up weakly and reached for her toothbrush. If one more person mentioned crackers as a cure for her morning, noon, and night sickness she was going to murder them.

"No thanks, Honey," she called sweetly, sticking her tongue out at her reflection. Her long brown hair was matted with bits of fresh vomit. Her cinnamon eyes were so red she looked like she had just come off a twelve day drunk. So much for the healthy glow of pregnancy. She brushed her teeth using the blue toothpaste with a happy shark on the tube. These days all other brands made her violently ill. Cautiously, she stepped into the shower, her thirty-four year old body feeling practically elderly. It was going to take a miracle to become somewhat presentable in the next hour and a half.

"Why don't you just call and tell them you can't make it? It's obvious you're sick." Jake sat across the table from her, his face a mask of concern. "It's not like this is your dream job."

"We need to save some money, Jake. You know I want to take some time off after the baby is born. If I have to accept crappy jobs that I'd normally not even consider, then so be it." In order to pay the fertility clinic's astronomical fees, they had gone heavily into debt. Until the baby was born, she was determined to work every job DeafMed would throw her way. Arin forced herself to think that the waffle in front of her was somehow edible. Cooper's head was planted in her lap, his huge brown eyes begging intensely. Lately he was getting the lion's share of her meals. The crackers were looming on the counter, but thankfully, Jake had not offered her any. She would hate to have to kill him, the father of her child and all.

"Well, don't forget to say a prayer for this heathen while you're there," Jake teased.

"You could use it," Arin snapped back, not appreciating his humor. Neither of them had been to a church since leaving the cult. They had sort of an unspoken agreement that church was not part of their plan. Been there, done that, been deprogrammed, no thanks. Now, when she was trying to build up their savings for the months after the baby was born, the thought of working an hour and a half on a Sunday for decent money appealed to her. Besides, the church was close and she needed something to distract her from her misery. She just hoped that she would not spew pea soup on anyone, inciting the need for an exorcism of some sort.

When Arin pulled in, the church parking lot was rapidly filling with cars and trucks, most with a fish slapped on the back of them. Stepping out of her fishless beat-up Explorer, she was relieved to see people in all manner of dress. There were squat old ladies dressed to the nines with sparkly hats, denim clad twenty-somethings casually strolling to the door sipping coffee, and all styles in between. Little ones were everywhere, giggling and darting in and out of the crowd. Arin preferred an understated style, or the "lazy look", as Jake liked to call it. She self-consciously ran her fingers through her unruly reddish-brown hair. Her work was promptly undone by a strong September breeze. In an attempt to blend in, Arin had chosen a simple cream colored sweater and black slacks. She hoped that it would be enough. Secretly, she yearned to wear her new shirt advertising, "Baby".

Even as a grown woman, childhood insecurities still haunted her. Her eyes were an unusual shade of brown. Her foster mother had once compared them to freshly ground cinnamon. A smattering of freckles sprinkled her forehead, nose and cheekbones, and her thick hair had an agenda of its own. Growing up with that combination, as well as the stigma of being a foster child, had made Arin open season for bullies. Bullies like Kevin Driver. Arin's jaw tightened at the mere mention of his name inside her head. Kevin Driver had done his very best to ensure that

Arin's middle and high school experience was as miserable as humanly possible. Unfortunately for Arin, Kevin had been quite the overachiever. Regardless of the miles and years that separated her from her pitiful adolescence, not a day passed that Arin did not think of Kevin Driver. Despite the fact that Jake considered her an absolute knockout and told her so often, a lonely and battered sixth grader still inhabited Arin Welsh's body.

An older gentleman wearing an ugly green jacket met her at the door. He greeted her heartily, pumping her hand and insisting that he was happy she was there. The sparkle in his blue eyes almost convinced Arin that he was sincere. As she entered the foyer, she was lost in the buzz of activity. Tight circles of people engaged in animated conversations, laughter erupted here and there, and children were herded down the hall to classes. She scanned the room but failed to see any signed conversations. Someone gently tapped her shoulder and she turned, grateful to see the pleasant greeter again.

"First time here, Darling?" he asked. Normally, Arin detested being called honey or darling or any assorted pet name by anyone other than her husband, and even that was iffy. Fortunately for this guy, he was just old and cute enough to get away with it.

"I'm the interpreter DeafMed sent for today's service, Arin Welsh." She stuck out her hand, and he shook it warmly. Arin felt a little sheepish, remembering they had already shaken hands once, but he did not seem to mind one bit. Shaking hands appeared to be this guy's forte, and she had to admit that he had a knack for it.

"Ed Webber," he announced, holding the handshake longer than was necessary, another pet peeve that Arin typically would have faulted him for. Again, she made concession for this charming old man in his ugly green blazer. "Follow me, Hon. I'll take you right where you need to be." He led her down the hallway and through a maze of people.

"We really appreciate you coming in," he called over his shoulder. "Our old interpreter, Betty, passed away just last week and we just didn't know what to do."

"I'm so sorry. That's terrible," Arin stammered, feeling incredibly awkward. Great. She gets to take the dead lady's place. Entering the quickly filling sanctuary, she recalled exactly why it was her general rule to turn down both convention and church assignments. She hated facing a huge room full of people while she interpreted. Paranoia always washed over her and she became fully convinced that every eye in the place was on her, critiquing her every movement. Of course, Mr. Webber led her directly to the front and indicated a single chair that faced the sanctuary. She wrestled with a strong urge to bolt. After all, she had been quite ill just this morning. Instead, she dutifully followed him to the front and sat.

"Haven't seen Rae yet," he said as he scanned the room. "She'll most likely be here." Arin's eyes lit up. Perhaps her services would not be required after all. DeafMed policy clearly stated that she was entitled to seventy-five percent of her fee if the client failed to show or cancel within the appropriate time. Perhaps this was her lucky day.

"Is there only one deaf member in the congregation?" she asked. In the interpreting world, churches were notorious for being cheap. It was highly unlikely that even a large church would be willing to pay the costly fee for a professional interpreter for only one member.

"Not even one, really. Rae's not a member, but she's been coming for a while and we all have kind of taken to her. Betty, the interpreter who passed, and Rae got on pretty well. None of us wanted her to stop coming, so we sent for you." He flashed a denture-filled smile that warmed Arin's heart. There was something special about this dear man. Arin found herself trying to imagine what it would be like to have him as a grandfather, and found the idea very appealing. A grandparent's love was not something Arin had ever been fortunate enough to experience. A pang of sorrow struck her when she considered that the child growing inside her would also have quite a void in the grandparent department.

"Well, I'll try not to disappoint," Arin promised half-heartedly. Ed nodded and excused himself to help an elderly lady find a seat. Behind her, music began to play. Conversations were cut short and people scurried to find their seats.

For a few long minutes, she sat facing the congregation, feeling very much like an exotic zoo specimen on display. When she had picked all the invisible lint from her slacks and was scanning for the nearest exit, Rae arrived. She was the polar opposite of what Arin had expected, although she was entirely unaware that she had been expecting anyone in particular. Rae Stewart was tall and slender, dressed simply in black with delicate sterling silver dripping from her neck and ears. Her most striking feature was her long shock of white hair, sharply contrasted by her wrinkle-free face. She appeared to be in her mid-thirties, but it was impossible to be certain. Arin studied Rae as she scanned her bulletin and determined that this woman must have been the very first baby ever to be born completely gray. It was impossible to picture her any other way.

Rae glanced up and smiled warmly at Arin, her silvery eyes brimming with intelligence. She exuded a peace and authenticity that Arin found intriguing. She had to fight the urge to unprofessionally pound her with personal questions. Instead, she introduced herself and as they conversed, she was pleasantly surprised to find that Rae was quite open and freely shared the details of her life.

Rae Stewart was the owner of the Silver Fox Nursery on the north side of town, a spot that Arin had frequented for years and thought was fantastic. There was an elevated gazebo in the center of the greenhouse surrounded by exotic birds in ornate wrought iron cages. The gazebo was encircled by sprawling plants that would take a truck to move if someone ever were to purchase them. Rae smiled and signed that she had created it as her own personal oasis. Each morning the gazebo served as her sanctuary as she prayed and studied her Bible. She spent a great deal of time at the greenhouse since her husband of twenty-four years had died the September before last. She joked that her oasis was as close to a vacation as she was ever going to get now that she managed The Silver Fox alone. Arin offered condolences on the loss of her husband, which Rae graciously accepted. He was a good man, she signed, and left it at that.

Absorbed in their conversation, Arin completely forgot that she sat in front of five hundred people. American Sign Language had always come naturally for Arin. She was fascinated by the animation and expression attached to each sign and the individual flair of each signer's style. She relished the privacy of a signed conversation amongst hearing people. Chatting with Rae Stewart was a breath of fresh air for Arin. At this point in her career she was bored to tears with doctor's office conversations. If she never participated in another question and answer session about bunions again it would be too soon. She could not recall the last time she had enjoyed a real conversation in the language she cherished.

They continued to chat like two old friends. Arin surprised herself when she freely offered to Rae that she was expecting, and was pleased with Rae's reaction. She bounced up and down with excitement and lunged forward, giving her a quick hug. When Rae asked if she had felt ill, Arin said a little and left it at that, afraid of risking the dreaded cracker advice since things were going so well. Normally, she made no effort to make friends and had nearly convinced herself that they were frivolous and unnecessary. Rae's enthusiasm regarding her pregnancy touched her, giving her a little taste of something she hadn't realized she had missed until then—another female to share her sorrows and delights with.

The sermon was not nearly as excruciating as Arin had expected it to be. In fact, the young bearded Pastor Wesley even made a bit of sense. He was teaching out of the Gospel of Mark where Jesus talked about how a house divided against itself could not stand. Arin thought of Jake and how poorly she had treated him lately, using her constant sickness as an excuse. She made a mental note to stop acting like a spoiled brat. She would not risk their house ever being divided.

When the message wrapped up and the final prayer was uttered, the worshipers started their slow shuffle out of the sanctuary. Arin and Rae made their way up the aisle to the foyer and then out into the bright September sun, all the while talking up a silent storm. Rae invited Arin to come to the greenhouse anytime for a visit, warning that she reserved the right to put her to work planting or watering. When asked if she would be back, Arin smiled and sincerely said she hoped so. Initially, she had considered Downsville Christian Fellowship a one-time only, grit-your-teeth-and-bear-it type assignment. She admitted to herself and to Rae that although church was not her thing, she wouldn't mind hanging around for a Sunday or two if they requested to have her back.

Contentment and hope filled Arin's thirsty soul as she made the trip home. She basked in the sunlight of connection and belonging she had enjoyed that morning, things she hadn't even acknowledged were missing in her life until now. Perhaps Arin Welsh, disconnected former foster child and cult member, had at last made a friend, and in church, of all places. Life is just chock-full of surprises.

Arin arrived at the Comprehensive Women's Medical Group more than an hour early for her scheduled appointment. She'd left early to make allowance for every conceivable emergency and to allow time for clean-up as needed. In the last eight weeks, she had learned to always have a few fresh sets of clothing and barf bags along. Experience had taught her that a regular old plastic grocery bag was not sufficient; instead, two plastic bags coupled with a heavy brown paper bag did the trick. She had even mastered the skill of driving while she lost her lunch in the bag which she constantly kept on her lap. It often crossed her mind that this was potentially a ticket-worthy offense.

As she struggled with the heavy double glass doors, it occurred to her how surreal it was to be entering the office for herself as opposed to meeting with one glowing pregnant client or another. Where she had full confidence before, now she felt a bit intimidated. Steeling her resolve and practicing her story, Arin strode to the front desk and waited patiently for Snippy, or Lisa as her name tag claimed, to slide the magic glass partition and grace her with her attention. Lisa, obviously on a personal call, swiveled her chair around and continued her chat, winding and unwinding the phone cord nonchalantly. After a minute, she snuck another peek over her shoulder and noticed that Arin was still there. Sighing, she abruptly ended the call and flashed Arin a look, communicating quite effectively that she did not appreciate being disturbed.

"Can I help you?"

"Hi. I have an appointment with Dr. Chen, Last name Welsh."

"You're an hour early," Lisa spat incredulously, as if this was the highest offense in all of doctor-office-dom. "You know you are going to have to wait," she said, impersonating an insolent child on the playground. Arin would not have been a bit surprised if she tacked on "Nanny-Nanny-Boo-Boo."

"No problem," Arin managed through clenched teeth, handing over the small mountain of paperwork and insurance information it had taken her an hour to complete. She stood submissively while Snippy scanned each page, hoping to find something out of order. Of course she wouldn't find anything. The long hours spent helping others fill out the tedious paperwork had basically error-proofed Arin when it came to brainless medical forms. The perfection with which Arin filled out her forms seemed to soften Snippy just a tad. She seemed impressed that a mere patient could possibly fill them out correctly the first time. Arin felt a twinge of pity for this poor creature, doomed to eight hours a day of fussing people for obscure mistakes on idiotic documents.

"You look familiar," she said, studying Arin's face.

"I've been here before." She felt her face flushing red. She was sure she had been found out. She scurried to the small waiting room and selected a large powder blue chair that looked comfortable enough to do some serious waiting in. Looks can sure be deceiving, she soon found, as she tried to position herself so that a spring was not cutting into her rear end. She started to read one baby magazine after another until she gave up. They were all full of paranoid articles such as, "Does Your Baby Have Tourette Syndrome?" Some pieces seemed clearly designed to scare young mothers directly to their pediatricians in hysterics. There were endless columns such as, "Is Your Baby at Risk for Developing Diabetes?" After a while, it became a baffling game of filling in the blank with obesity, schizophrenia, or a million other terrible maladies a baby was likely to develop. Arin gave up, closed her eyes, and focused on ignoring the spring that had undoubtedly punctured her jeans by now.

The waiting room filled around her with expectant mothers in all stages of pregnancy, some with cute little pooches, others swollen and lumbering painfully to their seats. Every time a nurse rounded the corner to call out a new name, all the women would lean forward in hopeful expectation. The winning patient would get up as quickly as she was able, and walk or waddle to the examination room. Those who remained let out deep sighs of discontent. The tension in the waiting room increased gradually as the minutes passed. Now and then someone would check her watch with an exaggerated motion, while several of the more outspoken women griped brashly. Finally, the bleached-blonde nurse, who looked to be approximately thirteen years old, called Arin's name. She hopped up even before the second syllable was pronounced. If she had sat any longer, she feared the spring would have to have been surgically removed.

"We'll need a clean catch urine specimen. Please write your name on the outside of the cup." The nurse rattled off information in a monotone voice as she led her to a bathroom down the hall. Arin dutifully filled the sterile cup and wrote her name on the label, opened the little window and placed it on the ledge. She jumped when a large gloved hand snatched it before she had even completely set it down. They sure didn't waste any time around here.

Donning a paper thin gown peppered with hearts and stars, she settled herself on the table, content to have a more comfortable place for the next round of waiting. At last, Dr. Chen and his assistant burst through the door. His head was down as he scanned her file for a name, and extended his small hand.

"Congratulations, Mrs. Welsh," he spoke slowly, enunciating every sound as best as his heavy Chinese accent would allow. He looked up and eyed Arin quizzically. "You my patient before? You translator for deaf women, right?"

"I'm your patient now," Arin said, much louder than was necessary. She chided herself. He was Chinese, not hard of hearing. "I'm thrilled to have you as my OB." A little flattery never hurt.

Dr. Chen was his usual self; humble and interested in what his patient had to say. He listened while Arin droned on and on about puking in the house, in the car, in the yard and other more unusual places. He took note of her extensive female problems and provided her with paperwork to sign, which would allow him to communicate with the fertility clinic. To his credit, Dr. Chen prescribed a powerful anti-nausea drug to be sparingly used instead of crackers. Finally, it was time for the much anticipated ultrasound.

The jelly the nurse liberally squirted on her belly had most certainly been retrieved directly from a deep freeze hidden somewhere in the room. Arin's heart fluttered inside her chest and she could not help but smile. She was dying to catch a glimpse of her little one. For a moment she regretted telling Jake not to come, but her practical side insisted that if he did not work, he did not make money. Simple as that.

With the lights dimmed, Dr. Chen went to work using his magic womb wand and ice cream belly-jelly to see the tiny life growing inside her. Arin's heart pounded with exhilaration when she first discerned the heartbeat, fast and strong. Dr. Chen indicated a pulsating circle of light on the otherwise dark screen. Arin felt the tears streaming down the sides of her face before she even realized she was crying. A million questions sprang to her mind, but she was mute with emotion. Dr. Chen measured the heart rate, stating that everything appeared to be completely normal. No words had ever sounded sweeter to her than *completely normal.*

Just as he was preparing to remove the wand from her slick belly, he paused, cocking his head slightly, and turned up the sound. The room was filled with the strong steady pounding of the baby's heart. Dr. Chen appeared to be nodding his head along with the beats, listening for something. After a moment, he applied more frosty jelly and searched her belly with renewed vigor. Arin found her voice to ask if something was wrong, but he held up a finger, signaling for her to wait. She studied his face, searching for any signs of concern or unease. At last, his face broke out into a huge toothy grin. Confused, she looked from him to the monitor and saw it - two circles of light, pulsating in unison.

***

They had been told, warned and informed to the hilt that multiple births were a real possibility. They'd signed the legal documents stating that they would not sue if Arin became pregnant with sextuplets. Never in a million years did they think it could actually happen. They never even joked about it. They considered conception a miracle in and of itself. Never did they even think to ask or hope for twins. Only one egg had been viable for transfer, which Dr. Chen explained meant the twins were identical, not fraternal. This news should have absolutely delighted Arin, but for some reason, which she did not yet understand, it had the extreme opposite effect. The realization that there were two human beings growing inside her settled on her like a cold wet blanket. Shell-shocked, she drove aimlessly, alternating between complete numbness and panic. If she did not have someone to talk to soon, she considered it a real possibility that she would implode. She could not bring herself to call Jake.

Lights flickered throughout the greenhouse, alerting Rae that someone had entered. She was on her hands and knees cleaning a display fountain in front near the cash register. When she saw Arin, her face brightened. She jumped up and removed her heavy rubber work gloves. For a few minutes, they made comfortable small talk. When Rae asked for the third time if everything was okay, Arin's face was a strange mask of raw emotion. She simply shrugged. Rae gently took her by the elbow and led the way to the gazebo, to her "oasis".

Rae's sanctuary was nothing less than spectacular. The sound of water rushing through the various fountains served to soothe Arin's frazzled nerves. Cockatoos, African Grey, and green Amazon parrots eyed them curiously as they were perched in their elaborate cages. They seemed to take turns calling out a "Hello there" or "Whatcha doing?" Thick vines and exotic trees with long Latin names encircled the elevated gazebo. The surface of each step was a mosaic of broken pottery and smooth colored glass. At the edge of the last step the initials RS were written in chunks of cobalt blue pottery. There was no doubt that Rae was an amazingly creative person. Arin began to feel completely clumsy and uninteresting, an ugly duckling in comparison to this silver fox of a woman.

It was clear that Rae was genuinely pleased to share this place and moment with her. Arin had come here with every intention of proclaiming the news that she was carrying twins, but her stiff hands stubbornly refused to make the signs. She had a strong premonition that something was horribly wrong. She could practically feel her dream child slipping away. There was no proof she could point to that would back up this feeling. In fact, all the evidence pointed in quite the other direction, to two healthy babies. Arin just knew.

Rae reached out and took both of Arin's hands in her own. Staring into her eyes, she searched her soul with her silvery pools of compassion. Arin blushed at the intimacy of the moment, but did not look away. She longed for this true connection. After a few moments, Rae released her hands and asked Arin once again if there was anything she needed to talk about. Arin mulled it over for a moment and decided to keep her secret for now. Rae did not push her for information, and for the better part of an hour they sat comfortably in the oasis. One thing Arin enjoyed about the company of the deaf was their level of comfort with extended breaks in conversation. Arin wished that Rae could hear the birds as they tossed around greetings and snide comments, savor the sound of the water flowing over the smooth stones. The beauty Rae had created was auditory as well as visual.

In the midst of the peaceful stillness, Rae turned to Arin and signed sympathetically that she knew there must be a lot on her mind, but that God was there and He would take care of her and the baby. She was sure everything was completely normal. There were those two wonderful words again. *Completely normal.* She assured Arin that children were a blessing from the Lord, and that every day she would faithfully pray for them.

Arin nodded politely. Suddenly, she was uncomfortable with all of this talk about the Lord. She had been sucked into believing a lie at another vulnerable point in her life. She was not going to make the same mistake. Where was the Lord when Arin's father was taken before her brain could even form a cohesive memory of him? Perhaps he was sleeping while Kevin Driver cornered her in the rarely traveled hallways of Fenwood Middle School, humiliating her and injecting yet another dose of poison to her already terminally ill spirit?

Rae sensed the sudden distance and turmoil, and she gently inquired about Arin's spiritual walk. Arin did not hold back and gave her the whole sordid cult story. Rae cut in here and there to ask a question or interject a comment. Arin concluded her story, justifying why she wanted nothing to do with religion. Rae appeared to be contemplating that for a moment, then signed in a matter-of-fact manner that it was a good thing that she was still a spiritual seeker. Arin shrugged indifferently and decided to let that one go. This intriguing woman was the closest thing she had to a friend at this point.

***

Arin knew beyond a shadow of a doubt that she had a moral obligation to share the news with Jake. After all, he was the father of the twins she was carrying. A cloud of negativity clung to her, and she was unable to force herself to tell him. She knew more than anyone how deeply Jake longed for a family. He would be nothing less than ecstatic with news of twins. She lie sandwiched between him and Cooper, each one snoring in one of her ears, and made a decision to keep her secret until his birthday. He was going to be thirty-five this year. For a milestone birthday, what better than a surprise of this magnitude? That was the excuse she selected to rationalize keeping this monumental news from her husband. Since the moment she witnessed those identical pulsating circles on the monitor, she knew something was going to go terribly wrong, despite Dr. Chen's assurances. Her body literally shook as she tried to free herself from these terrible thoughts, waking Jake and knocking Cooper clean off of the bed to the floor, where he belonged in the first place. "What's wrong, Hon? Do you need something?" Jake slurred, drunk with sleep.

"Just stop sawing logs, would you?" she whispered good-naturedly, and kissed his prickly cheek.

***

"I really don't know why you have to go now," Arin pouted as she poured herself a second cup of decaf. "Can't you learn that stuff another time? I am sure they are going to have the conference again next year."

"Sure, you're really going to want to be alone for two weeks with an infant."

She did not reply. He had a point there. For the next fifteen minutes, Jake railed against the foreign car makers who were designing their cars to discourage the owners and small shops from performing the simplest of tasks such as changing the oil. Even seasoned mechanics like Jake found themselves scratching their heads when a late model foreign car was brought in for routine maintenance. These days everything was controlled by a computer. It was nearly impossible anymore to simply lift the hood and diagnose the problem. The two week training course Jake was scheduled to attend promised to make him a pro, which had potential to significantly increase the caliber of jobs they could accept at D&J's. Arin knew this trip was a financial necessity.

"Dave just shelled out all that money for that expensive diagnostic equipment. I don't know why he doesn't go to Michigan himself and learn how to use it," Jake continued his rant.

"You're cute when you sulk," Arin teased, vainly attempting to lighten Jake's mood. "Dave doesn't trust anyone to take care of things at the shop without him."

Jake snickered and rolled his eyes. There was a certain amount of truth to that. Jake was close with his cousin Dave, but when it came to business, Dave trusted no one, not even his partner. He doubted Dave would allow Lee Iacocca run the place for five minutes for fear that it would fall into financial ruin. It was just Dave's obsessive nature. As an employee, Jake had to learn not to take it personally.

Arin was much more apprehensive about Jake going out of town than she let on. Despite the anti-nausea medication Dr. Chen had prescribed, she was rarely able to keep a whole meal down in a day. Somehow she continued to work, but she felt her strength steadily slipping away. It was all she could do to drag herself out of bed most mornings, and great restraint had to be exercised whenever she passed a couch or any other horizontal surface that had potential for lounging. Dr. Chen had explained several times that with twins, the hormone levels were greater; hence, the symptoms would be more severe. By the time she was into her second trimester, the nausea and fatigue would ease and she would enter into the salad days of pregnancy. Her second trimester was almost over and she was still eagerly waiting for her salad.

Arin timidly sipped her decaf and absentmindedly rifled through the stack of mail she had allowed to accumulate. Junk and bills, bills and junk, more junk and more bills. Her hand froze on an envelope with familiar handwriting. Her fingers traveled over the slanted print and she willed herself to feel nothing. After a quick rummage through the kitchen junk drawer, she found her red pen, a pen that she bought and used only for this purpose. It satisfied her greatly to scrawl *RETURN TO SENDER* across the front of the envelope in huge red letters. Jake eyed her from across the room. In the past he had encouraged her to at least open the letters to see what the old lady had to say. Since then, he had given up and no longer interjected when it came to Arin and her mother.

Arin noticed the time and cringed. There were only forty-five minutes until her first appointment across town. Jake pulled her close, wrapping his strong arms around her. For several minutes they stood and enjoyed the embrace, neither wanting it to end. Finally, he loosened his grip and placed his large hand gently on her rounded belly. "I love you," he whispered, his voice cracking. Arin was startled to see that his deep blue eyes were moist with tears. She allowed herself a brief and uncharacteristic cry. The tears quickly formed rivers of mascara down her face. They separated, and Jake cracked a few Tammy Faye jokes. Arin retaliated by kicking him in the shin. She glanced at the clock again and glowered. There was definitely no time for primping. She wiped her face on her shirt sleeve and headed out the door, yelling over her shoulder that she loved him, and wished him a safe flight.

***

Arin whipped into the parking lot of Orthopedic Associates fifteen minutes late to meet her client. She swore that she would never take another job this far from home again. She had to brace herself for a moment when she got out of the Explorer, gripping the door until she felt steady. After this job, she was going to cancel her afternoon appointments with DeafMed and go straight home to rest. As soon as she felt able, she stepped onto the cracked sidewalk and headed toward the building. A titanic wave of nausea and weakness struck her full force.

In an instant, her legs betrayed her and morphed into rubber. Attempting to muster her remaining strength and stay focused on the door twenty feet ahead, she tried to convince her swirling mind that she could reach it. She almost made it before crumpling in a heap on the sidewalk and succumbing to the blackness.

***

"Please," the skinny girl in a stained second hand outfit whimpered. "Please let me go today. Just today. I won't tell anyone."

"Why should I?" Kevin Driver snorted, not inclined to show mercy that particular morning, or any other. "What do you have to give me?" His pasty face flushed red and his icy blue eyes narrowed into hate-filled slits. One glance at the nasty bruise across his cheekbone told Arin that Kevin would be out for blood. That was the way it always had been with Kevin. The more his old man pounded on him, the more diligent and creative he had become in his deliberate and systematic torture of Arin. If he had applied that kind of dedication to his studies, Arin had no doubt that he would have graduated from medical school before he could legally drink a beer.

"You don't even have real parents, so you'll never have any money. I guess you'll have to find some other way to entertain me."

The familiar husky rasp in his voice elevated Arin's personal terror alert to red. Bright flaming fire-engine red. Her heart pounded its protest against her chest wall. She attempted to flatten herself against the cool tile wall of Fenwood Middle, wishing she could simply melt away and just be done. Her eyes flickered to the left and to the right, scanning the dark hallways for signs of life. On more than one occasion a random teacher or office worker strolling down the halls between classes had been Arin's salvation. Unfortunately, there was no salvation in sight and once again, Arin was at Kevin's mercy. A smug expression fixed on his face, he gripped Arin's second hand shirt and yanked, intent on taking whatever he wanted from this child whom no one loved.

***

A stinging at the bend of her arm ushered Arin from the familiar nightmare. Instinctively, she cried out and snatched her arm away.

Blinking hard, she concentrated on orienting her blurry eyes and clearing the fog from her head.

"Where am I?" she demanded, her words coming out clumsy and slurred. With much effort she was able to focus on a wild-haired nurse sitting next to her wielding a significant needle. She smiled sympathetically at Arin and put the needle down on a nearby stainless steel tray.

"Let me get your doctor, Honey." She disappeared behind the pale pink curtain that was drawn around the bed before Arin could pepper her with the questions swirling through her disjointed mind.

In an effort to grasp her current situation, Arin mentally retraced her steps. Had she passed out and hit her head? Cautiously, she examined her head and face with a trembling hand. She was relieved to detect no pain or other signs of injury. Her hands went to her rounded belly and rubbed it apprehensively. Her gown stuck to her stomach, which was sticky and wet with lubricant. Had someone performed an ultrasound? The curtain swished dramatically and Arin's heart leapt to her throat. A dark man invaded her pink cocoon and drew the curtain closed behind him. Arin sat up straight, protectively hugging her belly, spooked for some reason.

"Dr. Raines," he said coolly, extending his hand. After a few tense moments, Arin shook it firmly, hoping to convey strength and confidence, the antithesis of how she felt in reality. His hands were strangely cold and smooth, which caught her off guard. "I have been treating you this afternoon," he announced, as if to ensure Arin that she had no say in the matter. She looked at her wrist. Her watch was gone.

"It is three-thirty, Mrs. Welsh. You've been here for several hours," he reported, anticipating her question.

"Dr. Chen is my OB. I would like him called please."

"I'm sorry, Mrs. Welsh, but Dr. Chen does not have privileges to practice at this hospital." He spat out the name as if it disgusted him. "In the future, perhaps you should choose to collapse somewhere closer to Dr. Chen's office." Dr. Raines' speech was slow and deliberate. Obviously, he was unconcerned that his words were insensitive and cruel. He was tall with a dark olive complexion. Perfect ebony hair was neatly parted on the side, his inky eyes deep set and severe. If not for his offensive bedside manner and a strange coldness in his eyes, he might have been quite attractive.

"May I ask what I am being treated for?" Arin's eyes narrowed to slits, hating that this supposed doctor had touched her.

"Severe dehydration, for one thing," he explained as he studied his cuticles, as if to communicate that he was bored. "Janice was attempting to start another IV when you interrupted her. You yanked the old one out in one of your fits." Arin debated whether to kick him in the groin or ignore his offensive personality. She decided on the latter, figuring that she was too weak to cause the proper amount of discomfort his demeanor begged.

"Dehydration. Is that all?" Arin demanded, maintaining eye contact with Dr. Raines for a few seconds until he glanced away, which she considered a minor victory. With a wave of his well manicured hand he motioned for wild-haired Janice to continue with the IV. Arin acquiesced, holding her arm still and straight. She didn't allow herself to flinch as the needle searched for her shriveled vein. She would not give this arrogant doctor the pleasure. Evidently, Dr. Raines made Janice terribly nervous as well, and it took her several agonizing sticks to get the job done. With each stab she apologized profusely.

"When was your last sonogram, Mrs. Welsh?"

"Apparently sometime today, without my consent," Arin accused, gesturing to the thin gown clinging to her abdomen. The smile he flashed bordered on sinister. It seemed that what little patience he had was growing thin.

"I assume that you've had only one sonogram your first trimester?" he told her more than he asked her. Arin nodded curtly, not wanting to give this arrogant psycho any more information than was absolutely necessary. She just wanted to get on her feet and high tail it back to Dr. Chen. The contrast between this conceited creep and her beloved doctor with his humble servant's heart was enough to make her head spin.

"Well, there have been some unfortunate developments with your pregnancy, Mrs. Welsh." What he told her then would crush her and change her world forever, sealing in her heart a secret, an awful truth, a heavy burden she would carry alone.

Chapter Three

Five years later...

The air inside the greenhouse was thick and humid. Arin stopped running long enough to pull her sweatshirt over her head and tie it around her waist. She peered under a table overflowing with houseplants and spied Troy's trademark red sneakers about five rows over. She hummed the theme song from "Jaws" as she crept through the foliage to his hiding spot and pounced, enveloping him in her arms. Troy giggled breathlessly as Arin prodded and poked his armpits, drinking in his laughter and ignoring his pleas for mercy.

"I win again," Arin bragged.

"It's not all about winning, Mom," he panted.

"Thank you, Mr. Morals."

"Mr. Who?" Troy asked, obviously confused.

Arin rolled her eyes and tousled his hair. "Race you to Rae's office!" she blurted and took off, leaving Troy in the dust. She dodged plants that were randomly placed on the cement floor, weaving in and out of tables covered with exotic plants. Just before she got to Rae's open office door, she staged a fairly believable fall, allowing Troy to claim his victory.

Rae looked up from her desk strewn with plant catalogues and field guides and shook her head. "You guys need to grow up," she signed.

Troy and Arin replied with a unanimous, "Never!" Troy took off again, this time through the front area of the greenhouse that Rae had converted to a showroom and idea center for Koi ponds and fountains. Every conceivable shape and size fountain was represented. Rae's personal favorite was the cast rosin fountain shaped like a fox, which stood guard at the front near the cash register. A large sign that read Not For Sale hung around his neck. Rae had recently stocked her largest indoor display pond with Koi, much to Troy's delight.

"His signing improves every day," Rae commented, and Arin agreed. She was proud of Troy's progress. From infancy she had used sign with Troy, and now he was as fluent in American Sign Language as he was in English. When people saw Troy communicating with Rae they were amazed and often asked how he learned to sign so well. He simply answered that he did not know because he didn't remembered learning it.

Arin thanked Rae again for keeping an eye on Troy so she could work, and again Rae insisted that it was no problem. Arin called and he came running, simulating airplane noises, both arms straight out, and he landed and wrapped his arms around her legs.

"I'm getting ready to go. Daddy will pick you up when he gets off of work."

"Sure." Troy seemed completely untroubled that she was leaving, which tore at her heart a bit. She suspected that he wouldn't bat an eye if she went to the moon as long as he could stay at the greenhouse until she got back.

"Aunt Rae has some jobs for you. Do whatever she asks. Don't break anything and stay out of the customers' way, okay?"

"I know, Mom," Troy replied, his voice revealing a hint of childish impatience. With that, he once again became an airplane and flew to the fox fountain, circling it and patting the statues head before taking off toward the Koi pond display. Arin let Rae know that there were snacks in Troy's backpack, and encouraged her to put him to work. Jake should be there by six.

Arin halted at the nursery's entrance, absentmindedly digging in her purse for the keys. After she finally found them she made a mental note to trash her purse out at the next available opportunity. The knob turned easily and she pushed the heavy door open, stepping into the frosty February air. Out of the corner of her eye, Arin noticed a tall man approaching. Politely, she paused to hold the door for him as she searched her coat pockets for her gloves. The man passed by without as much as a thank you. Arin glowered at his back as he disappeared through the slowly closing door. She slipped the woven gloves on and headed toward her trusty old navy blue Explorer. Without warning or explanation, the hair on the back of her neck pricked up and a violent chill shook her. Her entire body broke out in a cold sweat. Suddenly, she felt conflicted about leaving Troy. She stood in the parking lot, halfway between the greenhouse and the Explorer.

"This is completely absurd. He is with his precious Aunt Rae for goodness sake!" she muttered, and forced herself to continue toward the vehicle. She did her best to rationalize the anxious feeling. It must be the harsh February air, or perhaps she was coming down with a virus. Just the other day at the grocery store, the clerk had warned her that a nasty bug was going around. Still, she could not shake the heavy cloud of trepidation that clung to her. She scolded herself for being so paranoid. As a mother, she was overprotective to a fault, and she knew she needed to relax unless she wanted to raise the next Norman Bates. She shoved the apprehension from her mind and hopped into the waiting Explorer, which loudly roared to life. The darn thing really needed a muffler; ironic, considering that she was married to a mechanic. The cobbler's children have no shoes. She understood that old adage all too well.

As she attempted to pull out of the parking lot, the Explorer was nearly broadsided by a huge red truck. In the nick of time, she kicked it in reverse, narrowly avoiding a potentially horrific collision. It took several long moments for her heartbeat and breathing to return to normal. How in the world had she not seen the truck coming? Again, her paranoid mind worked overtime. Was this a sign? Could it be that someone or something was trying to tell her that she shouldn't leave? A large and highly unusual opening in traffic appeared, and she pulled out of the Silver Fox Nursery, a little more cautiously this time, and headed to work. The nagging fear continued to plague her for the entire ride.

***

Troy's job was to water all the pathos on the table near the back of the greenhouse, and he was determined that he was going to do a great job. Aunt Rae had shown him which setting on the hose nozzle to use, and taught him to wait for the overspill containers to start filling before moving on to the next set of plants. He loved having such an important task. Aunt Rae had explained that if he did not give the pathos water, they would not be able to grow big and strong. Troy knew that growing was important. That's why he had to eat his dinner. Even the carrots, which he thought were gross. Happily, he relayed this message to the plants as he watered, figuring that some of them were probably not real fond of water and wouldn't mind a bit of conversation.

Every few minutes Aunt Rae would pop her head around the corner to make sure that he was still hard at work. She'd wave and smile, sometimes giving him a wink or sign that he was doing a good job. Helping Aunt Rae at the greenhouse was his very favorite thing to do. Sometimes she even let him use the cash register, especially if the customer was an old lady from her church who wouldn't get mad if he messed up and pressed the wrong button. If the lights flashed three times, he knew that Aunt Rae needed his help, and he was supposed to go to the front. It made Troy feel so big to help with important jobs, like watering the greenhouse plants and helping Daddy work on the car.

When Troy had finished with all but the last tray of pathos on the long table, he noticed a tall man a few rows ahead of him. The man looked straight ahead and had a strange slow walk. He seemed completely oblivious to the various trees and flats of plants all around him. Most customers made their way through the greenhouse at an unhurried pace, their faces expressive as they commented on the enormous variety of flora that Rae somehow convinced to flourish under one roof. This man was preoccupied. He ignored the plastic tags neatly stuck in the soil of each planter, and even failed to marvel at the heavy lemons that hung precariously on the spindly lemon trees. Hypnotically, he rounded each corner, weaving in and out of the long tables. He headed toward the very back of the greenhouse where larger plants and landscaping trees were kept.

Troy finished his watering and stood, hose in hand, mesmerized by this stranger. As the man neared Troy's row of pathos, he snapped his head sharply to the left and his dark eyes locked with Troy's. Instantly, Troy was hit with a sensation, like the jolt of electricity he remembered feeling when he'd touched a string of electric fence. It sent a shiver through his small body. The man fixed his head straight again, never missing a step in his deliberate, odd parade.

Shaken, Troy was about to run and find Aunt Rae, when something caught his eye. The man was not alone. Lagging behind was a little boy. Troy must not have been able to see him behind the tables before. In the boy's small hand was a long stick, which he held straight out, almost like an extended finger. It hit the man squarely between his shoulder blades. Troy sensed that the man was being nudged along, that the boy was forcing him to continue. As they passed, he noticed a trickle of blood in sharp contrast with the man's white button-down shirt. Troy felt sorry for him because he was hurt. The boy turned to Troy and flashed a huge smile, eyes wide and bright. He waved wildly with his free hand. His smile was wide and bright, just like Troy's. In fact, the boy looked identical to Troy in every way, from his silky reddish-brown hair and freckles, down to the red sneakers on his slowly marching feet.

The man and the boy disappeared into the tall shrubs and trees, and Troy could still hear their steady footsteps on the concrete. As he was turning to follow them, the lights flashed overhead, signaling that Rae needed him. Troy tried explaining to Aunt Rae what he had witnessed. His usually near perfect signs were frenzied and sloppy. Rae made him take a deep breath and tried to calm him down. When she finally understood his strange account, she cocked her head and eyed him incredulously. It had been a slow afternoon, and there was only one customer in the greenhouse-a man-and she was certain that he had been alone. She let Troy know that if he was bored, he did not have to make up stories. After all, there was plenty for him to do.

***

"I'm home!" Arin boomed, as she burst through the door of their ancient fixer -upper farmhouse. Cooper barked his greetings and wagged his stub, communicating his delight at her homecoming. Arin threw her cluttered purse down and scratched Cooper's back as he worshipped her with adoring eyes. If only the rest of the world was this warm and welcoming, Arin thought, as she often did after being so heartily greeted by her beloved dog.

"Where are my other boys, Cooper?" she asked in the baby talk that she reserved only for him. She was a little bent out of shape that Troy was not on Cooper's heels. Arin only accepted sporadic assignments these days because she hated to leave Troy. Normally, the best thing about being gone was the hugs and kisses he usually lavished on her when she returned. Her little boy was getting big, and soon he would not even want to hold her hand when crossing the street, she thought, sighing deeply. Next thing she knew he would be embarrassed to be seen with her at all.

"Hey, Hon," Jake called over his shoulder, and then he returned to slicing onions and olives to embellish his half of the frozen pizza. Arin and Troy preferred their half plain.

"Where's my welcoming committee?"

"Thanks a lot. What am I, chopped liver?" Jake asked, wiping his hands on a towel before he pulled her to him for a quick embrace.

"What about my boy?"

"He's in his room. He's been acting a little bizarre. Rae thinks he may be coming down with the flu or something." Jake tried his best to sound as nonchalant as humanly possible. He knew all too well how rapidly Arin could work herself up into a frenzy of worry when it came to Troy. She pulled away from him and searched his face with wide eyes.

"Strange how, did he throw up or something? Does he have a fever or a rash? Did you take his temperature or give him some Motrin? Have you called the doctor?" A list of potential illnesses paraded through her mind, including the nasty bug the cashier had warned her about.

"No, no, nothing like that, Honey. For some strange reason he decided to make up an imaginary friend, that's all. I'm sure it's a phase, just something most kids do. I remember my mother telling me that I had one when I was a kid, it bugged the heck out of her." Jake flashed a disarming smile and pecked his wife on the cheek before returning to decorate his half of the pizza.

Arin scanned her memory. She recently had read an article in some parenting magazine discussing the tendency of only children to create imaginary friends. She seemed to recall the author suggested that parents play along within reasonable limits in an effort not to stifle the child's creativity. There was a caution that the formation of imaginary playmates could be a sign of loneliness or stress in a child's life. Guilt stabbed at Arin's heart full force. She should have Troy involved in playgroups or Boy Scouts or karate or something. He was rarely around kids his age. Just because his parents preferred to keep to themselves did not mean that it was the best thing for Troy. Arin wondered if she had ever created a playmate to combat the loneliness she felt as a child. Troy is not going to go through that, she vowed. No matter what. Not ever.

"Maybe when I go to church on Sunday I'll take him along. There's a huge group of kids his age and a great play area. Sometimes they run around there for an hour after church laughing and playing in the sunshine. It would do him good to be around some other kids." Arin stated this more to herself than to Jake.

"Just don't bring him back born again. I prefer him the way he was born the first time." Jake was still extremely leery of any organized religion, church, and even most charities. Arin had been interpreting for Downsville Christian Fellowship for five years now and she considered herself a part of the family, although she was absolutely not willing to commit to their narrow-minded beliefs. Over those five years she had watched as Pastor Wesley blossomed into a confident, fervent and heartfelt teacher. Every Sunday she asked Jake to come along, and her invitations were always flatly refused.

"I'm going to change. Call me when the pizza is burned," Arin teased. Jake had a long history filled with charred pizzas. When she passed Troy's room, she heard his small voice coming from inside. Smiling, she tip-toed to the door and stood outside to listen.

***

"Do you want to play dinosaurs?" Troy asked his new friend, offering him the best of his extensive dinosaur collection. But the boy shook his head no. Troy sighed. Ever since his new friend had come home with him from the greenhouse, they hadn't had any fun at all. Troy gave the boy sitting opposite him on the floor a long look. "Why do you look just like me?" he finally worked up the nerve to ask.

"Because we're best friends now," he answered. His raspy voice was much deeper than Troy's.

"Why can't Aunt Rae and Daddy see you?" Troy asked, eyeing him warily. The boy's eyes jerked to the bedroom door, narrowed slightly, and returned to Troy. He put his pointer finger to his lips, signaling him to be quiet. Gesturing towards the door he winked and silently mouthed, "Mommy".

***

"Breakfast is ready. Come and get it while it's hot," Arin called, doing her best June Cleaver impression while flipping a perfectly browned pancake. She was determined that this was going to be a completely normal day, a picture of serene domestication, complete with a rare home cooked breakfast. Jake appeared in the doorway dressed for work in his old gray coveralls, sniffing the air wildly.

"You're cooking breakfast?" he asked, feigning disbelief, he held onto the doorframe to steady himself. "Is it my birthday?"

"Just sit down and shut up," Arin replied flatly, not appreciating his humor. "I'm cooking for my boy, but you can have some too. That is, if there is any after Cooper is finished." She winked at Cooper, who sat at her feet, a large puddle of drool forming on the kitchen tile. Of course he knew that she would not go through the trouble of making pancakes without flipping one or two his way.

"Did you make extra for Troy's new friend?"

41

Arin rolled her eyes and slammed Jake's plate of pancakes and eggs on the counter. He knew she was less than pleased with this whole invisible friend phenomenon. Troy was an outgoing well-adjusted kid. Why on earth would he need to resort to inventing an imaginary friend? It did not help that he had acted strangely secretive last night, leading Arin to wonder if he was in fact coming down with something. It was just so completely unlike him.

Either way, she was seriously going to consider joining one of those wretched playgroups, even if it meant discussing recipes and diaper rashes with a bunch of hens for a few hours each week. She needed things to be normal. Completely normal. Old invisible what's-his-name did not fit into the normal mold; hence, he had to go. Simple as that. Just as she was getting ready to climb the stairs to wake Troy, there was a knock on the door. At that point any promise of normalcy was fading fast.

***

"Mrs. Welsh?" A tall thin black man dressed in a navy blazer, golf shirt and dress pants wanted to know.

"Yes." Instinctively, Arin knew that this could not be good.

"I'm Detective Lyons of the Frederick County Police Department. I was wondering if I could have a word with you." He spoke gently, almost apologetically, as if he knew he was an unwanted blip on the radar of a pre-ordained completely normal day.

"Concerning?" She wanted to know, her knuckles white from the death grip she had on the doorknob.

"Come on in," Jake called from behind her, his voice calm and cordial as if a cop at their doorstep on a Friday morning was totally natural. When it seemed obvious that Arin was not going to move, Detective Lyons respectfully stepped around her and into the foyer, where Jake led him to the kitchen. Arin stood for a few moments holding the door, oblivious to the cold air flooding the room. What possible reason could there be for a detective to be in her kitchen at seven in the morning?

"Coffee," Jake offered, as he refilled his own cup.

"Sure. Cream, no sugar," Officer Lyons replied pleasantly. Arin patiently waited until Detective Lyons was seated comfortably at the breakfast bar with coffee in hand, before turning to him and bluntly demanding what in the heck he wanted. Jake almost choked on his coffee, astonished by her overall lack of couth.

"Of course, Ma'am. I apologize for interrupting your breakfast. I've just left the Silver Fox Nursery. It is my understanding that your son spent the afternoon there yesterday?"

"Why?" Arin demanded. "What's happened? Is Rae okay?"

"Ms. Stewart is absolutely fine," he quickly assured her. "I am investigating an incident that took place yesterday, and was wondering if I could ask your son a few questions."

"What incident would that be?" Jake pressed, his Mr. Nice Guy persona dissolving. "What incident could a four year old possibly have been involved in?"

Detective Lyons took a deep breath, set his coffee on the counter, and folded his hands together as if in prayer, taking a moment to collect his thoughts.

"There was a death at the Silver Fox last night. It appears to have been a suicide. Ms. Stewart found the body early this morning. There are no signs to indicate someone broke in, so it is possible that he may have been in the greenhouse at the same time as your son. The man had no identification, and no one matching his description has been reported missing. Any information your son could provide would be helpful at this point."

"Was he, I mean did he, you know-" Arin stammered, unable to properly form the question.

Detective Lyons kindly came to her rescue. "The cause of death was asphyxiation. Apparently, he climbed one of Ms. Stewart's ladders and hung himself from one of the ceiling joists." He paused for a moment, letting the information sink in. "According to Ms. Stewart, your son reported seeing a strange man yesterday. I just need to know if he has any information that would help us identify the victim."

Arin's mind raced. Unable to be still, she jumped off the barstool and began circling the kitchen. Troy had not told her anything about seeing a strange man. What if this man had done something to her boy? That would explain the sudden change in behavior.

"Was this guy some sort of pervert or something? What did he do to Troy?" She was frantically pacing now, her face flushed with rage. "Good thing that he is dead, because I swear if he touched one hair on that boy's head." Jake grabbed her by the shoulders and looked into her wild cinnamon-colored eyes.

"Arin, he's fine. I picked him up myself yesterday and everything was just fine." Arin snorted, and Jake looked away, acknowledging the truth that things had been a little off with Troy since yesterday. Neither of them admitted to this in front of Detective Lyons.

"I'll get him." Arin turned the corner to head up the stairs. She let out a shriek when she almost ran into Troy, who was completely dressed and sitting on the second step, intently listening in on their conversation.

The questioning started innocently enough. Jake and Arin both felt that Detective Lyons was handling their son with kid gloves, so they allowed him some leeway.

"The man didn't want to look at the plants," Troy said matter-of-factly. "I don't think he wanted to be there at all."

"What makes you think that, Troy?" Detective Lyons gently probed.

"He looked at me kind of funny. His eyes were scared or something. And his back-" Troy caught himself just in time. His new friend Jacob had warned him what would happen if he told anyone. His Aunt Rae did not believe him, and on the ride home in the truck, he could tell that his Dad didn't think that his friend was there at all. Jacob had told him not to say anything. Troy feared he had already said too much.

"What about his back, Troy? Take your time and think about it." Detective Lyons leaned in, obviously very interested in what Troy had to say.

"It had a little blood on it, that's all. I didn't talk to the man. I don't know why he murdered himself." Troy's cinnamon eyes filled with tears.

"We're done here," Arin pronounced, scooping her son up and whisking him into the living room, where she settled into their favorite rocking chair. On any normal day, he would curl up on her lap to play one of their ridiculous games. Airplane was Troy's personal favorite. Arin used her hand as an airplane to dive bomb him, going for the most ticklish spots such as his tummy and underarms. Airplane did not seem appropriate right now. Instead, she rocked and snuggled him, humming their special songs "You Are My Sunshine" and "Have I Told You Lately That I Love You?" Troy sniffled and smiled at the lyrics. He clung to Arin for a long time as they just rocked and hummed. Arin tested the waters.

"Was your new friend at the greenhouse?" Troy's eyes betrayed the conflict in his mind. He'd already told Aunt Rae the truth.

"Yeah, he was there," he admitted.

"Did something bad happen to you yesterday, baby?" Arin asked as calmly and rationally as possible. She realized that as she asked, she was squeezing Troy a little too tight, so she loosened up and played with his hair, forcing herself not to push for an answer.

"Something good happened to me, Mommy. I met a new friend who is just like me!" Troy smiled for the first time that morning.

"Is your new friend here right now?" Troy looked around and spied a short hand waving from behind the bathroom door.

"Not too far away," he said, "but I think I will wait until I have a pancake to play." Troy hopped off of her lap and headed for the kitchen. The Detective and Jake were gone, without as much as a goodbye. The detective's card was stuck on the refrigerator, his cell phone number scribbled in pen. Arin nuked a few pancakes for Troy and Cooper. When Troy finished with his breakfast, she sent him to brush his teeth and make his bed. The phone rang. The caller ID told her it was Jake.

"Hi, Hon."

"Hey, sorry I didn't get to say goodbye."

"Yeah, honeymoon is definitely over when you don't get a kiss goodbye. Not to mention cops in your kitchen first thing in the morning."

"Arin, something strange is going on," Jake said, completely serious. Arin longed to dub him Captain Obvious, but bit her tongue instead.

"Lyons told me that there were some markings on the back of the victim. He believes that Troy saw something, but is afraid to talk."

"What does he want us to do? Beat him? Slip some bamboo shoots under his nails? I think he is being honest. He remembers seeing blood on his back. What reason is there to assume there's any more to the story?" Arin felt herself growing increasingly protective of her precious cub. She was not going to let him get pulled into some insane creep's world. Sure, she was sorry the guy had offed himself and all, but her kid had nothing to do with it.

"I'm just saying, Hon, keep an extra close eye on him. If he is going to talk to anyone, it'll be you. I gotta go. Dave's giving me the evil eye. Love you."

The main problem with having a deaf person as a best friend is phone communication, or the lack thereof. Rae's preferred method of communication was her Blackberry, which she wielded skillfully. Arin, on the other hand, detested the Blackberry that DeafMed had provided for her to use to communicate with clients. Although occasionally she could lamely fumble through a message, she would never master the thing as Rae had. Deciding that this crisis was worth the trouble, she busted out the dreaded Blackberry and sent Rae an urgent and highly cryptic message. There were a handful of horticulture students who helped out at the Silver Fox on Fridays and Sundays. With any luck Rae could slip away for a while.

Arin padded silently through the house, peeking in on Troy as he played with cars and watched a video in the playroom, inspecting him carefully for signs of distress. Every once in a while, she would catch him chatting with an empty couch cushion, or offering a matchbox car to an unseen playmate. She knew she was losing it when she half expected the car to be snatched up and propelled across the room.

Arin sank into the old rocker in the corner of the large country kitchen. In an attempt to regain her sanity, she closed her eyes and massaged her temples. Relaxation had finally begun to wash over her when Cooper yelped, and she practically jumped out of her skin. Rae let herself in the front door as usual, tossing her bag on the counter. Rae delivered a much needed hug, communicating unconditional friendship without words. Burying her face in Rae's thick white ponytail, Arin was comforted by her familiar scent of ginger and white tea. When Troy realized Aunt Rae had arrived, he ran in to join the hug. Rae scooped him up and kissed his cheeks, snuggling him tightly for a few moments. When she finally set him down, he asked in perfect sign how she was feeling, and Rae replied that she was fine, thank you. He whirled around to return to his cars, and stopped suddenly, turning.

"Sorry about the man," he signed, and then headed back to his cars and video.

Over coffee, Arin and Rae hashed out the details of what had happened the night before at the greenhouse. Rae had flashed the lights as usual to alert any browsers who might have been out of sight that it was closing time. After performing the same cursory check of all the aisles, she had locked up the same way she did every night and set the alarm. Rae admitted feeling some sort of responsibility. After all, he had used her ladder and rope to do the deed. Of course Arin tried to assuage her friend's guilt, but understood that feelings such as these weren't rational and couldn't simply be argued away. Guilt, false or true, was a monster Arin also struggled with daily, a beast that hung over her head like a foul cloud. Rae explained what Troy had told her yesterday about the man and the boy who followed him. A shiver traveled down Rae's spine as Arin told her about the detective's visit that morning. Although she could not remember exactly what, she was sure that Troy had told her something about the man's back.

After a long pause in conversation, Rae stated that she prayed that the man, whoever he was, was now in heaven, out of whatever misery had driven him to such a brutal end. Under any other circumstances, Arin would have rolled her eyes at such a comment, but she was surprised to find herself nodding in agreement. At that point, Rae continued on and got a little too preachy for Arin's comfort. "We are all going to meet God one day," she warned, "to be judged or welcomed as his child." Bluntly, she asked Arin if she was through running from God.

"I am not running from anyone," Arin signed, standing abruptly and snatching the empty coffee cups. She busied herself with loading the dishwasher, knowing in her heart that was far from the truth.

***

"Vroom, vroom," Troy boomed, pretending that his red race car was the fastest one in the whole world. He pushed the car in circles around Jacob, who sat in the middle of the floor, his eyes fixed on the women in the kitchen.

"Don't you want to play cars anymore?" Troy asked, disappointed.

"They are talking about him," Jacob said in his deep, scratchy voice. His eyes turned dark, as he glared at Arin and Rae. Troy knew without asking that Jacob was talking about the man in the greenhouse.

"Why did he hurt himself?" Troy asked, nervously pushing his car back and forth across the carpet.

"He wanted to start his new life," Jacob answered.

"But he looked scared, and you pushed him with that stick. I saw you."

"He needed a little help, and I used the stick to help him, that's all," Jacob explained carefully. "Like when you help your Daddy work on the car. He uses tools, right?"

"Wrenches and a funnel," Troy responded proudly. "How did you know?" Troy's face remained a mask of confusion until a thought struck him. "Are you an angel?"

"I am," Jacob answered. "That's why you can't tell the grown-ups about me. They wouldn't understand. I'm your special angel, that's why I look just like you. Do you believe me?"

Troy nodded vigorously, hanging on every word.

***

Arin blindly stumbled through the blackness. Her hands protectively cradled her swollen belly. Desperately, she cried out for help, but only a pathetic croak managed to escape from her parched lips. She risked a glance over her shoulder and was gripped with panic. He was practically on top of her, his eyes sadistic and pitiless. He snorted and shrieked with the excitement of the chase. When he grew tired of the game, he pounced and together they tumbled forward. Arin drew herself tightly into a ball, protecting her hugely rounded belly. He raised the scalpel he held in his hands, already slick with blood, and plunged...

***

Arin bolted upright, her nightgown soaking wet and her heart drumming manically against her chest. Gasping, she swung her legs off the bed. She hung her head between her knees and willed her lungs to cooperate. Cooper put his head on her knee in an effort to comfort her, his eyes sad and sympathetic. That was more than she could say for Jake, who was doing quite a convincing impersonation of a log. When Arin regained control over her breathing, she quietly slipped out of her sweat soaked nightgown into an old Grateful Dead t-shirt and flannel pants. Remnants of the familiar dream still flashed before her eyes, raising gooseflesh on her forearms. She glanced at the clock on the nightstand. It screamed two forty-five in angry red.

The Intrusion

In an effort to trick her racing brain into sleeping again, Arin lay perfectly still, pacing her breathing with Jake's, hoping her mind would follow along. Apparently, she was too smart for herself, and she lay there motionless for what seemed like hours. For lack of anything better to do at three in the morning, she decided to keep up the charade. Just as her restless mind was about to throw in the towel, a faint noise snatched her back from near sleep. She sat up, and leaned in toward the door. There it was again, Troy's small sweet voice.

Arin loved hearing her little boy talk in his sleep, something he used to do nearly every night when he was a toddler. A smile tugged at her lips. Her mind traveled back to the times she and Jake used to make popcorn and sit next to the baby monitor, listening to Troy's sleepy babbling. Arin remembered sitting, pen in hand, recording his adorable phrases such as, "Bye-bye duck", or "Whatcha doin' moon?" Slipping out of bed, she padded across the room. For a moment, she considered waking Jake to spy with her, but decided against it, afraid that she would miss the moment altogether.

Soundlessly, she slinked across the hall, pausing at Troy's door. She strained to discern what he was mumbling, but his words were muffled through the closed door. Arin turned the knob and the door creaked open. She tip-toed into the room. It took a moment for her eyes to adjust to the darkness. Troy was lying on his side, eyes closed, with a troubled look on his sweet face. Concerned, Arin started toward the bed, intending to lie with him for a while in case he needed her. It was then that she noticed the intruder and stopped cold.

Sitting upright on the bed next to Troy was a boy, an exact duplicate of her son, except for the eyes. The eyes of this creature were entirely vile and black, with no light in them at all. It was obscene that such wicked eyes could look out from Troy's innocent face. The creature appeared stunned when Arin's eyes locked with his. She gasped in horror, afraid for Troy. The intruder's shocked expression quickly melted into one of revulsion. He lifted a small hand and began to gently stroke Troy's precious sleeping head. It was as if it was claiming ownership over him. Its wretched face scorned her son's innocence with evil its own intention. Troy began to whimper under the caress of this evil beast. Too petrified to move, Arin opened her mouth and a high-pitched scream shattered the silence. She continued the scream until her breath was spent.

Arin's scream ushered panic and confusion into the room. Cooper bounded in, snarling and barking uncharacteristically at the head of Troy's bed. Troy jolted awake, and began to bawl. Arin stood over him, lips trembling and face chalky, dumbly pointing to the empty space the specter had been just a moment ago. Jake burst through the doorway, clutching the Louisville slugger, which he kept under the bed. He was more than ready to protect his family, but from whom, or what? Blinking the sleep from his eyes, Jake wildly scanned the room, bewildered to say the least. He stood frozen between Arin and Troy, unsure which one needed his comfort and protection first.

"Did you see him, Mommy?" Troy asked through his tears, his voice trembling. Arin dropped to her knees by his bed, searching her son's eyes.

"Who is he, Troy?" she rasped. Troy stared at her for a long moment.

"Jacob," he whispered, almost inaudibly. That one word hit Arin with the force of a tidal wave. Instantly, she stood and stumbled backwards. Her eyes rolled back as she fell, smacking her head on the edge of Troy's antique dresser. Stunned and shell-shocked, Troy and Jake watched helplessly as a river of scarlet snaked through Arin's light brown hair.

Jake sprang to life and snatched her up. Adrenalin took over as he descended the stairs, two at a time, with Arin tucked in the safety of his arms. He flipped the kitchen light on, and laid her gently on the floor, examining the wound on her scalp. Relief flooded over him when he realized that her wound appeared to be superficial. He knew that even a minor head injury was likely to bleed excessively. Grabbing a clean cloth, he applied pressure, softly calling her name as she came to.

Troy stood at the bottom of the stairs, weeping uncontrollably. When Jake motioned for him to come over and be with his mother, he shook his head adamantly.

"I'm sorry, Mommy," was all he could manage to say through his heavy sobs.

A normal Saturday morning at the Welsh home was typically quite an event, or a non-event, you could say. It was the only day of the week that no one had to rush off to work or church. Jake and Troy thoroughly enjoyed their time together. It was an unwritten rule that everyone remained in their pajamas until at least noon, and ate whatever they wanted, whenever they wanted. Often Jake and Troy would devour brightly colored cereal while watching cartoons, sipping the leftover pink sugary milk directly from the bowls. Arin always enjoyed peeking in on them spending time together, even if they were just dribbling milk down the fronts of their pajamas.

Right now, Arin would have given anything in the world for that kind of Saturday. The throbbing in her head had dulled to a somewhat tolerable thud; fortunately the wound was not visible once the blood was gently rinsed from her hair. The carefree spirit of Saturday morning was replaced by an awkward, almost palpable tension. Troy watched cartoons alone. In the kitchen, Jake and Arin sat across from each other, obviously at odds. It hurt that he did not believe her. He pointed out that if the tables were turned, Arin would be the first to call him a complete nut. Silently, she agreed with him, but her pride would not allow her to openly admit it.

"Strange things can happen when you hit your head, Hon." Jake hesitantly explored this feeble line of reasoning for the tenth time. Arin's grip on her coffee cup tightened until she feared she would break it. Gently, she set it down while it was still intact and looked Jake dead in the eye.

"I saw him before I hit my head, Jake. And since when have you known me to make up crazy stories? When? Name one time?" She knew he couldn't.

"Maybe you were still asleep, and it was just a continuation of your nightmare. Did you think of that?" Jake raised the possibility, desperately seeking some explanation other than the one his wife had offered.

"I think I would know if I was awake or not, Jake."

"Arin," Jake spoke hesitantly, his spoon vigorously swirling his coffee, "there was that time when you were pregnant that you, you know, went through that really bad stretch. Maybe this can all be explained by some kind of hormonal imbalance, like the doctors told you back then. Don't you think that's possible?"

Arin physically recoiled and flashed him a fierce look, communicating in no uncertain terms that he had stepped on thin ice and fallen clean through. The several weeks before Troy was born had been an extremely dark and confusing time for Arin. She'd never shared the basis for her deep depression with Jake. Almost nightly she had suffered from terrible nightmares. Trapped in the prison of sleep, she would howl and scream hysterically. Jake had to shake her awake, and then gently rock her back to sleep. He begged Arin to confide in him about what was plaguing her, but she flatly refused to offer any explanation. Jake had longed for the ability to somehow peer into her soul, to grab hold of whatever or whoever dared cause her such anguish, and to rip them to shreds.

"I'm sorry," Jake fumbled his words like a greased football. "I shouldn't have brought it up."

Unwilling to even entertain the thought of having this long overdue conversation with her husband, Arin instead jumped up and snatched her jacket and purse. She'd always found that the most effective way to avoid conflict was simply to run away, and that was what she intended to do.

"I need to get out of here for a while. Don't let Troy out of your sight, not for one minute," she ordered before she sped away, leaving the echo of the slamming door in her wake.

Jake sat like a stone staring at the door. "Who is Jacob?" he finally asked Cooper, who eyed him sympathetically, cocked his head and offered Jake a paw instead of an explanation. Jake accepted the paw, and absentmindedly scratched Cooper's velvety ears. After a much deserved extended petting session, Jake washed the slightly unpleasant odor of Cooper from his hands and joined Troy in the playroom to watch cartoons. Try as he might, he could not shake the eerie sensation that they were not alone.

***

A torrent of expletives poured from Arin's mouth as she drove. Violently, she banged the Explorer's steering wheel, her foot pure lead on the accelerator. The SUV skidded around a sharp curve, missing the guardrail by mere inches. Rage that had long been simmering just below the surface finally boiled over. Arin needed to direct the flow to someone or something. She ranted and raved at passing motorists, gesturing wildly. A squirrel crossed her path and she actually sped up in an attempt to hit it, missing the fortunate rodent by a fraction of an inch. She cursed her mother for choosing the bottle over her, cursed her father for dying, and cursed Jake for calling her a liar and most of all, for bringing up that horrible time. A feral scream escaped her lips and she punched the wheel again. This time she yelped as her hand exploded in pain. Fat tears began to flow down her flushed cheeks. Her rage spent, it was replaced with powerful guilt and self-loathing. Kevin Driver's sadistic taunts from her childhood echoed in her brain. "You're ugly, Arin. I am doing you a favor by having anything do with you. Stop looking around for someone to save you. No one cares. No one is coming."

Why had she treated Jake so poorly? He had faithfully stood by her through thick and thin since the day they met. Suddenly, she was struck with the fear that he would grab Troy and leave her. She pictured him even now, snapping his suitcase shut and loading his truck, muttering under his breath as he did when he was livid that he was finally washing his hands of her. She would be totally alone. No one would care. No one would rush to save her. The evil prophesies Kevin Driver had spoken into her life would be fulfilled.

Then it was as if she entered the eye of the storm raging in her head. She experienced a strange sense of calm resolution. She knew what she must do. In her mind's eye, she could literally see herself driving the Explorer full speed ahead into the bridge abutment several hundred yards away. Blinking rapidly, she made an effort to resist the urge, to reject the vision. Unfamiliar voices mercilessly mocked, taunted and accused her at the same time. Jake and Troy would certainly be better off without her. After all, she was a horrible excuse for a wife and mother. She didn't deserve them. Impact with that bridge abutment was the greatest gift she could give them. Persuaded by the voices, she pressed the pedal until it hit the floor. Approaching traffic was forced to swerve wildly to avoid striking her. Bracing for impact, she squeezed her eyes shut and concentrated on a mental image of her beautiful family one last time. Ultimately, it was her love for them that prompted her to cry out for intervention from the depths of her soul. A barely audible request escaped her lips through clenched teeth.

"Help."

Unbeknownst to Arin, her desperate and broken utterance had been heard loud and clear by her Maker. The cab of the SUV had been packed to the gills with an unseen swirling frenzy, minions of the evil one. Gluttonously, they reveled in Arin's imminent demise, which they would have considered their ultimate victory. All it took was one holy moment and they were vanquished. They were replaced by mighty protectors, underlings of the Perfect One.

Arin's body was stiff and breathless as she anticipated impact. After several seconds of silent limbo, she allowed one eye to peek and was startled to find herself confronted with a wall of smooth grey concrete directly outside of the driver's side window. It was a miracle, which was the only possible explanation. Somehow, the Explorer had managed to land perfectly horizontal to the very wall that would have meant her death. There was only a half-inch gap between her driver's side mirror and the cement, if that. The realization of what she had almost done settled heavily on her chest, making it difficult to breathe. Knowing full well the anguish of growing up without a mother, it horrified her that she had almost ensured the same for her son. Arin shivered, wondering where she would be right now if she had succeeded in ending her life. Her thoughts and opinions concerning the afterlife were hazy to say the least, but the one thing she was sure of was that she was nowhere near ready to cross over.

Carefully, she considered the possibility that she might be going insane. Within twelve hours, she had seen her son's evil invisible friend and had come as close to offing herself as a person could. Yet here she was in one piece. She flipped the sun visor down and scanned her face in the mirror for any sign of lunacy, trying to be objective. After she studied her reflection at length, she decided to reject the insanity defense. She was forced to admit that she was as sane as she was on any given day and just plain terrified.

It took another minor miracle for Arin to maneuver the Explorer back onto the road without scraping the side on the cement. Apparently, today was her day to be the recipient of miracles, great and small. Her right hand still throbbed as she tightly gripped the wheel in an attempt to control the trembling which coursed through her entire body. Right now, she needed somewhere to think without being at the helm of a one-ton projectile that seemed hell bent on causing catastrophic damage.

***

Lights flashed in every corner of the greenhouse, announcing Arin's arrival. Arin waved across the room to Rae, who was assisting a well-dressed couple in the specialty fountain area. The man was scribbling his question or comment in the notebook Rae carried in her back pocket to communicate with the customers. Her eyes met Arin's and rolled, ever so slightly, indicating that the couple was less than cordial. Rae was used to dealing with these types. They migrated from the city because The Silver Fox boasted the most extensive fountain and Koi pond collection for hundreds of miles. Keeping Koi and creating exotic indoor ponds was a growing trend among D.C. businessman. Rae enjoyed creating the custom fountains as much as she relished the cash, but found the clients arrogant and at times downright obnoxious. Obviously, these self-important executives were used to being catered to. From across the room Arin signed that she needed some alone time, Rae waved her on to the oasis.

Norton, Rae's neurotic African Grey, greeted Arin as she ascended the mosaic steps to the heart of the gazebo.

"Whatcha doin', Cutie?" he asked in the voice of some female customer long gone, his bird head cocked in such a way that seemed to imply that he was waiting for an answer. Norton was quite the character. He could hear a voice just once and perfectly impersonate it. This was not something that one could force or even coax him to do. Norton alone chose whom he would mimic. Arin collapsed into one of the Adirondack chairs facing the back of the greenhouse and concentrated on breathing deeply. A smile tugged at the corners of her mouth. She recalled the time she had explained to Troy that the atmosphere was better here, because all of the plants worked so hard to make fresh air. Troy, who took all things literally, went plant to plant, thanking each one personally. The green tranquility around Arin permeated her troubled spirit. She tried to visualize the water flowing through the fountains, snatching her worries, and transporting them to the crest of the fountain before plunging them into the shallow pond, drowning them.

A half an hour or so later, she sat on the edge of the chair feeling strangely serene and unruffled, considering her day so far. She contemplated whether or not she was sane enough to return to her family. After lengthy self-evaluation, she issued herself a clean bill of mental health. At last she stood and stretched for a long moment. Rae's worn leather Bible on the floor of the gazebo caught her eye, a newspaper underneath. A bold headline grabbed her: "Greenhouse Suicide Victim Identified." She sat back down with a thud, the serenity draining from her pores. Snatching the paper from under the Bible, she unfolded it crisply. Unprepared, Arin found herself face to face with the supposed "Suicide Victim".

Struck silent with shock, Arin saw in malevolent detail the features she already knew entirely too well. Without even realizing it, she had memorized his face over the years, seeing him in perfect clarity when she obsessively replayed their disastrous meeting. Arin despised this man, and there was not an ounce of pity for him in her heart. *Good*, she thought. *I am glad he is dead. He deserves to be dead. Rotting in hell, in fact.* Since she left the cult, Arin rarely danced. It occurred to her that a little waltz on the fresh earth of this man's grave might be fun and even therapeutic. Under normal circumstances, Arin would have categorized herself as a compassionate sort, but the thoughts that currently invaded her mind certainly did not reflect it.

Still, the questions remained and reverberated through the corners of her mind. Why had he chosen to end his crummy life in this greenhouse of all places? Why had he appeared to her son, apparently bequeathing to him whatever creepy ghoul he had chosen to keep company with? Panic clutched her and she was overwhelmed by terror for her son. Tossing the paper, she sprinted out of the Silver Fox and blew past Rae without bothering to offer an explanation. She hopped into her Explorer and took off, gravel flying in her wake. The newsprint photo of Geoffrey Raines, M.D., smiling smugly for the camera, settled on the gazebo floor.

"Jacob, I am ready!" Norton called out in a distinctive voice, a voice that Arin would have instantly recognized as belonging to Dr. Geoffrey Raines.

Ben Wesley was ready to bite into a delectable roast beef sandwich when the loud and rather persistent pounding on his front door started. He paused, sandwich in midair, willing whoever it was to give up. No such luck. Instead his visitor discovered the doorbell and rang it frantically. Taylor shot him a look, communicating in her wordless way that yes, he did have to answer that. Ben lovingly set his sandwich down, promising it that he would return as soon as he dispensed of the Jehovah's Witness, Mormon, or fundraising child at their door.

Without bothering to check the peephole, he turned the knob. The door flew open and a frazzled woman spilled into his foyer. She insisted that she needed to confess to him and wouldn't take no for an answer. Recovering from his near fall, he eyed the woman and recognized her as the interpreter for the second Sunday service. Ben was more than a little embarrassed that he couldn't recall her name. For him, one of the most difficult parts of being the pastor of a growing church was matching names to faces.

"Of course, we can talk. I want to help in any way I can, Ms...."

"Welsh. Arin Welsh." Arin stuck out her hand awkwardly. They must think she was foolish and horribly rude. She noticed Pastor Wesley's wife at the kitchen table eating lunch, an untouched sandwich across from her.

"I've interrupted. I'm so sorry. I can just wait right here." Arin plopped on the wooden steps that led to the second floor, shooing Pastor Wesley to the kitchen to finish—or rather to start—his lunch.

"Nonsense," Taylor Wesley spoke up. "You will sit right here and have lunch with us."

Arin sensed that this was an order, not an invitation. Obediently, she slid into the chair that Taylor indicated. Her stomach reminded her that she had not eaten yet. Salivating and grateful, she watched as Taylor threw together another roast beef sandwich.

"Mayo?"

"Yes, please. I really didn't come here to eat. I just..." It occurred to her that they might believe she was nuts. They may even fire her from the Sunday interpreting job. Arin had come to rely on that income. Maybe this was a bad idea. Why, of all places, had she come here anyway? Taylor placed a scrumptious sandwich in front of her and Arin tried to restrain herself from hogging it down in huge bites. Instead, she hogged it down with smaller bites, finishing it off in no time. Content with her belly full, Arin was free to take notice of Taylor's slow deliberate bites. Instantly, she related.

"How far along are you now?"

"Almost six months." Taylor gave a wry smile. "But the nausea will suddenly go away after three months, right?"

Arin rolled her eyes and slapped the table, causing Taylor and Ben to jump.

"How many people have tried to shove Saltines on you?"

"Let's not go there," Pastor Wesley interjected. Apparently, Taylor appreciated this so-called remedy as much as Arin had. They enjoyed a moment of light-hearted laughter as Taylor and Ben concentrated on their sandwiches. Unlike Arin, they were taking time to chew. When Ben was finished, he set his plate in the sink and washed up.

"Would you like to chat in my office?" he asked softly, shifting into pastor mode.

"Sure," Arin answered. She followed him out of the kitchen, glancing back at Taylor, who was still tentatively eyeing her plate.

"It will get better. Hang in there. Thanks for lunch."

Taylor nodded appreciatively, inviting her to come anytime. Just leave the prescription for Saltines at home.

Pastor Wesley's office was not quite what she would have expected for an up and coming pastor. The walls were not lined with leather bound theological texts. The desk was not the mahogany giant she would have pictured him sitting at, fervently pounding out his sermons week after week. The room was actually in quite a state of disarray. Boxes were overflowing with documents. Books and office supplies were everywhere. The desk, old and small, was made of cheap particle board and the laminate was peeling from the corners. The ancient chair behind the desk protested loudly as he sat and squeaked with every movement he made. There were two chairs facing the shoddy desk. Arin chose the one that looked most likely to hold her.

"Sorry the office is such a disaster. It's in the process of being converted to a nursery," he explained. "The church keeps trying to allot me funds to replace my desk, but this dinosaur has been with me all through high school and college. Now it's sort of like an old friend." Arin nodded politely, knowing that if she were his wife, that desk would be in the trash heap, friend or no friend.

"You said you needed to confess. You do understand that we are not Catholic?"

"Protestant, Catholic, Moonie, whatever. The important thing is that you can't tell anyone anything about what I say to you, correct?" Arin looked him in the eye, searching for any hint of insincerity.

"Of course, I would never divulge anything you would choose to share with me in confidence. But I have to tell you that the difference between Protestants and Moonies is-"

"With all due respect," Arin snipped, "I didn't come here for a theology lesson. I used to be in a cult and I was thoroughly indoctrinated once, and I don't plan on falling for religious nonsense ever again." She cringed a bit at the bite of her words. Pastor Wesley didn't even flinch. He simply nodded.

"Fair enough," he said. "What is it that you feel you need to confess to me?"

At first Arin stumbled with her words, unsure of where to start and what to leave out. Finally, the words came and she unloaded most of the bag. She told him about the man Troy had seen in the greenhouse, who later committed suicide, and about Troy's invisible friend. Hesitantly, she described the scene last night in Troy's bedroom. Pastor Wesley listened to every word. He appeared absolutely riveted. Arin didn't detect any signs that he did not believe her, or that he thought she was insane, so she continued with her account. Still in shock, she explained the miracle of how she ended up perfectly horizontal with a concrete wall, instead of halfway through it and six feet under. Pastor Wesley closed his eyes briefly.

"Praise God. Thank you," he uttered.

Normally, this sort of thing would have made Arin very uncomfortable, but this time she glanced upward and lamely tacked on a, "Yeah, thanks," to his prayer. Concluding her story, Arin explained that the man who had committed suicide in the greenhouse was someone from her past, and she feared that he had targeted her son.

"What I really need is some sort of protection for my son," Arin explained desperately. "You guys do that sort of thing, right?"

"What kind of thing were you expecting?" Pastor Wesley asked, his face a mask of confusion.

"I don't know. Come over with some holy water, light a candle, baptize him or something. Isn't it your job to know what to do?" Again, her words were sharp, but the young pastor seemed unaffected. He sat rubbing his beard, eyeing her quizzically. It appeared that he was debating what to do about her. At last he spoke in a gentle tone.

"Arin, do you know the Lord?"

"Oh, lordy!" Arin replied irreverently, hoping to discourage him from this line of conversation.

"Have you even considered why God opened your eyes and allowed you a glimpse into the spirit realm, even if for just a brief second? Don't you agree that He could be trying to show you something?"

"Well, if that's what He wants to show me, I would just as soon not."

"May I show you some Scriptures?" he asked, reaching for his worn Bible without giving her a chance to weasel out of it. She decided to comply. After all, they had fed her and she'd just talked his ear off for the last forty-five minutes.

Efficiently, he flipped through his Bible, carefully choosing which verses to share. He sensed that Arin was only going to sit through so much, so he had better make it good. Already, she was jiggling her foot and drumming her fingers on the desk. She steeled herself against the barrage of "thou shalt nots" she knew were coming her way.

"Do you realize that you are in the middle of a spiritual battle, without any of the weapons you need to fight your enemy?"

"I don't have any enemies," Arin replied incredulously. She had not done any harm great enough to anyone to warrant full-fledged enemies.

"I am talking about the enemy of your soul. God's Word is very clear about this. No one is neutral. You are either for God, or you are against Him. Satan and his demons are going to do everything they can do to blind you to the fact that without Christ, you are dead in your sins. In the second chapter of the book of Ephesians, Paul is speaking to Christians when he says, 'Once you were dead, doomed forever because of your many sins. You used to live just like the rest of the world, full of sin, obeying Satan, the mighty prince of the power of the air. He is the spirit at work in the hearts of those who refuse to obey God. All of us used to live this way, following the passions and desires of our own evil nature. We were born with an evil nature, and were under God's wrath just like everyone else.'"

Pastor Wesley glanced up to make sure Arin was still with him. She was physically there, but had an openly defiant look on her face. He said a silent prayer for the right words and continued.

"Arin, these verses are clear. Think about your experience last night in your son's bedroom. The spirit you described to me could only come from the pit of hell. Think about what happened today. Satan is the father of lies, and the author of confusion. Praise God for intervening on your behalf."

Arin shifted uncomfortably. She was willing to concede that something supernatural had both driven her to the brink of disaster, and delivered her from it. She was not willing to accept this Jesus stuff.

"Let me continue in Ephesians," Pastor Wesley said urgently, fearing he was rapidly losing his audience. "Despite everything in the last few verses about our hearts refusing to obey God, and being dead in our sins, it says that God is so rich in mercy, and He loved us so very much, that even while we were dead because of our sins, He gave us life when he raised Christ from the dead. It is only by God's special favor that we can be saved. Arin, we are spiritual creatures made in the image of God himself. Our bodies are going to die and return to the earth, but our souls are eternal. We all have eternal life. The only question is where we will spend it."

Arin sighed deeply. "Look Pastor, I know it is your job, but I did not come here to be converted or for a Sunday School lesson. I just want these ghosts or whatever they are to leave my family alone."

"Demons, Arin. They are demons."

"Okay, whatever. You said something about spiritual warfare?"

"Yes, later in Ephesians, Paul writes about doing battle with the Devil. He says that we need to put on the full armor of God so that we will be able to stand firm against all strategies and tricks of the devil. We are not fighting against people made of flesh and blood, but against the evil rulers and authorities of the unseen world, and against wicked spirits in the heavenly realms."

"Sheesh," Arin uttered. "That doesn't sound good. What is the armor he is talking about? Holy water and crucifixes and stuff?"

Pastor Wesley chuckled for a moment, and quickly stopped when Arin shot him a withering look. Apparently, she had not been joking. It occurred to him that when she interpreted his sermons, his words must go in one ear and out of her hands without ever engaging her brain.

"Actually, Paul describes the armor of God in great detail. There are six things we need in order to have victory over Satan. First is the truth, which can defeat Satan's lies. Second is righteousness, which is really the righteousness of Jesus through his spirit in us. We need to be ready to share what Jesus has done for us, and what he can and will do for others. We need to have faith in God, to have assurance of our salvation. Lastly, we need the sword of the spirit, or the Word of God." He paused, willing his words to find some fertile soil to settle in. "You can have all of these things today if you will only say yes to Christ. He alone can protect you."

Arin felt like she was being pulled in several different directions. What he said made sense. She sure did not need much convincing that she was a sinner. She knew that if the good and bad of her heart were set on the scales, she would be found lacking. Something in her desperately desired to just open up, to embrace it. Another part of her mocked the message that had been presented, and cursed the exclusivity of Jesus. How could only one religion be right? How can there only be one way to God? It seemed so unfair.

"Arin, the Scriptures also say, 'Today is the day of your salvation. Do not harden your heart to this message.' You may think you will consider it, but I promise you, as soon as you walk out the door, your mind will be flooded with worldly things, crowding His message out." He was pleading with her now, his eyes brimming with compassion. "Do you need a Bible?" he asked.

She assured him that she already had a few on the shelf gathering dust, but thanks anyway. Arin's heart was touched to see how genuinely he cared about her and her family, but she stubbornly refused to commit to a God who had given her such a luckless lot in life. Every time she saw a boy Troy's age spending time with his grandpa, she railed against the idea of a loving God, wondering why her father was taken before she ever had a chance to know if he was even worth having. She hated shopping at the mall because she was always faced with women her age shopping with their mothers. Her mother had never even fought for her, yet she made sure that she would never belong to an actual family by refusing to sign away her parental rights and release her for adoption. If

God loved her so much, how could he have allowed Kevin Driver to trap her like a scared rabbit day after day, using her as an outlet for his anger as well as his sexual plaything? A supposed God who would allow things like this to happen could not be trusted, and she would not bend to his will. Not today, and maybe not ever.

"I'm going to give it some thought. I will," Arin lied. Her mind was already made up. "Right now I need to go. My husband probably thinks I left the country, and I've taken up way too much of your time." As Arin rose to leave, she noticed a newspaper on the desk. "Do you mind if I look at that a minute?" she asked.

"Take it. I'm finished." Pastor Wesley handed her the paper. He seemed reluctant for her to go. "Call me anytime, day or night. Taylor and I will be praying for you."

Arin thanked him and turned to go. She felt bad for the young pastor. He looked forlorn as she left. Apparently, he held himself personally responsible for Arin's rebellious soul. He meant well and was likeable enough, but Arin was just not going to allow herself to be gullible and cave into some rigid spiritual philosophy. She was almost to her car when Ben called her name from the doorway.

"This doctor. How did you say you know him?" he asked, still trying to fit the puzzle pieces together.

"I didn't say. It's a long story," she replied with a wave of her hand, and escaped into the Explorer, grateful to have dodged that bullet. After a moment of scanning the paper, she found Dr. Raines' obituary, noting that the funeral was scheduled for the following evening.

A rin returned to a vacant house. Not even Cooper rushed to greet her. She tossed the newspaper and keys on the counter and her heart sunk when she noticed the note. The earlier image of Jake packing his suitcase and leaving flashed through her mind. She snatched the paper and promptly sat, preparing herself for the worst. After scanning Jake's slanted script the third time, she still could not make sense of it.

Took Cooper to Dr. Brummel. Where are you?

Cooper hadn't seemed sick this morning and wasn't due for shots until August. Arin got up and walked across the kitchen to the phone. With any luck, Jake had the cell on and she could reach him for some sort of clarification. She absentmindedly reached for the receiver mounted on the wall as her gaze shifted into the playroom adjacent to the kitchen. The white walls in the far corner of the playroom were covered with dark red streaks, and pools of crimson coated the carpet underneath. Blood spatter sprinkled the toy cars and dinosaurs that were strewn throughout the room. When the metallic scent of blood finally hit her nostrils, it sent her into full panic mode. After four attempts, she was finally able to dial Jake's cell phone correctly. Her heart leapt when he picked up on the first ring.

"Where have you been?" he demanded, his tone cold and accusatory.

"What happened in the playroom?" Arin demanded, answering his question with one of her own. She could hear Jake telling Troy to stay put. He came back on the line, this time hushed, his voice breaking.

"Troy tried to kill Cooper."

"What?" Jake had to be yanking her chain. "Why would he do such a thing? He loves Cooper!"

"Troy may love Cooper, but apparently Jacob isn't a big fan."

Arin was speechless. Her mind was working overtime to comprehend Jake's strange words.

After a long silent stretch, Jake continued. "I was upstairs changing when I heard Cooper growling. By the time I made it to the playroom, Troy had already stabbed Cooper several times with one of the steak knives." Jake hesitated, his voice tight with emotion. Cooper was more than a dog. Before they conceived, they suspected that he would be the only baby they'd ever hope to have. True, they lavished him with love and affection, but what they received in return was far greater. He was a member of the Welsh family and was fiercely loved. "He didn't even snap at Troy. He was backed into the corner, and Troy just kept knifing him. He cried and took it without trying to defend himself." Emotions overcame Jake and he was unable to continue.

"Is he going to be okay?" Arin's nails bit into the flesh of her palms and she held her breath anticipating his reply.

"Probably not. He's injured pretty bad, Arin. Dr. Brummel's working on him now."

Arin's hand went to her mouth. It was not possible for her to comprehend what had taken place in the blood spattered playroom.

"How could this happen? How could Troy do something like this?"

"He didn't do it." Jake's tone had morphed from vulnerable to sarcastic. "Jacob did." Again, the very mention of that name stunned Arin into silence. "Maybe someday soon you can clue me in Arin, because right now I feel like I don't know what the heck is going on. Quite frankly, I'm sick and tired of the secrets." There was a long laundry list of things Jake longed to tack on, questions he wanted to ask. He stopped short, however, when his conscience reminded him that he was harboring a secret or two of his own.

A vice grip on the wheel and jaw clamped tight, Arin drove like an absolute maniac. All things considered, she could hardly believe her fortune to have avoided a major traffic violation or collision so far today. Her entire life seemed to be falling apart in huge chunks all around her. She desperately desired something solid to cling to. Overnight, it seemed that her husband had grown resentful and cold. No doubt he probably would blame her for Troy's actions. One way or another, she felt she was responsible. After all, she was his mother. It was her job to have her finger soundly on the pulse of his little life, to weed out evil when it sprouted up with the potential to harm him. The image of Jacob stroking Troy's sleeping head haunted her. Now she realized that he had been challenging her. This spirit, demon, whatever he was, intended to steal Troy away from her. He'd better get geared up for a fight, Arin snickered, because she was not about to let her son go. Not ever. She tried to replay her conversation with Pastor Wesley, but oddly the more she tried, the cloudier her recollection became.

Spiritual warfare. That's what he'd called it. He'd said to fight the enemy, she needed the truth. But the truth about what? She pictured herself making a cross with her fingers and yelling "TRUTH!" which would not quite be effective. He'd said something about sharing Jesus, which was not an option for her. Thanks, but no thanks. Somehow, she did not think this Jacob character would be interested in converting. Then there was righteousness. A quick review of her history would instantly rule that one out. She had to admit, she was not one hundred percent sure what it even meant to be a righteous person. Next, there was faith. But faith in what? The last thing Pastor Wesley had mentioned was the sword of the spirit. At least this involved a weapon. Arin could use a weapon or two to smear this ghost, or demon, whatever it was.

She parked next to Jake's truck and jumped out of the Explorer almost before it had come to a complete stop. The vet's office was locked, and Arin pounded fitfully on the glass door. An older lady in modest Mennonite attire appeared and ushered her in. Arin apologized for intruding on their day off. They exchanged rushed niceties and the woman insisted that it was no trouble at all. Arin's stomach twisted in a thousand knots as she trailed the woman down the hall, which was scented with wet dog and disinfectant. When she turned the corner and laid eyes on Cooper, her heart sank. There he was, stretched out on a stainless steel exam table, white gauze covering most of his midsection. The snow white bandages were spotted with crimson where blood had seeped through. Troy perched next to him on the table. Cooper's head limply rested in his lap. Jake sat on a stool, his back to Arin. His shoulders shook as he wept soundlessly.

The vet emerged from a back room and noticed Arin. He pulled her aside to an exam room, gently shutting the door behind him. Dr. Brummel was a hardworking and highly ethical Mennonite man who specialized in large animals. After years of treating the cats and dogs of local cattle farmers, he begrudgingly agreed to devote two office days a week to caring for small animals. Even he had to admit that the change was refreshing. Most people didn't share the same emotional connection with their cows as they did their dogs. It felt good when he was able to rescue the family pet. Today, however, Dr. Brummel was not feeling so good.

"It doesn't look good for the old boy, Mrs. Welsh."

"What can we do?" Arin would be willing to take out a second mortgage or sell a kidney to save Cooper at this point. She knew that his death was inevitable, but not like this.

"He'd lost quite a bit of blood by the time he got here. We tried a transfusion and thought that he was improving until I explored his wounds. His intestine is badly punctured and there is some damage to his spinal cord." He shook his head solemnly. "The most humane thing would be to put him down. I'm so sorry."

"That's our only option?"

"I am afraid so." Dr. Brummel wrung his hands and cleared his throat, obviously uncomfortable. "Mrs. Welsh, I am required to report all incidents of animal cruelty."

Arin groaned, her eyes pleading for him to make an exception.

"I hate to do it. I've treated Cooper for years. Heck, we live right down the street from you guys. I see you out on wagon rides all the time. I feel confident that there was no long term abuse, but something must have triggered Troy to do this."

Arin was unsure how to respond, and decided on a simple plea. "Dr. Brummel, please don't report this. Our family has been going through a rough time. I don't know how much more we can take." Her eyes welled with tears and her voice wavered. "Troy has never been violent. Something must have scared him. I promise we will find him a therapist right away. We will do whatever it takes to get him help." Her words trailed off. Try as she might to convince him, she knew her defense was flimsy at best. Her son had stabbed their dog. Not once, but repeatedly. How could she possibly defend that? Blame it on a renegade demon? For a moment she considered that argument, but decided that the-devil-made-him-do-it defense only had the potential to make things worse. She threw up her hands and implored him with her eyes, her family completely at his mercy.

Dr. Brummell was clearly conflicted. He knew that he should report this incident, but he also knew the Welsh family reasonably well. Jake worked on his wife's car, and always did a great job for a very reasonable rate. It was obvious that the animal had never been neglected or abandoned, as was usually the case with animal cruelty incidents. It chilled him to his core that the same little boy in the other room, gently stroking the dying boxer's head, had repetitively stabbed him just hours earlier. If not for the bloody pajamas, they all would have been happy to deny what happened and blame it on some anonymous dog-stabbing stranger.

"Go, say good-bye," Dr. Brummel urged. "I'm not going to make the call. Just promise me you'll get your boy some help." Arin nodded thankfully, gave him a quick hug, and started toward her family on legs of jelly.

Tentatively, Arin placed her hand on Jake's back. He turned to face her, tears streaming down his cheeks and settling in his beard. Arin sat on the stool next to him and buried her face in his neck. "I am so sorry, Jake. So sorry…"

"Mommy, Cooper doesn't feel good." Troy's small voice was sad, but there was nothing to indicate that he accepted any sort of responsibility for the state Cooper was in. In fact, he was the picture of innocence, except, of course, for the gore that covered his shirt and pants. Even the bright white strings laced through his red sneakers were sprinkled with deep burgundy.

"That's because of you. You hurt him," Arin snapped. "How could you do this?" The words flew out before she had time to think.

"Jacob hates Cooper, Mommy," Troy cried. "He told me to get the knife, or he would do something really bad. Cooper kept growling at Jacob. I tried to tell him to stop, but he wouldn't listen. That's why Jacob hates him so much."

"Well, I hate Jacob," Jake spat, "and it's about time for him to go." Troy's eyes darted around the room, his small face a mask of fright.

"Daddy, please don't talk that way. He might hear you." His bottom lip began to quiver. "I don't want Jacob to be mad at you." They dropped the subject when Dr. Brummel walked in, a syringe in his gloved hand. Apologetically, he indicated that it was time.

Jake, Arin and Troy huddled together and sobbed in unison as they said their goodbyes to their old friend. Cooper stared at them sadly with his huge brown eyes. He seemed to intuitively know what was coming. Arin kissed his velvety muzzle for the last time, her tears wetting his black leathery nose. Less than a minute after the injection, Cooper exhaled deeply and slipped away. Jake gently scooped his warm body up and wordlessly carried him from the room. Troy wiped his nose on his bloodstained sleeve and jumped down to follow. Dr. Brummel handed Arin a tissue, and she leaned on his shoulder and wept. Awkwardly, he tried to console her, which did not come naturally to him. It occurred to him that perhaps he should have stuck with livestock after all.

***

The Intrusion

Jake buried Cooper in the back yard the next day. Troy marked the grave with special rocks he had scavenged from Cooper's favorite place in the yard to play fetch. He sat cross-legged in the grass in front of his makeshift memorial, recalling some of the silly times he and the boxer had shared. It disturbed Jake that he didn't show any signs of remorse. Not an inkling of guilt. Unable to deal with witnessing her old friend covered forever with earth, Arin focused her energy instead on erasing all evidence of her faithful friend's violent end. The tears liberally rolled as she vigorously scrubbed the blood from the playroom walls and carpet. She sniffled and scoured for over an hour, the whole time oblivious that Jacob lounged on the playroom sofa, a pleased expression on his face.

***

That night, for the first time in what felt like weeks, Jake and Arin held each other close. She carefully recounted the condensed version of her conversation with Pastor Wesley. To her surprise, Jake allowed her to finish without interrupting or even so much as a sarcastic grunt. After much hemming and hawing, Arin worked up the nerve to ask if he would attend church with her the next day. She steeled herself against the bite of his rejection, and instead, she was amazed when he readily agreed. They enjoyed a few peaceful moments of silence before sleep mercifully came.

J ake sat in the front row studying his bulletin. So far, he'd managed to avoid eye contact with any of the "churchers," as he liked to call them. Just the sight of the hymnals and pews was enough to give him flashbacks to his childhood. The atmosphere at Downsville Christian Fellowship was surprisingly warm, the polar opposite of the lifeless church of his parents. The sanctuary was filled with lighthearted banter, even an occasional belly laugh. Such exchanges would have instantly been hushed at Richard and Anne Welsh's formal Lutheran congregation.

The bitterness inside him squelched any positive feelings he might have otherwise had about this place. No matter how great it looked on the surface, deep down he was convinced that every church sought to control people through guilt and social pressure. He had grown up tightly under the thumb of organized religion. For reasons even he never understood, when he had escaped his parents, he jumped right into the hungry arms of the cult. Again, he had become the puppet of those in spiritual authority. After the cult experience, Jake had resolved to decide for himself and his family what was right and wrong. He was a decent man, he had a good head on his shoulders, and he worked hard to provide for his family. Church had nothing to offer him. Yet, here he sat. Glancing up from the safety of his tightly clutched bulletin, he caught Arin's eye. She winked and flashed a supportive smile.

Arin had been interpreting for the Downsville Christian Fellowship for over five years now, and she seemed very much at home. An older man in the rattiest blazer Jake had ever seen approached her, grinning broadly.

"Hey, Darling, I saw that boy of yours this mornin'." Jake was amazed that Arin would allow anyone to call her 'Darling'. "That one's a pistol, ain't he? He'll be in the wife's class for Sunday School. I think we'd better pray for her!" His laughter was easy and contagious.

"Hey, Ed, I want you to meet my husband." Arin made the introduction. Ed Webber pumped Jake's hand enthusiastically until Jake was fully convinced that Ed was pleased that he was visiting. The guy was a natural born greeter if there ever was one. He could easily put the blue vests at Wal-Mart to shame.

Rae was fashionably late, as usual, slipping in well after the music started. The band was passionate and upbeat, yet reverent. Arin tapped her foot and unconsciously sang along. Rae did a double take when she saw Jake sitting on the pew next to her. She sprang up and hugged him. Although Jake had never learned to sign, he and Rae had shared some good conversations via Rae's handy notebook. He'd helped her out at the greenhouse from time to time, tinkering with a malfunctioning fountain pump, or unloading an especially cumbersome shipment of shrubs. Although Jake was cynical at best in regard to anyone who labeled themselves as Christian, he respected Rae, and appreciated the friendship she had shown Arin.

He studied Arin as she interpreted, surprised at how comfortable she appeared. Begrudgingly, he admitted to himself that this was not the church of his youth, and maybe he was the one being judgmental. The band was clearly talented. It puzzled Jake that they didn't try to get some gigs playing real music and drop this church performance. As Arin's hands sang words of praise in unison with Rae, Jake was filled with a renewed love for his wife. It amazed him how her fingers flowed with beauty and precision. Her face was expressive and alive. She was in her element, and Jake was proud to be her husband. Pastor Wesley stepped behind the podium after the last song. Jake sighed deeply and picked a spot on the floor to concentrate on, resolving not to hear a word. After a somewhat awkward silence, the young bearded pastor began.

"I had the message all planned out for this morning. I worked on it all week." Pastor Wesley shook his head and set his Bible down on the podium, flipping to a marked page. "God had other plans. On my way here this morning, He laid a message on my heart so strongly that I feel I would be in direct disobedience if I did not preach it. So, please forgive me if I seem unprepared. I am. My prayer is that He will give me the words, because I believe that there is someone here today who needs this message." He bowed his head and fumbled through a prayer, obviously nervous at the idea of veering from his prepared sermon. Without even realizing it, Jake had broken his own rule and was all ears. He was riveted by this man's humility, a quality he wasn't aware a pastor or spiritual authority figure could possess.

When the simple prayer was finished, a resounding "Amen!" rose from the congregation, emboldening the young pastor.

"Please turn to Proverbs, chapter 28 verse 13." The sound of flipping onionskin pages filled the sanctuary. Pastor Wesley did not continue until everyone had found the passage. He read the verse from a modern version.

"People who cover over their sins will not prosper. But if they confess and forsake them, they will receive mercy." He allowed the congregation to sit with that statement for a moment, letting it soak in before starting again. "Can any of us claim that we haven't covered our sins? Is there anyone here who has a secret so dark that they are in constant fear of being found out?"

Jake had the eerie suspicion that the young pastor could somehow read his mind. He had worked hard over the years to cover his own sinful secret, and lately his conscience hounded him night and day. He tried to discern what the hidden motives of the pastor could be. He seemed sincere. Jake was touched at one point when Pastor Wesley tearfully shared an illustration about anticipating their first child after years of trying. He and Arin exchanged knowing glances. They understood that struggle all too well.

Pastor Wesley became animated, circling the stage, arms waving. "Any prosperity you may achieve, without knowing God, is useless and temporary. He is waiting for you to confess your sins and come to Him. Not come to church, not be a good person, simply come to Him. You may think you are successful at covering your sins. You may even do a fair job of keeping the truth from your wife, your kids, your boss, friends, or church family. The truth is you can never conceal a single thing from the Lord. He sees it all. He knows it all."

Pastor Wesley paused then, and touched his clenched fist to his lips, eyes closed. "Imagine with me now that someone knew everything about you. I mean each and every wretched thing, every lie, every lustful and selfish thought, false motive, slanderous thought and word, every insincerity, hatred and betrayal. Now, think about what that person must think of you, feel about you, what sort of relationship that person would want to have with you." He allowed the scenario to settle over the congregation, which hung on his every word. "Now consider the Lord Jesus Christ who sacrificed Himself, gave Himself up to death, even the horrible and humiliating death on a cross, for you, so that He could have a relationship with you! He was not ignorant of your sins, private or public. He knew it all. He paid the penalty for those sins so you would not have to live in bondage to them, so that you could walk in freedom and peace, with the joy that only He can give ruling your hearts."

Ben's heartfelt sermon halted a moment, and he paced back and forth on the stage, apparently measuring his words.

"God paid for your sins on the cross so that you can confess your sins and find forgiveness. He does, however, not make the decision for you. Please, please choose Christ. Choose life and purpose in Him. Consider the alternative, in this life and in the life to come." Pastor Wesley concluded with a sober warning. "Please, think about your eternity without Christ, an eternity of torment and regret, and choose another option now, while you still can. Christians are constantly defending the gospel against fools who insist that a loving God would not send anyone to hell. I wholeheartedly agree. He provided a way for us to enter heaven. There is only one way, and that is Jesus. Call it narrow minded, intolerant or exclusive, but it's the truth. If He had provided us with twelve ways, man's arrogant heart would question why not thirteen. Accept Jesus, the one and only provision for our sins today, now. Receive the mercy He longs to extend to you." Pastor Wesley stepped off the stage and the band silently returned to their instruments and began to play.

Jake sat entranced. When he finally noticed the congregation standing around him, he numbly rose to join them. He observed Arin brushing tears from her eyes as she interpreted the concluding song. He understood that she harbored secrets too, and wondered if he would ever know the reason behind the sorrow she tried to hide from him. Perhaps she, like him, had a dark and terrible secret.

After an invitation, several people came forward for prayer and to rededicate their lives to God. Then the congregation was dismissed. Arin and Rae huddled together, and Arin described the horrid events of the previous day. Rae was broken-hearted when she heard the news about poor old Cooper. There had always been a special place in her heart for that goofy dog. Grief was quickly replaced with shock and disbelief that Troy was even capable of such a violent act. Arin reminded her that according to Troy, Jacob had been responsible for Cooper's death. Flipping her Bible open to the Old Testament, Rae pointed out a passage in the twenty-fifth chapter of Genesis. Arin read along as Rae's pointer finger moved across the page: *"After his brother came out, his hand took hold of Esau's heel: so his name was called Jacob."*

Puzzled, Arin glanced up. Again, Rae directed her attention to the page, this time to the footnotes for the passage. She drew in a sharp breath upon reading an alternative meaning of the name Jacob– "Deceiver."

***

Lunch proved to be a silent affair at the Welsh house. The kitchen overflowed with the void of Cooper's absence. Arin half expected to look down and see his huge brown eyes negotiating for the crusts of her sandwich. It was impossible to believe that he was gone. Bravely, she decided to attempt to lighten the mood. "What did you learn about in Sunday School?" Troy bit his lip and took a long time to answer.

"I couldn't hear what Mrs. Webber was saying."

"Why not," Arin probed. Troy's eyes were glued to his plate.

"Jacob was yelling in my ear."

With that, Jake set his scarcely touched sandwich down, stood up and muttered an expletive as he exited the room.

When the last dish was loaded and the counter was wiped clean, Arin settled on a stool to sort out the mail that had accumulated over the last few days. The familiar handwriting and ivory envelope caught her off guard. Running her fingers over the slanted script, for a split second she contemplated opening it. A huge part of her yearned to tear it open and to gobble her mother's words. What could she possibly have to say to the daughter she had traded so carelessly for the bottle all those years ago? During Arin's first few years in foster care, she often daydreamed about her beautiful mother. Perhaps she was being held hostage by a jilted suitor, but she fought to escape night and day so she could be reunited with her waiting daughter. Or she could be lying in some pristine hospital bed deep in a coma, unable to awaken and find her way back to her. Once the nightmare named Kevin Driver became her unfortunate reality, Arin no longer had time for foolish fantasies. Her life became a game of survival. Before curiosity could get the better of her, she retrieved the red pen from the junk drawer and scribbled her rejection across the envelope. But this time she did not experience any satisfaction. She just felt empty.

A rin glanced up and down Burnside Boulevard before exiting the Explorer. Although she did not exactly understand why, she was leery of anyone seeing her enter The Divine Connection. For years she had driven by the battered Victorian on her way into Hagerstown, and it had always roused her curiosity. The makeshift sign in the front yard featured an aqua palm with an eye in the center, which Troy inquired about whenever they drove by. Mortified by the thought of being spotted by a passing motorist, Arin briskly strode to the front door and tried it. She groaned when the knob failed to turn. A note indicated that she was to ring the bell and wait, and she complied. Just as she was preparing to make a break back to the Explorer, she noticed the popping and scraping of someone working the abundant locks. The impressively fortified wooden door swung open and she was greeted by a tall thin woman in a long purple dress.

"Hello, child," she said. Arin had not been called a child in a very long time, and she wasn't entirely sure how she felt about it.

"I wanted to see if... I mean, are you open right now?"

"Of course, Sister Amber is always available to help a child of God find her way." Arin bit her lip and stepped over the threshold. One of the things she despised most in the world was when people spoke of themselves in the third person. As she entered, Sister Amber began to hum—another thing on Arin's top ten most hated habits list. Arin vowed that if Sister Amber started square dancing, she was out of there. The line had to be drawn somewhere. Once inside, the smell of cat urine, Indian food, and too much patchouli hit her like a brick wall. She coughed and fought against the urge to gag. Upon observing her obvious distress, Sister Amber graciously crossed the room and lit a stick of incense, which only served to intensify the problem.

"The energy in the house is heavy today," she said apologetically, as if this explained the wretched odors. It was on the tip of Arin's tongue to suggest that the cat box was perhaps the thing that was a little on the heavy side and that someone should put some of that voracious mental energy into changing it once in a while. She studied her host as she adjusted to the noxious stench. Sister Amber's hair was ridiculously similar to that of a dandelion long past its prime. White and about two inches long, it fluffed out in every direction, except for the back of her head, where it was smashed and matted. Her long dress was a cotton mass of wrinkles and bunches. Arin suspected that it doubled as pajamas.

"Although the universe gives gifts freely to her children, the establishment forces even ministers like me to request compensation."

"Come again?"

"I don't take credit cards or checks," Sister Amber stated matter-of-factly.

"I have cash."

"Good," she smiled, her green eyes wide and beaming. "Would you like to talk in the chapel?"

"Sure," Arin agreed. That sounded tame enough. She was led through a maze of dimly lit hallways. She ceased counting cats after the tenth one. To her, owning ten cats was just as crazy as owning a hundred. Sister Amber halted in front of a dazzling yellow door adorned with an eyed-palm identical to the one on the sign in the yard. She hummed as she opened the door and ushered Arin inside. The first thing Arin noticed upon entering was that this room was considerably colder than the rest of the house, and thankfully, it was relatively clear of rank odors. The room was devoid of furniture except for a small oak table with folding metal chairs in the center. An impressive geode was positioned in the heart of the table.

"This room is kept absolutely pure of any negative energy," the dandelion-headed guru bragged.

"That's nice… I guess," Arin fumbled lamely, unsure of how to respond. "Should I sit?"

"Please do." Sister Amber sat across from Arin and studied her closely. "You are here out of concern for a loved one, isn't that right?"

Arin's heart skipped a beat and her palms began to sweat. What was she doing here? "I need to know what I can do to help my son."

Sister Amber's eyes closed and she began to caress the geode on the table as she rocked back and forth. Arin was horrified when she started to hum again. This time there was no melody, only a low flat drone. The humming ceased only long enough for her to draw another breath. Arin wondered if Sister Amber was charging by the hour, because she sure wasn't going to pay good money to sit on a hard chair in a cold room and listen to her hum. After fifteen minutes, Arin couldn't take it anymore. Just as she opened her mouth to interrupt, Sister Amber's mint green eyes burst open and she slapped the table with her open palm. Arin shrieked and practically fell out of her chair.

"Sorry, I didn't intend to startle you, child." She pulled the geode close to her chest, her fingers exploring the jagged quartz in the center. "The spirits have wonderful plans for your son. You must be very proud of him."

Images of the monster Arin had witnessed in Troy's room several nights before and of Cooper's lifeless body flashed across her mind. Wonderful things? She thought not. "No, you don't understand. – They—the spirits—whatever they are. How do I get them to just leave him alone, please?"

"Why would you want to do that?"

"I just do. I need them to go away. Please, just tell me what I can do. I've already talked to a Christian pastor and he was no help at all."

Sister Amber snorted and leaned back, folding her arms across her chest. "I don't know why you'd search for answers from a dead religion like Christianity." She stood and motioned for Arin to do the same. "Besides," she added as they exited the chapel, "you don't have the power to make the spirits obey you. The harder you resist, the more difficult this transition will be for your son."

Sister Amber led the way back down the dingy hallway to the foyer. She collected fifty dollars, turned on her heels, and resumed her humming. Unable to tolerate another second of this place or Sister Amber, Arin got out of there as fast as her feet would take her. Despite the fact that she had, in essence, tossed fifty dollars into a toilet and flushed, she was grateful that no familiar cars had passed, and she entered the safety of the Explorer undetected. Admittedly, she was shaken by Sister Amber's statements. She did her best to write her off as a flake and press on in search of help for her son. Now she fully realized how silly it had been to seek assistance from a psychic. Still, as much as she loved Downsville Christian Fellowship, she was an outsider there, spiritually speaking. Her mind wandered to her only church experience as a child.

"I just want something that I can believe in," she explained to the empty seat beside her. "And someone who believes in me." Arin thought back to a church she had visited as a child with her friend Hannah. When it came to spiritual matters, her foster parents, the Duvalls, had been sincere in their belief that Sunday was a day of rest, and that commandment had trumped them all. As a child, Arin remembered being giddy with excitement as she stood at the window in her only dress suitable for church. When the Stone family station wagon pulled into her driveway, she would tear down the stairs and hop in the backseat with Hannah. All the way to the church they would giggle and compliment each other on their hair and various accessories. Mr. Stone would peek at them in the rear view mirror. His eyes were always full of smiles.

Although Arin could not remember one simple detail about the outside or inside of the church she had attended faithfully for an entire summer, she could most impressively expound on the things she did care enough to drink in. Mr. Stone had always let Mrs. Stone and the girls out at the door before finding a parking spot. When the last song was sung and a kindly old farmer prayed over the offering with his thick Virginia drawl, like clockwork, Mr. Stone would wrap his strong arm around his wife's shoulders and she would lean into him ever so slightly. To most people, and virtually all children, this act was regarded as meaningless or not regarded at all. But to Arin, the consistent, predictable affection and consideration the Stone family showed for each other was like an anchor on a boat she longed to climb aboard. Her heart ached to sit next to her very own mother and father; to observe her father protectively grip her mother's shoulder; to observe her appreciation for all his hard work, expressed simply yet clearly as she leaned into him. The exchange was subtle yet undeniable. She accepted his loving protection. He accepted her loving adoration.

So basically, the pastor could have been preaching about cabbages and kings for all Arin knew. She was really there as a fly on the wall of sorts, desperate to witness what actually happened when a real family spent time together. To her, church was nothing more than a primo opportunity to do just that. Sometimes, as she interpreted a particularly passionate sermon of Ben's, Arin longed for that passion to burn within her own soul. She had even tried parroting the prayer at the end of the service, although she had no faith in any of it to work for her. Parts of her wanted to believe, but she felt that there was a thick impenetrable fog obscuring the truth from her understanding. There was no way she could have known how real that unseen fog was in the spiritual realm.

T he parking lot of the Wells Funeral Home was jam-packed with luxury cars. Nearly every spot was occupied by a Mercedes, Lexus, Beamer, or a Cadillac. There was not a Ford or Chevy in sight. Arin tucked the Explorer away in the far corner of the lot, under the cover of a sagging willow tree. She felt more than a little guilty about lying to Jake. She had told him that she was interpreting for a funeral tonight, and had failed to mention her unfortunate and costly visit with Sister Amber. He just would not understand. Heck, she didn't understand either. The draw to attend Dr. Raines' funeral had been irresistible. She sensed that if she attended the ceremony, she might find answers to some of the nagging issues.

Arin slipped into a plush lavender seat near the back of the room. She spent the next few minutes observing the action around her. This gathering had the feel of a business meeting rather than a funeral. She eavesdropped on different conversations around her. She heard about expense reports, profit-loss summaries, even office drama and gossip. There was not one anecdote about the bereaved. No one expressed sadness or even surprise that he had hung himself in a public place without even leaving a note. This funeral was reminiscent of Ebenezer Scrooge's vision presented by the Ghost of Christmas Future. Unlike Ebenezer, it was too late for Dr. Geoffrey Raines.

After observing for a while, it dawned on Arin that there were a disproportionate number of women to men. Probably two-thirds of the crowd of a hundred or so was female. Many of them were young and quite beautiful. There were blondes, brunettes, redheads of all shapes and sizes. But they all had one thing in common. Each of them sported a pink button on the front of their fashionable gray and black funeral clothes. A blonde finally got close enough for Arin to make out what it said. "My Body, My Choice." How tacky, Arin thought. A funeral sure seemed like an odd setting to make a political statement.

Shifting into detective mode, she listened in on the conversation a pair of women was having to her left.

"He was so devoted to the cause. Losing him is going to be a real setback."

"Don't be so naïve," the second woman scolded. "He couldn't have cared less about the cause. I often thought that he hated women altogether. I don't know why he even went into obstetrics in the first place."

"He was always so kind to me…" the first woman's voice trailed off.

"Dr. Raines was never kind to a person a day in his life, unless there was something in it for him. The only reason he even worked at the clinic was the money he made selling parts and tissue. The man had dollar signs in his eyes, plain and simple."

Their conversation ended abruptly when a woman stepped up to the podium and asked for everyone to take their seats. She introduced herself simply as "Allie, Geoffrey's spiritual advisor." She was a striking woman in her mid- to late thirties with long platinum hair and crystal blue eyes. The standard pink button was attached to the right side of her bright blue peasant blouse. Wrinkled khakis, striped socks, and Birkenstocks completed her ensemble. Intrigued by her unconventional funeral attire, Arin sat up and craned her neck in an effort to see past the big hair of the woman in front of her. It took a few moments for the crowd to choose seats and settle. Allie waited, smiling benevolently at her audience.

"I feel so blessed that everyone is able to be here tonight to honor the earthly life of Dr. Geoffrey Raines." She must not have known him well, Arin thought. "Geoffrey was not only our dear friend; he was a champion for women's rights as well as one of the most spiritually evolved people I have ever had the pleasure of working with." She droned on and on extolling all Geoffrey's fine attributes when her speech took another course. "In the past year alone, he had mastered the art of channeling, and was in frequent communication with several spirits." This was the strangest eulogy Arin had ever heard. She observed heads nodding in agreement all around her. This must be a spiritually evolved group of people, whatever that meant. Sister Amber would be right at home with this crowd.

"This afternoon, Geoffrey visited me while I was meditating. The purpose of his visitation was to reassure his family and friends that the next world is beautiful. Our souls are finally free to explore our own divinity, without the baggage of our inhibitions. There is no need for religion, no lake of fire to be saved from."

Arin crossed her arms skeptically.

"Geoffrey told me about the profound joy he experienced when he met the spirits he had channeled. They greeted him like old friends, ushering him into his new world." An attractive brunette in the front row jerked to her feet and hurried out of the room, obviously upset. Something about her face was so familiar. Arin racked her brain, but could not place her. Between Sister Amber and Allie, she too had heard more than enough. Arin also rose and headed for the door.

"Get your pajamas and tubby toys. It's bath time," Jake called over his shoulder as he crossed the kitchen to answer the phone. "Hello?"

"Hey, Jake. It's Dawn from DeafMed. Is Arin around?" Jake was confused. If anyone should know Arin's interpreting schedule it would be Dawn.

"She's working tonight." Jake could hear Dawn flipping through papers.

"No, she's not scheduled for anything until Tuesday."

"Oh."

"Can you just let her know that Mrs. Miller cancelled her three o'clock next week, and I will call her when we reschedule?"

"Sure. Will do," Jake responded, trying to sound pleasant. Anger burned within him and he slammed the cordless back into the receiver.

Arin spied the back of the brunette's head as the bathroom door was closing. On impulse, she made the decision to follow her. The woman stood bracing herself at the sink, her head down, quietly sniffling. Feeling awkward, Arin grabbed a tissue and offered it to her. She met Arin's gaze with familiar, sparkling blue eyes.

"Thank you," she said, taking the tissue and blowing her nose.

"Lose your button?" Arin asked. They were probably the only two women in the room without a pink button advertising their popular pro-choice stance. The woman just shook her head and rolled her eyes.

"Were you his…"

"We were separated," she said. She sighed deeply and sat in one of the plush arm chairs near the mirrors.

Arin sat next to her. "I'm sorry."

"Thanks. That's very kind of you." She eyed Arin thoughtfully for a moment. "Have we met?"

"Arin Welsh. I sort of knew your husband. I was his patient once." Arin carefully worded her response.

"Emily Raines." She extended her hand. "I'm surprised that a patient of Geoffrey's would bother to come. He wasn't exactly the warm, fuzzy type."

Arin nodded. Boy, was that an understatement.

"At least he was spiritually evolved," Arin said, risking a joke. Anger flashed across Emily's stunning face.

"That was the biggest load of horse crap I have ever heard."

"That's one way to put it," Arin laughed. "I guess Allie isn't your spiritual guru."

"No way," Emily shook her head emphatically. "When I became a Christian, she advised Geoffrey to leave me. Not that our marriage was all peaches and cream, but-"

Arin interrupted, finally remembering where she had seen Emily before. "You go to Downsville Christian Fellowship, right?"

"Yeah, for about the past year," Emily replied. She studied Arin carefully for a moment. "Are you the sign language interpreter?" Arin smiled and nodded.

"While Allie was talking, I kept thinking about Pastor Wesley. He would've had a whole herd of cows if he'd had to sit through that nonsense." They both laughed, releasing some nervous tension. Out of the blue, Emily tossed out a question that Arin was not prepared to answer.

"So, why in the world are you here? I doubt you came out as a tribute to Geoffrey's bedside manner, or his dedication to women." Arin sat frozen, clueless how to answer. After trying several stories on for size, she opted for the truth. Just as she was deciding where to start, a herd of pink-buttoned attendees burst through the door.

"Can we grab a beer or something?" Arin asked.

"Make it a cup of coffee and you've got yourself a deal," Emily bargained. Together they stood and walked out, drawing the gazes of the other women. On their way to the parking lot, Emily was practically bowled over by Allie McIntyre. Emily muttered an apology, and Allie regarded her coldly, her crystal eyes pure ice.

***

Jake knelt at the edge of the tub. He tested the water temperature and plugged the drain. His face flushed red with anger, and it was a struggle for him to act as if everything was ordinary. Not that it mattered. Troy showed little to no desire to interact with him. Instead, he remained stoic and withdrawn, even during bath time. Typically, Troy would balk at the idea of bathing with less than a million of his favorite toys. Arin or Jake would force him to choose four or five that he couldn't live without, which would take another ten or fifteen minutes—just long enough for the water to get cold. Tonight, Troy stood quietly behind his father, a plastic snake in one hand, a red soap crayon in the other.

"That's it?" Jake asked with exaggerated astonishment. Troy just shrugged. He silently removed his socks and underwear and allowed his dad to help him step into the tub. Jake put the lid of the toilet down and sat. He had hoped that some bath time play would inspire some happy feelings. No matter what Arin had done, or may be doing right at that moment, his son was innocent. Troy showed no interest in playing, at least not with his father. He situated himself with his back to Jake, and began to whisper to the empty space at the other side of the tub. Jake felt the sting of rejection from his wife as well as his son. He snatched a motorcycle magazine from the rack and searched for an article to get lost in.

While Troy chatted with thin air, Jake read an article about a man, his free-spirited wife, and their journey around the country on matching motorcycles. Although Jake Welsh loved his family and would give his life for them in a heartbeat, he sometimes yearned for that kind of freedom and adventure. His mind traveled back to their days in the cult. While in Hawaii, they had lived in a tent for several months. Jake loved waking every morning to the sound and smell of the ocean. Neither cult nor tent living was something he had any desire to relive, but he did yearn for the joy of exploration, the strange sense of freedom that came from living hand-to-mouth, no house, job, or even a car to tie him down. More than anything, he ached for the bond that he and Arin had shared back then.

The exact moment that Jake had first laid eyes on Arin was perfectly preserved in his memory. Like a favorite library book, he checked it out and reviewed it on occasion when he needed a reminder of what he was working for. He had been in Troy, New York, bunking in a converted barn owned by a cult sympathizer. The shepherd of the group had announced that some new recruits would soon be arriving from Virginia and asked that they be made to feel welcomed. As an introvert, Jake usually left the initial meeting and greeting to the more sanguine members. Historically, more than half of the newbies would be running home to mommy before the week was over, so he preferred to hold off and get to know the ones who were in it for the long haul. His standard greeting protocol was out the window the second that his eyes locked on Arin Gruber.

Her gaze had been fixed on her feet as she and the other Virginia members had been ushered in. Her waist length brown hair was parted in the middle and tucked neatly behind her ears. She wore a stained white t-shirt and torn blue jeans. Nothing about her was showy or flashy. When she finally dared to lift her sun-kissed face, Jake's breath was taken from him. Her eyes were a gorgeous warm brown, her cheekbones high and heavily accented with freckles. Jake had always had a thing for a girl with freckles. As Arin scanned her new surroundings, their eyes met. She held his gaze for a few seconds before she looked away, her freckled cheeks flushing and a smile tugging at the corners of her mauve lips. They both just knew. By the end of the evening, they had traded life stories and enjoyed an easy exchange of thoughts and ideas. In a month, they were engaged. The rest was history.

It occurred to Jake that Troy had been unusually quiet for the last few minutes. Troy still sat with his back to Jake, absolutely motionless. The hairs on the back of Jake's neck began to prick and his heart picked up its pace. Something was not right.

"Buddy, are you okay?"

Troy did not acknowledge that Jake had spoken to him. The magazine slipped from Jake's fingers and he fell to his knees in front of the tub. A startled gasp escaped from his lips when he saw Troy's face. A large red X had been carefully drawn entirely across it with a soap crayon. His lips were completely blue. Jake took hold of Troy and pulled him from the tub. Jake drew in a sharp breath. The water was ice cold. Troy's small body was freezing, and as soon as he was out of water he began to shake violently. Jake grabbed a few thick towels and snuggled his son next to his chest. Fear, frustration, and a sense of powerlessness ripped at his soul, and he began to cry. Troy looked up at his father, some pinkness finally returning to his lips. The disturbing red marks on his face were smudged from Jake's efforts to warm him.

"What happened, Daddy?" he asked.

"How did the water get so cold? I just checked it a few minutes ago. Why didn't you tell me you were so cold, Buddy? I was right here."

Troy looked at his father with eyes full of misery. "I'm so cold all the time now, Daddy." Jake hugged his shivering son close to his chest and sobbed. Never in his life had he felt so completely helpless.

Hours later, Troy had finally slipped into a fitful sleep. Restless and angry, Jake walked the floors, checking the time obsessively. It was nearly ten o'clock. What kind of funeral goes on past eight o'clock, let alone ten? One that did not exist, he decided, answering his own question. His wife had been lying to him, and her timing could not have been worse considering what was going on with Troy, with their *son*. Jake approached the wall-mounted phone several times and spun around each time, abandoning the idea. He checked the clock again. Ten-thirty. Anger sparked within him and he marched to the phone with fresh resolve. He needed to talk to someone, to know that someone cared. His fingers quickly raced across the keypad, tapping in the ten digits that were as clear in his mind now as they had been twenty-five years ago. Ring. Ring. Ring. Ring. Jake was ready to abort his mission when the ringing stopped.

"Hello? Who is this?"

Jake's lips might as well have been sewn shut.

"Hello?" his mother's irritation and disapproval supernaturally shone through the receiver.

"I, uh, I'm sorry," was all he could get out before hanging up.

As he tossed and turned in bed that night, he could not help but wonder if she had recognized his voice. Was it possible for a mother to simply forget her son's voice if she chose to? Deep down, he ached for something soft and maternal to guide him, to allow him to rest his head in her lap and weep without shame.

Arin sat across the table from Emily Raines, estranged wife of her former doctor and nemesis. Emily settled in, explaining that she had all night, so Arin started at the beginning. This would be the first time that she would share the whole truth with another human being. Not even her best friend, Rae, knew what she was about to tell this stranger. Initially, her words were slow and clumsy, and then they came in a torrent, in an absolute rush to get out. Reliving that day was sickening as well as exhilarating, similar to lancing an angry boil—excruciating yet necessary.

Dr. Raines had been on call at Franklin Memorial when Arin had collapsed and was rushed in. She described his caustic demeanor, and how cruelly he had delivered the tragic news. A significant issue had developed with her pregnancy. The twins were diagnosed with Twin-to-Twin-Transfusion Syndrome, which normally affected only identical twins. In his usual detached clinical manner, he had informed her that Baby A, or the recipient, was receiving most of the nutrients from the placenta, which was overwhelming the still-forming organs, while Baby B, the donor, was in essence starving.

He clarified the gravity of the situation, spouting off statistics for which she lacked the capacity to absorb. He warned that for every six-thousand babies diagnosed with TTTS, only two-thousand babies survived. A large percentage of that number had significant health problems for the remainder of their lives. Fetal reduction was the only option, he insisted, and it must be carried out immediately if the donor twin was to be saved. She was already seventeen weeks along, and he swore that by waiting she would be signing the death certificates of both her babies.

Desperate to salvage at least one of the struggling lives inside of her, Arin numbly consented to the treatment. Before the ink was dry on the consent form, she was whisked down the hall to a bitter cold operating room and prepped for the procedure. She recalled the compassion in the nurse's voice when she asked who she could call for her. Arin lied, saying that the father was not in the picture. There was no one to call.

Guided by ultrasound, Dr. Raines injected Baby B with a lethal saline solution. He then cauterized the umbilical cord, cutting off the blood flow from the placenta. He made no effort to hide the screen from Arin as he plunged the needle into her numb belly. Horrified, she watched as Baby B wildly flailed his arms and legs, attempting to avoid the needle. The image was permanently ingrained in her mind. She was absolutely helpless as she watched Baby B, the twin she had secretly named Jacob, cease his frantic movement and die.

Hours later, in the middle if the night, Arin called Dr. Chen from her hospital bed, completely hysterical. He'd agreed to see her the next day after she was released from Franklin Memorial. Thank God it was a Saturday and the office was deserted.

"Why Dr. Raines not call me?" Dr. Chen had asked in broken English. "There are other treatment options with TTTS. We could have tried laser surgery to correct the blood flow. It would have been more logical. Why you not call me?" Dr. Chen had seemed as devastated as if it had been his own child. Arin tried to explain that she had been given no other options. Dr. Chen was sympathetic. It was obvious to her that he was holding his tongue in regard to his true feelings about Dr. Raines. She would never forget the tenderness and depth of concern he had shown her that day. On her way out the door, he had patted her shoulder and made her a promise. "Your baby will be healthy and strong. Do not worry."

It took a lot of explaining to help Dr. Chen comprehend that Jake was unaware of the surgery, or even the fact that she was pregnant with twins at all. Arin doubted that he'd ever really understood her reasons for keeping it from Jake. She wasn't even sure she did. In the end, he'd graciously agreed be discreet when she delivered. When the moment finally came and Troy was born, he was inspected, cleaned, and immediately presented to Jake. Distracted by his beautiful brand new baby boy, Jake did not notice when Dr. Chen quickly delivered Jacob. For one brief moment, Arin saw his gray, lifeless body before it was placed in a red biohazard bag and whisked away.

Her story spilled into the present. She explained to Emily that Troy had witnessed Dr. Raines at the Silver Fox Nursery on the day of his suicide. Going for broke, she revealed how Troy had adopted a so-called imaginary friend, and then had proceeded to viciously murder the family dog.

"All this has happened since Geoffrey's death?" Emily asked, her eyes wide with disbelief.

"There's more." Arin closed her eyes and rubbed her temples for a few moments. She needed to get it out. She needed to say the words out loud to another human being. She needed to hear that she wasn't crazy.

"A few nights ago, in my son's room..." her voice broke and her lips began to quiver.

"Take a minute, Honey."

"No," Arin refused. Afraid that she would lose her nerve, she continued, her voice a whisper. "I saw something, or someone, in my son's room. I think it was a demon."

Emily leaned in intently, captivated by Arin's story. Fat tears rolled down her freckled cheeks as she described her near miss with the concrete wall the day before, her talk with Pastor Wesley, and finally the bloody details of Cooper's death. When Arin could find no more words, the women just sat silently with the truth for a few moments. Clinking dishes and the laughter of diners filled the air around them. Finally, Emily spoke.

"That's quite a heavy load to carry all by yourself." Her tone was warm, yet candid. Her sympathetic words touched Arin, and the tears continued to roll.

"I'm sorry," she sniffed, embarrassed. "I am not usually much of a crier."

Emily reached across the table and squeezed Arin's trembling hand. She decided that the time had come to share her own experience, that perhaps God could use it for his good.

"I was Geoffrey's nurse. He was married at the time. Of course I knew it was wrong, but he was so charming and I was sure he loved me. Next thing you know, I'm pregnant." The waitress fluttered over to refill their coffee, apologizing profusely for her inattention. Emily poured her cream and stirred, fighting to keep her composure. When she was able to continue, her voice was slightly strained. "Geoffrey insisted that the baby be aborted, and in the end I went along with it. He performed the procedure himself. I could never shake the feeling that he derived some sick pleasure from it." Arin shivered, vividly remembering the smug look on his face as he performed her procedure.

"He was an awful man. I honestly don't see how you could have ever thought he was charming." Arin regretted the words as soon as they left her mouth.

"You would be surprised, Arin. He wasn't always like that," Emily explained. Thankfully, she did not appear to have felt the sting of her harsh words. Apparently, neither of them minded speaking ill of the dead. "Before we were married, he was exciting and charismatic to say the least. Of course, he always had an arrogant way about him, but you come to expect that when you work with enough doctors. It was soon after he met Allie that he started pulling his Jeckle and Hyde act. It was incredibly naïve of me to think that he would treat me any better than he had treated his first wife."

"One morning, I woke up and suddenly Allie McIntyre was his constant companion, or his spiritual advisor, as she referred to herself. In a matter of months, Geoffrey was learning to channel the dead. That was where I drew the line in the sand. Candles, incense and meditation were one thing, but I wanted no part of conversing with dead folks. I grew up Southern Baptist, and although at that time in my life I was not exactly walking on the straight and narrow, I knew that stuff was absolutely evil. Obviously, Geoffrey disagreed. It was difficult to watch him sink into the bondage of the occult, but he wouldn't even discuss it with me." Emily set her empty coffee cup on its matching porcelain saucer and pushed it toward the center of the table. When she lifted her eyes to meet Arin's, her expression was deadly serious. "Strange things began to happen."

***

"God help me!" Geoffrey Raines screamed, anguished by the knowledge that there would be no rescue. His agony was so great that he could not help but cry out to the God he had mocked and rejected, even though he knew it was futile. His tormenters thrashed around him, jeering and tearing at his soul in strips, reveling that their victim shared their eternal misery. Relentlessly he begged, even prayed for death, and the hideous voices assured him that this unbearable existence would never end. Never. He was cursed to spend eternity apart from the only One who could have saved him, the One who had given all to save him. Seconds after the spirits had convinced him to tighten the noose and jump, Geoffrey knew he had been deceived. But by then, it was too late.

***

Arin rocked rhythmically as she stared into space. Random thoughts swirled around her weary mind. If she tried to grab onto one long enough to inspect it, undoubtedly it would wiggle free and rejoin the tornado of ideas. The fact that she was nursing her second vodka and orange juice probably didn't help her thought processes any. Although she rarely drank, Arin had guzzled her first screwdriver. She'd almost dropped the dusty vodka bottle as she poured her second with trembling hands.

Arin had grown up avoiding alcohol like the plague. She knew all too well exactly what it had taken from her, and she had no plans of bowing to a bottle when it came to her loved ones. In fact, it wasn't until she was married and out of the cult that she had enjoyed her first sip of red wine. As the wine warmed her throat and stomach, Arin knew in her heart that she had the potential for enjoying it way, way too much. After the extended coffee break with Emily Raines, Arin felt restless and vulnerable. She just needed a little something to take the edge off, to smooth away the rough patches. When she'd arrived home late, the house was pitch black. Not even the porch light was left on to welcome her, which was highly abnormal. Typically, Jake would have waited up for her or, at the very least, left all the outside lights blazing. Her mood was foul as she felt her way to the light switch, and it declined further when she noticed the note Jake had left her on the kitchen counter stating DeafMed had called. Most likely, she had been caught in her lie. Arin rested her head against the high back of the old rocker.

For the next fifteen minutes, she racked her brain for a believable account. She was intent on coming up with a bigger and better lie to replace the first. At this point, she stubbornly refused to consider the truth as her last resort. Jake would never understand why she had felt compelled to attend Dr. Raines' funeral. And after successfully keeping her secret for all of these years, Arin was unwilling to spill it now. Especially not twice in the same evening.

Merely allowing the words to pass from her brain to her lips had ripped the scabs from emotional wounds long left untouched. She gripped the wooden arm of the rocking chair with one hand and the half empty glass with the other. As a child, she had found solace in an old swing set. As an adult, she exchanged the swing for the rocker.

Something about the slow steady back and forth always soothed her. The vodka didn't hurt either.

"I had two babies," Arin whispered to the empty room. "But I had one of them killed." She drained the remaining screwdriver and tossed the empty glass across the room. It hit the brick chimney and shattered, peppering the room with iridescent green shards.

The bookshelf on the far wall next to the chimney caught her attention. Something seemed out of place. It took her fuzzy mind a moment to realize that Troy's baby book was on its side. Every now and then Troy liked to take it down, and they would look through it together. He loved reciting his first word, or the date he took his first step, or had his first tractor ride with Daddy. Arin rose and stumbled across the room, taking care to avoid the scattered glass. She stopped and braced herself against the back of a recliner. For the first time in her adult life, she was downright drunk. The room stopped swirling, and a flash of color on the floor grabbed her attention. She bent down for a closer look and lost her balance, landing squarely on her rear end. Irritated, she grabbed the item and held it close to her face for inspection.

Somehow, her red pen had made it from the kitchen to the floor in front of the bookshelf. This was not any ordinary pen, it was *the* red pen. The one she had bought for and used only to return the unwanted letters her mother refused to quit sending. Jake and Troy both knew better than to touch it. Roughly, she snatched the blue baby book to restore it to its proper space on the shelf next to the other family albums.

A piece of paper escaped from between the pages of Troy's baby book and lazily traveled to the carpet. Even in her altered state, Arin somehow managed to snatch it from the air before it landed. For the second time in so many days, she found herself staring into the cold dark eyes of Dr. Geoffrey Raines. Someone must have cut his picture from the newspaper and slipped it inside. But why? Who? Arin's heart frantically knocked against her chest. Cautiously, she opened the book. Fresh waves of sorrow and terror washed over her as she turned page after page. A red X had been slashed over Arin, Jake and Troy's faces in each and every photo.

The next morning, Arin felt it was necessary to make good on her promise to Dr. Brummell and find a therapist for Troy. She could no longer stand by and wring her hands as her precious little boy became strange and withdrawn. There were moments that Troy seemed to be his old self, but especially since Cooper's death, they were becoming few and far between. It frustrated her to no end that their insurance company participated with only one local psychologist whose specialty was pediatrics. A. McIntyre, M.D. Arin had not heard anything good or bad about this doctor, or any other mental health worker for that matter. Head-shrinking was one specialty that did not often call on interpreters.

"Dr. McIntyre's office. Hope speaking. May I help you?" Arin fought the urge to say that she hoped so.

"I need to make an appointment for my son."

"When would you like him to be seen?"

"As soon as possible, please." Arin looked at the clock. It was nine-thirty. They could be there by ten.

"It looks like the soonest we could get him in would be the middle of next month. Are Tuesdays good for you?" Arin sighed heavily and tried to get control of her emotions before opening her mouth, something she rarely had the self control to do.

"Hope, if I could just share with you a little of what has been going on, perhaps that would help." Before Hope could protest, she started. "Several days ago my son, who is four-and-a-half years old, was possibly a witness to a suicide. Since then, he's adopted an evil imaginary friend and stabbed the family dog. My husband and I are at a loss. We need to get him some help. Under the circumstances, I don't feel that he can wait until the middle of next month. I realize that your schedule is crowded, but Dr. McIntyre is the only psychologist our worthless insurance participates with." Arin paused to steady her rising voice. No need to yell at poor Hope. "I'm extremely concerned about my son. Is there any possibility at all that we could be squeezed in today?"

Arin gently massaged her thumping temples, firmly resolving to abstain from alcohol for the rest of her life. While on hold, she mentally reviewed her morning. Jake had been frosty and short with her. She wasn't sure if it was because she'd passed out on the couch of the glass-littered family room, or if he knew she'd lied to him about her whereabouts the previous night. Either way, the distance and tension between them was palpable and frightening. In the past, when they were faced with issues, it had always seemed to bring them closer together. Now the opposite was true. Thankfully, Hope returned on the line and interrupted her troubled thoughts.

"Ma'am?"

"Still here."

"Given the urgent nature of your son's problems, Dr. McIntyre has agreed to meet with him today at 11:30, if that is convenient." Hope sounded darn proud of herself.

"We'll be there."

Arin eyed Troy from the Explorer's rear-view mirror. He was uncharacteristically agitated and restless. He had made it clear in no uncertain terms that he did not want to go to the doctor. He felt fine, and it didn't matter that he wasn't getting a shot. When her attempts at bribery had failed, Arin had resorted to physical force and had literally dragged him from his room, down the stairs, and into the car. Breathless, she strapped him in and took off before he had a chance to escape. Thank God for child safety locks, she thought, or he probably would have bailed out at the first stop sign. They rode in uncomfortable silence until she pulled into the medical complex and scanned the directory for the correct suite.

"What's the doctor's name?" Troy asked, his voice ripe with rebellion.

"Dr. McIntyre," Arin answered, attempting to keep her tone light. When she peeked at Troy in the rear view, it surprised her to see a smile on his face. "What's so funny?"

"It will be fun to see her. Jacob knows her. He says that she's a good doctor and that she's nice," Troy answered. At that point Arin should have put it in reverse and high-tailed it out of there.

Dr. McIntyre had obviously spent a lot of time and money to ensure that her waiting room was one that children would take pleasure in. Two bright yellow walls featured a meticulously painted landscape with trees, flowers, and a pond complete with ducks. The two opposite walls were a brilliant blue and boasted a grinning moon and hundreds of pinpoint stars. The big and little dippers and Milky Way made for a breathtaking display. In the far corner of the room where night and day met was the Kids Corner. A half wall sectioned the area off from the rest of the waiting room. Troy's eyes lit up like a Christmas tree when he noticed the train table.

"Mommy, can we go play trains?"

Arin cringed when he referred to himself in the plural. "Sure."

After breezing through four pages of paperwork, Arin sat in the otherwise empty waiting room and watched Troy play. Without a doubt, Jacob had come along for the ride. Troy gestured and whispered to him, smiling secretively. Her skin crawled as the reality sank in that for some reason, this thing had attached itself to her son. She prayed, something she caught herself doing more lately, despite the fact that she was still unsure of who exactly she was praying to. Her prayers were always simple and to the point. Please, keep him safe. Make it stop.

"Mrs. Welsh?" Hope poked her head out of the sliding glass window. "Dr. McIntyre is ready for you. You can go right on in." She gestured to the door bearing the doctor's name.

Arin managed to coax a reluctant Troy away from a wooden train. She felt unreasonably sheepish as the heavy oak door swung open. Her gaze was met by the distinctive crystal blue eyes of the previous night. Allie McIntyre sat in an overstuffed maroon chair. Her legs were crossed and her left foot wagged lazily. Her expression was mildly curious as she examined Arin with her intelligent crystal pools. After a moment of internal panic, Arin doubted that Allie would recognize her. She had been so intent on staring Emily down that she never even glanced her way. Troy broke away from Arin, and had a seat in one of the modern chairs opposite Dr. McIntyre. Arin hesitated for a moment before sliding into the chair next to him.

"You must be Troy." Allie's voice was warm and non-threatening. He smiled and nodded.

"Mrs. Welsh, it's a pleasure to meet you as well." Arin mumbled something in reply, still in shock that Dr. A. McIntyre was Allie, Geoffrey Raines' spiritual advisor and deliverer of his bizarre eulogy.

"Mrs. Welsh, would you be comfortable with having Troy play in the waiting room with Hope for a few moments so we could talk privately?" Troy's eyes lit up. He relished the idea of a few more minutes with the wooden train he hadn't wanted to abandon.

"Can I, Mom?" Arin shrugged, and he bolted out the door before she could definitively answer.

"Hope?" Allie rose from her impressive chair and walked to her office door. "Please get Troy something to drink, and keep an eye on him, okay?" Of course Hope was falling all over herself to please the boss. She assured her that she would not let him out of her sight. Allie closed the heavy door and strode back to her chair. The air thickened with sudden tension.

"So, I am anxious to hear about your concerns. You certainly convinced Hope that your son is in some type of life or death situation." Her voice was pleasant enough, but Arin perceived that she was being patronized. Instantly her guard was up. Something about this woman seemed positively cat-like. Before she spoke, Arin reminded herself that this was the only psychologist that her insurance participated with. Her only option was to suck it up and give her a chance. Perhaps her flaky spiritual ideals did not spill over into her work. Arin took a deep breath and did her best to paint an accurate picture of the chaos of the last few days.

"Troy has always been quite a character, a carefree and outgoing sort of kid," Arin started. She went into great detail about her son's personality, how compliant and affectionate he had always been. She contrasted that with Troy since he had adopted his imaginary friend. When Arin gave the gory details about Cooper's death, Allie's eyes widened in surprise. Matter-of-factly, she listed some of the other odd happenings of the last week, including Troy's explanation for why he had not been able to hear Betty Webber's Sunday School lesson. Lastly, she explained the state in which she had found Troy's beloved baby book. Although she knew without a doubt that it was relevant to tie Troy's odd behavior with its genesis, she left out his connection with Dr. Raines' suicide, as well as the fact that she had seen this Jacob character with her own eyes. Alarms were sounding and red flags were waving. A powerful sensation in her gut told her not to put all her cards on the table, at least not yet. She did not trust this woman.

"Can you associate any trauma or change in his behavior with the timing of the imaginary friend?" Allie asked, leaning back in her chair and toying with a pencil.

"Some family stress, perhaps." Arin tried to be as vague as possible, which appeared to irritate Allie just a bit.

"How does your husband interact with Troy?"

Arin quickly jumped to Jake's defense. "Jake is great with him. He works a lot and isn't around as much as Troy would like, but when he is home, Troy has his full attention. He is an extremely hands-on dad."

"Would it be possible to get a more detailed account of what happened between Troy and your dog? What events led up to his violent episode?" Arin relayed Jake's somewhat sketchy account of Cooper's injury. She expressed how difficult it had been to witness Troy grieving for Cooper, yet accepting none of the responsibility for his death and placing the blame squarely on the non-existent shoulders of Jacob. Unexpectedly, Arin's eyes were wet with tears. She still could not grasp the fact that dear sweet Cooper was dead, and in such a horrific way. Simply speaking, his name was enough to get the waterworks going. Allie plucked a Kleenex from a box on an end table and offered it.

"Thanks." There was a long pause. Arin was aware that Allie was sizing her up, chewing on what she had heard and passing judgment.

"In your opinion, what possible reason could your son's spiritual companion have had to try to keep him from hearing the Sunday School lesson?" Allie asked, her head cocked slightly. Long blonde tresses danced on the desk. The question caught Arin completely off guard. Of all the information she had presented so far, she expected to be discussing the murder of domesticated animals or ghouls who doubled as imaginary friends, not some old lady's flannel graph lesson. Could Arin have possibly heard wrong? Had she, in all seriousness, referred to Jacob as a "spiritual companion"?

"What do you mean?" Arin asked, doing her very best to give Allie the benefit of the doubt. Perhaps she had heard incorrectly.

"Why would Jacob attempt to block your son from hearing the message presented at...?"

"We go to Downsville Christian Fellowship." Although Arin was actually more of an adjunct staff member at this point rather than a part of the congregation, this was technically not a lie. Arin attended every Sunday, Troy, sporadically, and Jake once. As soon as the words were out of Arin's mouth, Allie began to nod in an exaggerated fashion. Her face broke out into a knowing grin, which Arin wanted to smack off of her face so badly her palm itched. This woman's condescension was beyond insulting.

"I am quite familiar with your church, Mrs. Welsh, and I have to be candid with you. Pastor Wesley preaches some of the most narrow-minded philosophies I have ever heard. I imagine you have taken the time to read a few of the letters to the editor that he writes every now and then, railing against everything from a woman's right to choose to condemning hard-working educators from teaching children about safe sex. Honestly, Mrs. Welsh, in our day and age, what place does hateful teaching like his have in our culture?" Arin's head was spinning. Before she could even begin to formulate a cohesive reply, Allie continued. "Based on what I know about Downsville Christian Fellowship and what your son has been going through, I believe that your child's guiding spirit was attempting to shield him from the hateful indoctrination. He was attempting to keep him pure, in a way."

"Wait just a minute. You truly believe that this *guiding spirit* was trying to keep my son *pure* by slashing our dog to death? That is the most absurd thing I have ever heard." Blood rushed to Arin's face, and she felt her fingers begin to tremble.

Instantly, Allie began to backpedal. "That was a separate incident, which I agree is extremely disturbing. It is likely that I'll need several in-depth sessions with Troy and his spirit guide before I know what was behind that unfortunate event. I do believe that there is a purpose behind it, and when it is discovered, it will hopefully give your family some closure."

"So, let me see if I am hearing you correctly," Arin started, her voice wavering slightly. "You would encourage my son to embrace this, this spirit guide?"

"I see absolutely no reason to discourage it at this point. At the very least, we should explore the possibility that this could be a positive thing for your son." Allie leaned forward, her elbows on her knees and her hands clasped under her chin. "Mrs. Welsh, some children are born with a special gift, and they can easily sense things on a spiritual level that others are not even aware of. Please hear me on this. The worst thing a parent could do to a child such as this would be to squash his gift with an old tired religion."

That settled it for Arin. She knew what she had to do. Insurance coverage or not, she had to get out of there before this woman could get her hooks into Troy. Although she did not agree with many of the doctrines of Ben Wesley and his church, she sensed that this woman was pure evil and was attempting to manipulate Arin into giving her carte blanche control over her son.

"I appreciate your time, Dr. McIntyre, I really do. I know that you squeezed me into your schedule today, and that was very kind of you." Flustered, Arin stood. Allie stayed sitting, a mix of anger and confusion on her beautiful face. "After speaking with you and hearing about your treatment methods, I just don't feel that this would be a good match." Seeing no need for further discussion with this ice queen, Arin turned on her heels and headed to the waiting room to collect her child. Troy, however, was not in such a hurry to bolt. As she pleaded with Troy, she felt increasingly uncomfortable. Finally, she was able to coax him into parting with the wooden train and they inched toward the door.

"I thought I was going to get to talk to Allie," he whined. It shocked Arin that he so comfortably used her first name.

"Well, she doesn't have any more time today," Arin lied. They were almost out the door when Allie appeared.

"Goodbye, Troy," she called. His freckled face broke out into a charming smile, and Arin's cheeks flushed with jealousy. She could not remember the last time Troy had smiled at her in such a way.

They'd almost made it out the door before Troy called out to Dr. McIntyre, "Jacob really loves your swimming pool." Allie's jaw dropped. Arin snatched Troy and threw him over her shoulder, refusing to let him down until they had exited the building and stepped out into the parking lot.

"Your hands are shaky, Mommy." Arin forced a humorless smile and helped Troy buckle up, then slid into the driver's seat and prepared to get the heck out of Dodge. Allie appeared out of nowhere, pounding frantically on the driver's side glass. Arin reluctantly rolled down the window, figuring she had forgotten her co-pay or something.

"Please, Mrs. Welsh, may I just have a few moments with your son. I believe he may have an amazing gift-" Her words were cut off by the closing window. Thanks, but no thanks. Arin burned rubber and headed for home. Troy spent the rest of the afternoon sulking insolently, refusing to answer Arin's questions about his strange statement to Allie McIntyre. Arin nursed her wounded mother's heart. More than anything, she hated the feeling that she was iced out of her baby's life.

In an attempt to diminish the rage seething within her, Allie dimmed the lights in her office and lit a ceremonial candle she kept on her desk for occasions such as this. She forced her eyes to shut and concentrated on taking deep, deliberate breaths. She drew on her visceral hatred of Taylor and Ben Wesley as well as the rest of the fundamentalists. She focused on her hatred, nurtured it, endeavoring to transform it into energy that could be harnessed and used to accomplish her purposes. Allie despised all organized religions. As much as she hated anything remotely Christian, she equally looked down upon those who practiced Buddhism, and even outright Satanists, whom she felt were crass and their methods ineffective. As far as she was concerned, anyone involved in organized religion of any sort was weak and spiritually stunted.

For her, power was the ultimate goal. She knew that there was unlimited power available to her through the spirit realm, and once she got a taste of it, she was hungry for more. In the beginning, she had been more than a little frightened by some of the spirits that allowed her to channel them. She couldn't deny that some of them were evil, but they showed her favor and blessed her with such energy and spiritual awareness that she no longer cared. After all, she did not notice any sweet little cherubs flying around attempting to endow her with spiritual gifts or knowledge. Through much meditation and time spent with her wise old spirit guide Sayger, she had come to realize that good and evil were completely irrelevant. What really mattered was control, and Allie intended to have it all. Over a year ago, Sayger had ordered her to search for a gifted child. He insisted that the child would be the only way to increase her awareness and control in the spirit realm. Troy Welsh was this child. Of that, she was absolutely positive. She was desperate to get to him before he was spoiled by the fairy tale god of the Wesley's.

Her mind wandered back to the secret worship meeting held at her home the night before Geoffrey crossed over. Throughout the community, Allie had come to know a few select spiritual seekers who shared her pursuit of power and knowledge. They were men and women from all walks of life: a stay-at-home mom, a lawyer, a couple of dentists, a high school principal, and three science teachers as well as a coffee shop owner and a literary agent. Each member had been hand-picked by Allie and sworn to secrecy. Nearly all of the members had attended that night. The brisk air crackled with the electricity of their combined spiritual authority. Her massive heated pool was surrounded with flickering candles on tall wrought iron holders. The smell of incense permeated the air. Scentedtorches burned around the perimeter of the yard, casting an eerie glow on the unlikely gathering.

Geoffrey's mood that night had been uncharacteristically jovial. He bragged that he had attained spiritual powers beyond his wildest dreams. Allie called them to order and they stood in a perfect circle around the pool. They chanted, and each slipped into an altered state of consciousness. Then they performed their individual rites. They offered their worship to the earth, the wind, the moon, and the spirits that connected with and led them daily. Benevolently, their spirit guides rewarded their worship uniquely and personally. Each member felt that they had been anointed with divine knowledge and power that night.

Some swam naked deep into the night. Others performed sexual rites or recited incantations, inviting spirits to inhabit them. Geoffrey and Allie swam together, their long slow strokes synchronized. It excited them to feel the spirits swimming alongside, gently nudging and brushing up against their skin. Geoffrey told her that his spirit guide had presented himself visibly to him in the form of a young male child, with ancient eyes full of wisdom. Geoffrey had been jealous of Allie's spirit guide Sayger, who had visibly appeared to her several years ago as an old man with hollow eyes who smelled of fresh earth. Sayger had promised Allie that she would attain great influence and understanding. All she needed was an innocent one with the gift to unlock the doors for her.

Allie's eyes snapped open. Geoffrey's guiding spirit had manifested itself as a child. A child named Jacob. Now it all made sense. Jacob had sacrificed the animal as a way of insuring that Troy and Allie would meet. This boy must be the innocent one Sayger had promised would take her to the next level. She blew out the candle and watched as the twirling smoke ascended from the wick. Her painted lips curled into a triumphant smile. She had a plan.

***

The underlings of the Eternal One had also been there that black night. The spiritual stench had kept them at quite a distance, yet they still had a perfect view of the vulgar event. The sparkling waters of the pool were teeming with yellow-eyed demons, their razor sharp teeth shredding the souls of the deceived, although the deceived felt nothing. Not yet. Emboldened by the welcome of their worshipers, the cunning spirits swarmed from all corners of the globe. They whispered into the mortals' itching ears all the things they hungered to hear, and then cackled hysterically at their blind acceptance. Their hatred of these damned ones was visceral; nonetheless, the nefarious spirits greedily accepted their adoration. They fully intended to reward their worshippers with an unspeakable eternity from which there would be no escape.

***

Jake pounded on his wrench, willing the stubborn bolt to give way. When it finally did, his knuckles grazed the transmission. He cried out in pain and cursed at the top of his voice. He wiped the blood on his grease-stained shirt and attacked the bolt once again, ignoring his stinging knuckle and the ringing phone.

"Dave, are you going to get that?" Jake called out, obviously irritated. After another ring, he threw his wrench down and sighed. He rolled out from under the car and rushed to grab the phone. Apparently, Dave had stepped out. *Thanks for letting me know, Buddy*, Jake thought.

"D & J's Auto. Jake speaking."

"Mr. Welsh?" a sultry female voice asked.

"Speaking."

"I'm sorry to call you at work. I was wondering if I could have a few moments of your time."

Jake leaned against the wall. "We're really not interested in whatever you're selling."

"It's about Troy."

Jake pulled up a stool and sat. "You have my attention."

"My name is Allie McIntyre. I am a therapist. Your wife called this morning and insisted that your son needed to be seen immediately. I cleared my schedule and squeezed her in because of the violent episode she reported involving your son and the dog."

Jake winced. He hadn't planned on sharing that story with anyone, especially a mental health worker.

"After I briefly spoke with your wife, she decided that she didn't want your son to be evaluated after all and left in quite a hurry." Allie sighed, choosing her words carefully. "Frankly, Mr. Welsh, I am concerned that your wife may be psychologically unstable, and that her mental illness could be a contributing factor in your son's recent behavior." She gave this statement a few moments to sink in.

"She seems to be going through a rough patch," Jake admitted cautiously, uncomfortable with the direction this conversation was going.

"I thought as much." A sinister smile spread across Allie's face. She fought to keep her tone serious and sympathetic. "I really would hate to get social services involved if there is no need. That can be a huge mess for everyone."

"Why on earth would you call social services? Arin may be having a difficult time, but she has never raised a hand to hurt Troy."

"Mr. Welsh, I am required by law to report all types of abuse, neglect or child endangerment. The fact that your son killed your dog is a huge red flag for me to say the least. A sign that immediate intervention may be necessary." Allie paused for effect. All she had to do now was reel him in. "Professionally, I would feel much more comfortable with not alerting the authorities if I had an opportunity to meet with Troy privately and make sure that he is not a danger to himself or others."

Jake answered quickly, obviously relieved that there was a simple resolution. "Fine, whatever we need to do. I'll call Arin and have her set up another appointment."

"Under normal circumstances, that would certainly suffice. But I don't think you fully appreciate the inappropriateness of your wife's behavior today. She was extremely irrational and upset when she left, and I am not exactly sure what could have set her off. In my opinion, it would be best if you and Troy could come alone. I would hate for Troy to be subjected to another emotionally distressing scene."

Jake sighed. He simply did not have time for this. On the other hand, the thought of a social worker picking through their personal business was one of his worst nightmares, especially with Troy, and now Arin, behaving so bizarrely. Jake began to wonder if they were all losing their marbles.

"Give me the time and place and I'll be there."

"Actually, I plan on working late tomorrow evening. Would seven work for you?"

***

Allie gently placed the receiver back in its cradle, astonished at how effortless that had been. She stood in front of a full-length mirror and studied her reflection. She tossed her silky blonde hair and practiced faces of concern and sincerity, reciting her lines like an expert actress. Something about the sound of Jake Welsh's voice intrigued her—rugged and capable. Not since Geoffrey, whom she had grown easily bored with, had she had the arms of a strong man wrapped around her. Allie wondered if Jake Welsh shared his wife's archaic religious views. Something she picked up in the tone of his voice told her no.

"Mr. Welsh, I'll just need a few moments with Troy in private," she purred, her voice a strong undertow of seduction that was sure to carry any man away. Whispering, she finished her thought. "A few moments is all I'll need."

All four burners and both ovens were in use as Arin endeavored to prepare the perfect dinner for Jake. In the past, food had always been an easy way to recapture his heart. Arin, who was raised on corn chips and cereal, tried her best when it came to cooking. But she knew she had to try and do better. As she was covering the final layer of lasagna noodles with spinach and meat sauce, the phone rang. She snatched the portable from the wall, held the phone with her shoulder and continued her chore, seamlessly multi-tasking as only women seem to be equipped to do.

"Hello?"

"Arin?"

"Yeah."

"Hey, it's Taylor. Is this a bad time?"

"Not at all," Arin insisted, genuinely pleased to hear her voice. "How are you feeling?"

"The nausea should be over by the second trimester, right?" Taylor's voice dripped with sarcasm.

"You know, I have heard that Saltines are really helpful-"

"Don't you dare finish that sentence."

Arin smiled. It was a relief to enjoy some light-hearted banter. The heaviness of the last week was weighing her down. Taylor was just calling to check in on her. Arin peeked around the corner to make sure Troy was not in earshot before giving her a condensed version of Cooper's unfortunate demise. When Taylor gently inquired whether Arin was seeking some help for Troy, she explained her strange trip to Dr. McIntyre's office that morning. Taylor gasped at the mere mention of her name.

"Arin, please tell me you are not going to allow that woman to have access to your son."

"You know her?"

"I am a therapist. I mostly work with Christians for grief and marriage counseling. This is a small community, and mental health professionals get to know each other. Dr. McIntyre is-" Taylor stopped mid-sentence.

"Is what?" Arin prodded.

"I don't want to act like a stereotypical pastor's wife and gossip or assassinate her character. Please just take my word for it, okay? She is not the sort of person that you want involved with your son." Arin agreed, although she was a bit disappointed. She wouldn't have minded a little juicy gossip right now to take her mind off of everything else. An idea suddenly came to her.

"How much do you charge for therapy? After my experience today, I would much rather Troy talk to someone I know and trust, even if I do have to pay out of pocket."

"Arin, I would be happy to meet Troy and work together with you and Jake to figure out what's going on. No charge. I consider it a ministry opportunity to help out where I can, especially within the body of Christ."

Arin wasn't exactly sure that she could technically be considered a part of Christ's body, and found the whole concept slightly creepy, but either way she was grateful. They decided to meet the next afternoon for Troy's first session. Arin felt a heavy burden lift from her shoulders. Perhaps there was an end to this nightmare in sight and they could return to some sense of normalcy.

***

Troy sat in the very back of his closet behind all the hanging clothes and old toys. He hugged his knees and concentrated on keeping his sobbing silent. He was terrified of what Jacob could do to his Mommy or Daddy. Pressing his palms tightly against his ears, he tried to block the sound of Jacob's deep raspy voice as he spouted bad words and made bloody threats. Troy began to rock and cry harder, his thoughts turning to poor Cooper and what Jacob had made him do. He could not clearly remember hurting Cooper, but his hand had held the bloody knife. Dimly, he recalled the look of disbelief in Cooper's eyes as the knife plunged in again and again.

He shuttered at Jacob's violent threats to hurt Mommy. Jacob was very upset at Mommy for not letting him talk to Ms. Allie, and he called Mrs. Taylor a very bad word. Troy closed his eyes and pressed his palms tighter against his ears. He struggled to remember something Mrs.

Webber had said in Sunday School. Jacob had done his best to make sure that Troy did not hear a word of it, but Troy had grabbed onto something the sweet old lady had said. It had been in some book called Psalm twenty-three. In his mind, where Jacob could not go, he repeated the line over and over. It comforted him and calmed his breathing. I will fear no evil, for You are with me. I will fear no evil, for You are with me. Troy didn't even know for sure who the You in the passage was, but he knew down deep that whoever it was, He had the power to rescue him from Jacob.

The horrific threats continued. Jacob had worked himself into a frenzied tantrum. He ranted and raved, promising bloody retribution to Arin, as well as Taylor Wesley, and anyone else who stood in his way. He was so caught up in his fury that he was completely unaware that deep within the closet, the Eternal One's peace had flooded his captive's soul.

***

The champagne Mercedes convertible brazenly rolled into the only handicapped spot in the parking lot of the Silver Fox Nursery. The shapely and obviously able-bodied Allie McIntyre emerged. She had an hour to kill before her next appointment. Geoffrey had failed to come to her, despite multiple efforts at channeling him. One of her wisest spirit guides suggested that she go to the place where his soul and body had been separated in hopes of enticing him.

She was startled by the flashing lights as she entered the balmy greenhouse, and understood their purpose as soon as she saw a striking silver-haired woman rapidly signing with an employee. Allie rolled her eyes. She found dealing with the deaf tedious and rather excruciating. Smiling sweetly in their direction, she turned and focused her attention on discerning the exact spot Geoffrey had chosen for his ascension. She was led past the vast expanse of the greenhouse and its impressive collection of plants and trees. The mosaic steps that led to the gazebo and exotic birds were marked with a "Private" sign. The spirits within her became anxious as they neared the gazebo. Powerful unseen forces urged her to hurry past.

Allie continued on until she had reached the very back of the greenhouse. It was completely secluded by rows of tall trees and shrubs and, lucky for her, devoid of customers at the time. The spirit guiding her strongly implied that this was the place. She glanced up at the rafters and was startled to see Geoffrey's body hanging limply, his tongue blue and thick, his hideous eyes wide and bulging. Closing her eyes tightly, she asked the spirit to take the unpleasant image away. She was horrified that it was still there when she opened them again. Sitting Indian style on the cold concrete floor, Allie listened and did exactly what her spirit guide instructed. When she awakened from her trance thirty minutes later, the image was gone. She stood and exited the greenhouse quickly. She knew exactly what she had to do.

***

Rae flashed the lights throughout the greenhouse to alert any stragglers that it was closing time. Her newest employee headed home. He was a sweet teenager from the Maryland School for the Deaf with a green thumb and an uncommon work ethic. With all the out of town business coming her way, Rae could finally afford to hire some help. She was giddy at the prospect of actually having a life again. She missed spending time with Arin and Troy. During her prayer time every morning in the oasis, she prayed fervently as she had for years, and resolved to do for as long as it was necessary. She sensed that Arin was on the verge of a breakthrough . . . or a breakdown. Rae prayed for the former. She feared for Troy and prayed that God would protect his innocence.

Since finding the body of Geoffrey Raines, she cautiously inspected every row. She was now hyper-vigilant in making sure that no one remained in the huge greenhouse when she locked up. Forcing her feet ahead, she neared the end of the building where the body had been found. It still gave her the creeps. Turning the corner, she stopped dead in her tracks. The sight before her caused bile to rise in her throat. On the concrete floor, directly below where the body had been hanging was a huge perfectly circular pentagram. Inside of it was an upside down cross facing south. It appeared to have been roughly drawn with fresh soil. When Rae was finally able to remove her eyes from the unwelcome symbol, she noticed something that turned her blood to ice. She sprinted out of there as fast as her long legs would take her. The circle of trees and shrubs surrounding the pentagram, which had been perfectly healthy just hours before, had since dried up. Leaves, brown and frail with death, were scattered around the circle on the concrete floor.

J ake slinked through the back door, hoping that without Cooper to announce his arrival, he could just grab a shower and go to bed. The last thing he needed right now was a barrage of questions about where he'd been and why he was late. It wasn't like he had intentionally worked so late. If he was going to take off early the next night to get Troy to Dr. McIntyre's office to patch up the mess Arin had created, he had to finish a few jobs. Arin would never understand that. His cell phone had rung incessantly. He ignored it and finally put it on silent. He just couldn't deal with her right now. There was a note for him on the counter, which seemed to be the only way either of them was communicating these days.

Jake, homemade lasagna in the fridge. Sorry it got a little dry. I thought you would be home. I tried your cell. I guess you must have been busy. Love you.

A wave of guilt rushed toward him and he expertly shoved it away. He crumpled the note and scored two points when it sailed into the trash. He showered and slipped into bed, his back to Arin, who feigned sleep beside him. Her was pillow damp with tears. The rift between them widened with each passing day, and neither one of them had a clue about how to fix it, or if it was even fixable.

Jacob casually leaned against the doorframe of their bedroom, the corners of his mouth turned up in an evil half-smile of satisfaction. The deeper the wedge was driven between this husband and wife, the closer he was to a complete victory.

***

Rae Stewart was normally an incredibly laid back individual, often to a fault. She was blessed with the ability to blow off offenses and allow insults and rejection to roll off her like water on a duck's back. Anger, practically a foreign emotion for her, had unexpectedly washed over her and filled her to the brim. Restless, she paced around her condo, cleaning rag in one hand, furniture polish in the other. She viciously obliterated the innocent dust bunnies and cobwebs that had been allowed to thrive for far too long. Rae spent virtually all day, every day, at the Silver Fox and had essentially no time at home. At least not when she was awake and vertical. When she did have a few spare moments, dusting was hardly at the top of her list of things to do.

Rae's flurry of activity halted when she picked up the framed picture of Sam, her late husband. With great care she wiped the glass and pewter frame. The main reason she rarely stopped long enough to think these days was because every time she paused, her thoughts would always turn to Sam. They had met in a horticulture class. The college had provided an interpreter for Rae, but on the first day, Sam had asked if he could do the honors. He was a CODA—a child of a deaf adult—and he insisted that he needed the practice. The school certainly didn't mind saving the money.

They grabbed a cup of coffee together after class. Sam was quite a catch, a handsome man with integrity as well as a fantastic sense of humor. Rae, a new Christian herself, was thrilled when she discovered that he shared her faith in Christ. In addition, he shared Rae's passion for exotic plants and birds. A year later to the day, they married in a simple ceremony held at the small church Sam had grown up in. The wordless service was performed by a young deaf minister and attended by a small group of close friends and family. For years, they had scrimped and saved in hopes of making their dream of owning a greenhouse come to fruition. In the early days things were tight, but they doggedly pursued their dream until the greenhouse was up and running. Sam insisted on dubbing their business The Silver Fox, which was his pet name for his young silver-haired bride.

Her thoughts returned to the present. The fact that someone had defiled the place that she and Sam had worked so hard to build together made Rae so livid she could spit nails. Gently, she touched Sam's mouth with her finger and stared into his kind eyes. How she yearned for him right now. Sam always knew what to do.

The heavy frame vibrated slightly in her hands and the glass shattered. Rae recoiled and dropped it in shock. Cautiously, she knelt by the portrait of her beloved Sam, the glass now cracked and spread out like a spider's web. Sam's bright blue eyes blinked and turned dark and menacing. Horrified, she stumbled backwards in an attempt to get away from the animated photo, and tripped over a magazine rack. On her hands and knees, she scurried across the room and huddled in the corner. Like a frightened child, she shielded her eyes with her hands. Every few seconds, she peeked at the picture frame from between her fingers, expecting it to somehow pursue her.

She resolved to get a grip and tried to push the terror away. There was a fierce spiritual battle raging right now. For some reason beyond her comprehension, she, as well as Arin and Troy, were smack dab in the middle of it. Her hands fervently poured out her fear and petitions for spiritual protection for herself and her loved ones. Her Heavenly Father heard her requests without the need of an interpreter and granted them immediately. The evil ones were banished and a strong warrior was dispatched to comfort the Holy One's dear child. Immediately, her spirit was calmed. Although Rae was still frightened, she was comforted by her steadfast faith in the Almighty One, and the fact that she was safe and secure in His embrace.

***

Emily Raines rose with the sun as usual. She was determined that today was the day that she would finally sort through the boxes of things Geoffrey had left behind. Ever since they had separated, she had been putting off this unpleasant task. Now that he was dead, she could no longer justify her procrastination. Kira, her regal yet quirky Akita, ran in circles ahead of her, anxious for her romp outside. Emily threw on some sweats and they headed out the door with her scooper and bag dutifully in tow. Kira led the way down the driveway to the sidewalk and turned left, as they did every morning. Emily and Kira thoroughly enjoyed their daily walk, although when it came time to cross the street, Emily had to practically drag the pup across. Emily had decided that Kira must suffer from a touch of dromophobia, the fear of crossing the street. Even at this early hour, the sidewalks outside her house were bustling with runners, joggers, cyclists, walkers, and an odd elderly stroller here and there.

Emily and Kira started their jaunt around Baker Park and settled into their pace. Emily nodded hello to the other park patrons who made eye contact. Silently she prayed, thanking God for this beautiful day and for His unconditional love. Her thoughts and prayers turned to Arin Welsh. Talking with her the previous night had been a powerful experience for her. Sharing her story had helped her heal in some respects, but it also brought her own shame and guilt to the surface. They were emotions she'd thought she was long past. Emily shook her head and picked up speed. As she had on countless occasions, she asked God to continue His perfect healing in her heart. Without a doubt, she knew that He had forgiven her. But this did not change the fact that every time she saw a child the age that her child would have been, she couldn't help but wonder. She longed to have a family one day. She was haunted by the familiar fear that she would never marry again, she wound never be a mother. Her biological clock was more like a bomb ticking away.

It took some emotional gymnastics on her part, but Emily was able to shove the fear aside and make the decision to put her trust in God. He knew her past as well as her future, and had a special plan for her. Fear was a tricky thing, and she knew that if she caved into it, she would no doubt divert from the path that God had for her to follow. She had to learn to trust that He had given her the desire to be a mother not to torture her, but to help her to be a great one when the time was right.

Another tool she used to combat her fear was to remember Ronnie Clark, an unfortunate soul she had befriended when she was a freshman in college. He was handsome enough, but he was plagued by fear and paranoia to the point that the last Emily had heard, he no longer left his house. Strictly out of compassion, Emily had continued to correspond with him over the years. His letters taught her quite a bit about mental illness and phobias, in particular. It amazed her that there were so many of them, and with each of his letters Ronnie would inform her that he had been diagnosed with another. It started with pyrophobia, or fear of fire. That seemed reasonable enough to Emily, who also had a healthy fear of fire. A week later, poor Ronnie confessed that, in addition, he suffered with heliophobia, the fear of the sun, catoptrophobia, the fear of mirrors, and even bathmorphobia, the fear of stairs or a sharp incline. Emily had done her best to console him while trying to suggest that perhaps he needed a new therapist. She wondered if Ronnie had developed papyrphobia, or fear of paper, since his letters suddenly stopped after she suggested that the various phobias were psychosomatic. To this day, phobias held great interest to her. She prided herself on knowing all of them, even the strangest and most rare phobias such as lutraphobia, or fear of otters. She used the exaggerated story of Ronnie Clark to keep herself from stepping into a prison of fear and doubt.

Invigorated by her walk, Emily thanked the Lord that she did not suffer from agoraphobia. She trudged up the stone walkway to the brick Cape Cod that she'd shared with Geoffrey. After depositing Kira's morning constitutional in the trash can, she changed and got to work. Geoffrey had taken most everything of any value when he'd left her.

Only one corner of the musty basement attested to the fact that he'd ever lived there at all. She stood for a few moments, hands on hips, surveying the various boxes and garment bags. Kira sat at her side with her head cocked, one ear up, one ear down. For a brief moment, Emily considered trashing all of it. However, guilt prevailed and she rolled up her sleeves and got to work.

Wading through Geoffrey's expensive but out of style suits, golf clubs, and watches, Emily found herself mourning for the first time since his death. Not necessarily because she would miss him, but for the emptiness of the life he had led. Tossing his once valued belongings in the Goodwill pile intensified the feeling. Geoffrey had been a brilliant man. Medicine had always seemed to come naturally for him. He often remarked that he snoozed through medical school, waking only for tests and internships. He was gifted with an amazing mind, yet he never used his God-given intellect for the good of others. In the end, he had wasted his talent and left a legacy of aborted babies and hurting women. Emily prayed that she would not waste her life. With each passing day, it became increasingly vital to her that after she was gone, there would be someone whose life was better because she had lived. There was a sudden primal urge in her heart to use the time she had left wisely, to make it count for eternity. She prayed that this time the urge would not ebb and flow like the tide, as emotions usually do. Instead, she wanted it to impact every aspect of her daily life. She was young, but she knew that her next breath was not guaranteed to her. Tomorrow was not a sure thing.

The last box she came to was old and practically falling apart. It had been underneath some heavier boxes of books and golf trophies. Emily seriously doubted that Geoffrey had meant to leave it behind. It was labeled "Patient Files. Confidential". Geoffrey had always been extremely secretive when it came to his files. Emily was conflicted for a moment about what she should do with the contents of this box. They were, after all, private medical documents, and patients deserved their privacy. Inspired, she ran upstairs and grabbed her professional grade shredder, which she affectionately referred to as "Jaws". Her paranoia about being the victim of identity theft was finally paying off.

Before opening the box, she promised herself that she would shred everything without peeking. She would fight the urge to invade anyone's privacy. Happily, she shredded one file after another. There was something about the sound and feel of the powerful iron teeth chewing the manila files, staples and all, that intrigued her. Jaws was indeed an awesome shredding machine, just as the salesman at the office superstore had promised. As the files in the box dwindled, she felt a spark of sadness. Surely there must be something else around the house that needed shredding.

"Almost finished, girl," she called over her shoulder to Kira, who sat nearby. She lacked her owner's obvious enthusiasm for the noisy machine and eyed it warily. As she loaded the last file into the mouth of the powerful shredder, something caught her eye. She flipped the reverse switch, and rescued the file from the razor sharp teeth just in time. Gasping, her hand flew to her mouth. In her shaking hands, she held a confidential medical file for patient Arin Welsh.

S harp rapping at the door was a welcome interruption of Jake and Arin's less than cordial conversation.

"Expecting someone?" Jake asked in a severe tone.

"No, are you?" Arin's tone was equally snappish. She padded to the door in her slippers, coffee in hand. When she opened the door she was hit with such an overwhelming wave of déjà vu that she stumbled backwards. She grabbed the doorknob for support and regained her composure. Again, a tall, thin, black man in a button-down shirt and dress pants holding a notebook stood at her door. Arin blinked wordlessly, attempting to fathom what on earth could have brought him to her home yet again.

"Good morning, Mrs. Welsh," he offered respectfully. "I don't know if you remember me. Detective Lyons with the Frederick County Police Department."

Arin snapped out of it in time to invite him in. Jake flashed a questioning look and she simply shrugged. Jake poured the detective a cup of coffee, stirred in a bit of creamer and set it in front of him at the breakfast bar without bothering to ask if he even wanted any. All three of them settled into the exact positions they had been in during his last visit. It was actually quite eerie. It would not have surprised Arin to hear "The Twilight Zone" theme song followed by Rod Serling strolling into the kitchen.

This morning, Detective Lyons did not waste any time getting to the point. "There has been another incident at the Silver Fox," he started, his voice gentle and soothing. Before Arin could get the words out, he reassured her. "Ms. Stewart is fine. Absolutely fine. Someone vandalized a portion of the greenhouse. It was probably just some kids fascinated by the suicide." Arin and Jake exchanged glances. If that's all there was to the story, then why was he here?

"I just wanted to stop by and check in. I thought perhaps your son had mentioned something else about that day at the greenhouse. Often a witness feels that something they remember is too insignificant to warrant contacting the officer, but what they have to say can actually be extremely helpful." The kitchen was filled with flat silence. Jake studied a scratch in the counter and Arin fiddled self-consciously with her hair, which was so full of tangles it was more like a nest than a head of hair. Neither could think of anything concrete to tell the detective, but they also could not discount that the day of the suicide had been the day all their lives took a strange turn for the worse.

"Vandalized how?" Arin asked, more to end the silence than out of curiosity. Now Detective Lyons seemed uncomfortable.

"May I inquire about your spiritual beliefs?" he asked unexpectedly.

"What could that possibly have to do with the vandalism at The Silver Fox?" It was an understatement to say that Jake easily went on the defense when it came to religion.

"You could say that the message left by the vandals was spiritual in nature."

Now Arin was completely baffled. Was there a band of renegade Christian youth out there, boom boxes blasting Jesus rock into their heavily pierced ears, crosses dangling from their necks as they busted into greenhouses, scrawling scripture and prayer requests in spray paint?

"Huh?"

Detective Lyons spoke deliberately, carefully choosing his words. "An occult symbol was left at the site of the suicide. I don't know if the two incidents are related or not, but I didn't think there was any harm in checking back with you folks."

"Thanks for checking in," Jake said, standing abruptly. "Our son has not given us any more information about that day, but he has been deeply affected by the suicide. He's seeing a counselor now to help him get through it. If he shares any information with us, even if it seems unimportant, we will certainly let you know." Jakes voice was firm and his message clear. Don't call us, we'll call you. Detective Lyons politely thanked them and showed himself to the door.

They stared after him a moment. Finally, Arin broke the silence.

"Taylor is going to meet with Troy today. I wasn't aware before that she's a counselor, and she said that she is willing to work with Troy without even charging us. Isn't that great?"

"Taylor who?"

"Taylor Wesley, Pastor Wesley's wife. You would know her if you saw her. Long red hair."

Jake nodded. He remembered meeting her the previous Sunday. "What sort of counselor is she? She isn't going to try and convert him or make him join the church or something, is she? Don't get me wrong. It is a very nice offer and all, but why would she want to work for free? It just doesn't make sense, Arin."

"Relax, Jake. She's a professional, but she's also a Christian and just wants to help. I wouldn't worry about Taylor. You should have heard some of the nonsense that Dr. McIntyre was spouting off today, though. Boy, did we dodge a bullet with her. That woman is certifiable."

Jake winced when he noticed the time. He gulped his coffee and grabbed his jacket. "Gotta run. I'm already late." The door slammed, and he was gone without so much as a peck on the cheek.

"Good bye and I love you too, Honey," Arin spat sarcastically at the door. What had she done to earn Jake's sudden disdain? She was not ignorant of or in denial of her faults. She had a whole plethora of them. She was aware that she was not always the easiest person to live with. In the past, they had worked hard to keep the lines of communication open and made allowances for each other's quirks and character flaws. He had even confessed at various times that he thought some of her faults and quirks were cute, like when she wiggled her toes all night long or ate one thing at a time before moving on to the next thing. She highly doubted that he considered anything she did these days to be cute.

Arin paused at the mirror over the sofa and cringed. Her reddish hair was matted and unruly. Dark blotches under her red rimmed eyes betrayed the fact that she had not slept well for quite some time. Her cheeks flushed red with embarrassment. It was bad enough that her husband had seen her in such a state. Detective Lyons must think she just came off of a ten day drunk. Arin turned away from her reflection, disgusted and ashamed. She felt completely unlovable. No wonder Jake had absolutely no desire to touch her these days. Groaning, she headed for the shower, hoping to wash away the weary wretch the mirror had reflected to reveal a younger, fresher version.

***

Couch cushions and pillows flew as Arin dug for her keys. She knew without question that they had been in her purse the night before. Yet when she had emptied her purse on the counter, tossed the trash, and returned the countless items she insisted on carrying around for no good reason, her search was fruitless. Her keys were nowhere to be found. As absentminded as Arin knew she could be, and she admitted that she was in pretty much the same boat as the folks in the Alzheimer's unit when it came to memory, she had a fairly good track record with keys. For nearly an hour she paced the house, looking in the same places that she had already checked twelve times, hoping that the keys might have somehow snuck there when her back was turned.

At the end of her rope and intent on enlisting Troy in the search, she burst into his room. She found him sitting on the edge of his bed. He stuffed something behind his back as she entered and hung his head.

"Troy, baby, have you seen my keys? If we don't get going soon we're going to be late for our visit with Mrs. Taylor. I have looked everywhere and would really appreciate your help."

"I don't want to go."

"You don't want to go, or Jacob doesn't want you to go?" Arin asked softly, hating the fact that the bratty specter was probably right next to her.

"Neither one of us wants to go. We want to talk to Ms. Allie."

Arin felt like smacking the surly child. Instead, she grabbed Troy and tickled his underarms and tummy until he allowed a weak giggle to escape. As Arin put him down, she noticed her keys in plain view on the bed where Troy had been sitting a moment ago. Arin snatched them up and fought to gain control over her tongue. Kneeling to his level, she looked Troy sternly in the eye, clearly communicating to him that she meant business.

"Let's go. Now." Troy held his stare, his eyes insolent. "Move," Arin bellowed.

They marched down the hallway toward the stairs. Arin glanced over her shoulder to make sure that Troy was following. He was, his shoulders hunched and head hanging low, obviously unenthusiastic. His reluctance added fuel to the fire of Arin's smoldering anger. She intended to have a talk with him on the way to Taylor's house. She would not tolerate him acting disrespectfully toward her while she was doing them such a huge favor.

Arin took the first step and shrieked when her foot slipped. A second later, she was bouncing down the steep wooden stairs like a rag doll. Her body banged painfully against each step, all the way down. At last she landed, her battered body splayed on the floor. Desperately, she fought to maintain consciousness, but the blackness came for her and would not be denied. Everything faded and slipped away...

***

"Mom, push me, push me!" Troy begged, situating himself on an old black rubber swing. Arin happily padded barefoot across the lush emerald grass toward her son. The sun was high and bright in the cloudless sky. What a perfect day, she thought.

"Push me, too!" said another boy, as he climbed onto the swing next to Troy, his back to Arin. Arin searched for the boy's mother, but there was not another adult or child in sight.

"Hold on, guys!" she warned, as she began to push them hard, high, and fast, exactly the way she knew that little boys liked it. Troy squealed with delight, and the other boy parroted his squeal. Arin continued to push the boys for several minutes, until they declared that they could maintain on their own. By that time, they were going equally fast and high, the chain jumping each time it ascended or descended. Most mothers would probably frown on her allowing her boy and his friend to swing so high and fast. Arin trusted that Troy would hold on tightly.

She sat on an old blanket under an Ash tree. The boys' giggles mixed with the jumping chain were music to her ears. She was transported back in time to the old rusty swing set that had been in the run down park near her foster parents' home. Many an evening, she would run from the soundless house for the sanctuary the swing offered her. For hours on end, she would swing as hard and high as the old rusty thing would allow, her big toe aiming for the clouds, for the sky, for the Milky Way. The motion always calmed her and temporarily soothed her lonely heart. Often times she would scream at the top of her lungs, begging someone to hear, someone who could make a difference in her empty life. She had channeled her longing for a mother and father into that old rusty swing. Although nothing externally ever changed for her as a child, Arin could not pass by an old swing set without a moment of fond remembrance.

"What's for lunch?" Troy asked, finished with swinging. A strange echo accompanied his voice.

"I don't know," Arin stammered, suddenly feeling panicked and unprepared. "I didn't pack anything."

"How could you be that stupid?" The harsh comment echoed inside Arin's mind and shame washed over her. She was shocked that her son would speak to her with such disrespect. As she decided what punishment would be most appropriate for his surliness and lack of respect, it occurred to her how completely unlike Troy that comment really was.

Arin bolted upright, determined to discipline her son before his attitude got any further out of control. Troy sat directly across from her, and next to him was… his twin. Arin gasped at the impossibility of what she saw. How could she know which one truly belonged to her? Did they both belong to her? She examined each boy. They each wore identical Thomas the Tank Engine t-shirts, blue sweatpants, and Thomas velcro sneakers. The cautiously optimistic dreams she had clung to when she had been carrying twins came rushing back to her. She had dreamed of dressing them alike. They would play together, bathe together, eat and sleep together, and they would love each other in the special and mysterious way that only twins can. Those months that she had secretly carried the twins had been bittersweet for Arin. Although she desperately wanted them both, from the very beginning she had known in her gut that it was not possible. Still her mind had allowed her to dream about what it would have been like to carry and deliver twins. Of course, after her encounter with Dr. Raines, the dreams and speculation came to an abrupt end.

"Mommy, I love you," said the first boy. His sweet voice baited the hook that reeled Arin back from the depths of her thoughts.

"Mommy, I own you," declared the second. Jacob.

"Please don't be angry with me, Jacob," Arin pleaded. "I didn't know what else to do. I really did want you. God, I am so sorry Jacob. I wanted you so badly…"

***

"Mommy? Mommy, are you okay?" Troy's little face was bunched with worry. The concern in his voice brought her back from her heart wrenching dream to her physically excruciating reality.

Arin's vision was blurry, pain exploded from her head, wrist, side, and hip. She attempted to shake the eerie dream out of her head, but when she tried, brand new pain erupted from her neck and traveled down both arms. Cautiously, Arin moved her legs until she was relatively sure they were not broken. Next, she rotated her wrist painfully, but easily enough to reason that it was just a sprain. Gingerly, she turned her head and looked to the top of the stairs. Several of Troy's toy cars were scattered on the first few steps. Arin knew wither certainty that they had not been there when she climbed those stairs just moments before.

***

Emily paced around her kitchen island for perhaps the hundredth time. Kira observed her curiously from the doorway. Her mistress was acting strangely today.

"I just need to call her and get it over with," Emily decisively declared to Kira, who blinked in agreement. She purposefully strode over to the phone. When she got there, she hesitated. Indecision inundated her again.

"It is really none of my business." She performed this strange dance for at least twenty minutes before she finally decided to call. What was the harm? She'd been wanting to follow up with Arin since their last conversation. Emily sensed that she needed the Lord, and hoped that the chaos in her life would lead her to letting go of the reins and giving her life over to God. She snatched the napkin Arin had scribbled her name and number on, grabbed the phone, and dialed before she had a chance to change her mind again.

***

Arin lay completely still at the foot of the steps. Troy sat faithfully by her side, stroking her hand and brushing the hair from her eyes. Disoriented and vulnerable, Arin felt something that was completely foreign to her relationship with her son until this moment- fear. She tried to focus on his small face looming over her. Was it possible that she had a concrete reason to fear him? A preschooler? Scenes flashed in her mind of the bloody playroom wall, the red slash marks across the faces in Troy's baby book, and the conspicuously placed toy cars on the first step. The ringing phone startled them both. Arin whimpered as she stood and pathetically limped across the room, answering on the seventh ring.

"Hello?" she managed weakly.

"Arin, it's Emily. Is this a bad time?"

Arin waded through the clouds of confusion that had formed in her brain. Emily, Emily…the former Mrs. Raines. Finally the name and face registered. It clicked in her mind that Emily was a registered nurse.

"I need your help," she whispered, her jaw clenched as a sharp pain shot down her neck to her left arm. "Please come. Right now." Arin struggled to give the address.

Emily had her keys and trauma bag in hand before she even hung up the phone. Recognizing the panic and urgency in Arin's voice, she knew there was no time to waste.

"Not this time, girl," Emily cooed. Kira, who was always energized by the jiggling of her mistresses keys, was more than a little put out that she was being left behind. Emily made good time through town and only sat through one red light.

***

"I'm sure that they're fine," Ben insisted. "Are you certain that you guys didn't get your days confused or something? You know that pregnancy can do some crazy things to your memory," he teased.

"I'm sure," Taylor shot back, a little annoyed.

"Maybe you should call?"

"Maybe," Taylor had a bad feeling she could not shake. Hunger pangs reminded her that, more than anything, Arin and her family needed prayer. Following the Bibles teaching that some spirits can only be removed with fasting and prayer, Taylor and Ben had decided to fast and pray today. From what Taylor had heard was going on in the Welsh household, there were some spirits that needed to be removed. Fasting was something that held great mystery for Taylor. She had been practicing the principle once or twice a month for the last few years and felt that she had grown spiritually through it. At first, she figured that the whole point was to be disciplined and to deny yourself of something in order to devote your attention more wholly to prayer. In the last few months, though, Taylor had learned through fasting that it was a way of learning how to deny the appetites of the flesh—physical, spiritual, and emotional—and to feed on the pure spiritual food that God has for each of us. Fasting is simply a way to bring the mind and body to a place where they are able to receive nourishment for our souls from the hand of God. Of course, since she was eating for two now, she had revised her fast to include juice, veggies, and fruit.

"Let's pray," Taylor said softly. Ben smiled, grateful for a godly wife and soon-to-be mother of their baby. He slid into the chair beside her and gently clasped her hand. In unison they sought their Heavenly Father in prayer. They begged for a strong hedge of protection, both physical and spiritual for Arin, Troy and Jake.

***

Emily banged on the Welsh's locked front door. An adorable little boy boasting Arin's unusual brown eyes let her in. The look on his freckled face bordered on panic.

"Mommy's hurt. She fell down the stairs." He grabbed her hand and tugged, pulling her to the living room where Arin had managed to collapse on the couch.

"Hi," Arin said faintly, her eyes grateful.

"Is Mommy okay?"

"Of course she is." Emily's voice was strong and confident. She easily shifted into the familiar role as a trauma nurse. "I'm going to need a few minutes to help her feel better." Emily reached into the large leather bag slung over her shoulder. "I bet you like Thomas the Tank Engine." Troy nodded, a hint of a smile forming on his lips. "I brought this coloring book. Do you think you could color Mommy a nice picture? I think that would really help her a lot, wouldn't it, Mommy?"

"That would be wonderful," Arin squeaked.

Troy's eyes lit up. He grabbed the coloring book and took off to create another masterpiece for their refrigerator gallery.

"You're a genius."

"I know," Emily agreed. She searched her bag for her stethoscope. "What happened to you?"

Arin did her best to explain her painful down-the-stairs fall due to the toys that had been placed on the first step. It would have been impossible for Troy to have placed them there. He had been behind her the entire time and simply didn't have the opportunity. No one else had been in the house at the time. No one, she thought, except Jacob.

A half an hour later, Emily was satisfied that no major bones were broken, although she was certain that Arin had probably cracked a rib or two. She explained unless the bone interfered with the function of the lung, there was really no treatment for rib fractures other than bandages and ice. She'd listened to Arin's lung sounds intently until she was convinced that she was not in danger. Emily was, however, quite concerned that Arin may have suffered a concussion. She shined her tiny flashlight into Arin's eyes and was relieved that the pupils were equal and reactive. Arin denied any nausea, ringing in her ears, or headache. She was aware that she had lost consciousness, but she had no clue how long she had been out. Late for her shift at the local hospital, Emily hastily gathered her things. She stood, hands on hips, scrutinizing her patient.

"Well, you are going to make it. But I think after today, you are likely to suffer from a serious case of climacaphobia."

"What?" Arin asked. "It sounds serious."

Emily smiled and winked as she turned to leave. "Fear of falling down the stairs, she called over her shoulder. "I don't feel good about leaving you. Can't I give your husband a call?" Emily urged from the kitchen.

"Jake will be home anytime," Arin lied. "Troy can help me out with pretty much anything I need. I know he'll take great care of me."

Emily caught herself before she could say that was what she was afraid of. She scribbled her cell phone number on a Post-it in the kitchen and gently hugged Arin before she left. A green truck was pulling into Arin's driveway as Emily jogged to her car. A tall silver haired woman whom she recognized from Downsville Christian Fellowship hopped out. Emily waved and offered a friendly hello, but the woman did not look up. Emily tossed her bag on the seat beside her and sped off. For now, the medical file lying on the seat was completely forgotten.

***

Rae sat on the floor next to the couch, her long fingers skillfully rubbing medicated ointment into Arin's stiff neck and shoulders. Since Arin's wrist was out of commission, Rae did most of the talking. Arin's eyes widened as Rae described the chilling scene at the greenhouse the day before. Arin had not known what to think when the detective said the vandals had left some sort of an occult symbol. It was obvious to Arin that Rae had been deeply affected by the second incident at The Silver Fox. As she recounted it, her signs had a blunt characteristic to them that was unlike her typical fluid style.

Conflicted, Arin wrestled with the urge to tell Rae everything about Dr. Raines and Jacob. It had been nearly impossible to keep so many secrets from her dearest friend. If not for the burning pain in her wrist, she probably would have come clean. At the same time, Arin knew that it would hurt Rae deeply to know that she had kept such important things from her for all of these years. She was the best friend Arin had ever had, completely loyal and compassionate.

Rae, who lived to serve, busied herself with various tasks in the kitchen. She grilled a cheese sandwich for Troy and heated up a can of vegetable soup for Arin. She arranged the soup and crackers on a TV tray in front of the couch and gently lifted her to a sitting position. Generally, Arin was fiercely independent and would have despised being babied. At this point, the pain and stiffness were such that she was grateful for any and all help she could get. After lunch, Rae put on Troy's favorite Thomas video. He was overjoyed. Arin rarely let him watch TV during the week unless he was sick. After the pillows had been fluffed and she had removed Arin's shoes, Rae insisted on signing some of her favorite Psalms for Arin. She implored her to open her mind and pay attention. Though Arin rolled her eyes in protest, Rae was not discouraged in the least. She knew that God was screaming to Arin through her struggles right now. Her daily prayer for the past five years was that Arin would just take that first step towards her Creator. She knew from personal experience that He would do the rest, and that Arin would never, ever regret it.

Without further complaint, Arin observed as Rae signed with a more dramatic flair than she would usually use with normal conversation. She found herself being drawn in, intrigued. Even as a non-believer, Arin had to admit that the Psalms were beautiful. They had a haunting and somewhat enigmatic quality to them. She could easily relate to the down-and-out theme that ran through many of the Psalms of David. Rae paused between each one to set the stage for Arin, informing her that David wrote this one when Saul was trying to kill him, or he wrote that one after he killed someone. It came as a surprise to Arin that David that the same boy who had slain a giant with a single stone had also committed adultery and murder. It made him seem more like an actual human than some fairy tale character. In particular, she was fond of Psalm 103, and even asked Rae to repeat a certain part that she found especially appealing. Rae did so gladly, encouraged by Arin's interest.

"His unfailing love toward those who fear him is as high as the heavens above the earth; He has removed our rebellious acts as far away from us as the east is from the west." Rae's hands were transformed to beautiful instruments charged with delivering the very message of God.

The Intrusion

"Thanks, Rae," she said aloud, although she knew that Rae would never hear her words. Arin yawned. She allowed her eyes to close, and slipped into a peaceful sleep. Rae rocked vigilantly beside her, praying for her friend, oblivious to the ringing phone.

"Yo Mamma is so stupid, it takes her two hours to watch '60 Minutes'," Dave called from underneath a Cadillac. It took Jake a few minutes to respond. He had to admit that one was pretty good.

"Yo Mamma is so fat, when she steps on the scale it says 'to be continued'." Dave whistled, amazed by Jake's comeback. It would take him some time to one up him, but he always did.

While Jake finished up on a brake job, he stressed about his appointment that evening with Dr. McIntyre. He still had not settled on what story would be best to tell Arin in order to get out of the house with Troy. Of one thing he was certain: he could not tell her where he was really going. Arin had made it very clear how she felt about Dr. McIntyre. Briefly, Jake considered canceling the appointment, but decided against it after just a moment's consideration. The fear of social workers, which may even have qualified as a phobia, was too great. Ever since the incident with Cooper, Jake had felt like his family was spiraling downward, spinning out of control. He would not risk losing Troy.

For perhaps the thousandth time, he replayed in his mind the conversation with Dr. McIntyre. Jake was sure he had not imagined the seductive tone in her sultry voice. He found himself wondering what she might look like and eagerly anticipating their meeting later that evening. He hoped that he had time to shower and shave. Suddenly ashamed of the path his thoughts had taken, he attempted to focus on the job in front of him rather than fantasizing about a woman he had never even seen. He had sworn that he would never betray Arin again, and so far, just the thought of her discovering his indiscretion had kept him planted firmly on the straight and narrow.

Jake's thoughts rarely traveled back to that night anymore. The whole thing had started out innocently enough, as trysts often do. The seminar he was scheduled to attend did not start until late the following morning. After several hours in his hotel room channel surfing, he was ready for a change of scenery. Bored and restless, he wandered the halls of the large hotel. In the gift shop, he had bought an outfit for the baby, who was slowly becoming a reality in his mind. Hungry, he made his way to the hotel's upscale restaurant and bar. Jake felt awkward sitting at a table alone, so he opted for a seat at the bar. He struck up a lively conversation about sports with the bartender and enjoyed a cold beer.

He had been nursing his third beer when a black-haired beauty slid onto the stool next to him. She ordered a vodka martini before turning her full attention to him. With a husky voice she'd introduced herself as Kate. They sat at the bar and chatted for hours. She laughed uproariously at his jokes. Jolts of electricity flowed through her fingertips when she lightly touched his arm, his back, his knee. She was exciting and alive, and by his fifth drink, Jake had been intoxicated and completely enamored with her.

When the bartender politely announced that it was closing time, Jake protested loudly, not wanting the night to end. He remembered the resolve on her tanned face as Kate had stared hard at the band on his left ring finger. She hadn't bother to ask the obvious question; instead she stood and discreetly slipped her room key onto the bar next to him before turning away and exiting the restaurant. The bartender caught the act, his eyebrow raised and he winked at Jake. It took him a matter of seconds to decide, and he stumbled to the elevator and made his way to room two-sixteen.

Heart pounding against his chest, he grasped the doorknob and paused. For a brief moment he considered Arin, his wife, pregnant with their child, sick and waiting for him in their home, in their bed. A fresh wave of lust washed over him and he slipped the plastic card into the slot and entered Kate's room. There was no turning back. There was no way that she would ever find out. Jake enjoyed a night of passion and pleasure in Kate's arms, out of which was born five years of tremendous guilt and shame. He awoke the next morning with a pounding head and betrayal stabbing at his heart. He swore then that he would never be unfaithful to Arin again. Until now, he had not even allowed himself to entertain the idea. Since his conversation with Allie McIntyre, he had thought of little else, and that scared him.

"Yo Mamma's so old, she owes Moses a dollar," Dave hollered, interrupting Jakes thoughts. He rolled his eyes and focused his brain on coming up with an original "Yo Mamma" joke, grateful for the distraction.

***

Allie brushed her long thick hair, not satisfied until it shone. Standing in front of her full length mirror, she eyed her reflection critically. It was absolutely necessary for her to look perfect tonight for her meeting with Jake and Troy Welsh. She played her mental tape of their conversation the day before. She had not missed the faint interest in his voice. Allie knew how to read men. She smiled broadly, exposing perfect teeth. Although she was not easily impressed with males in general, she had to admit that the rugged tone of Jake's voice had intrigued her. The skirt of her tailored heather-grey business suit was cut well above the knee, showing off her slender legs nicely. She slipped into black leather pumps and dabbed her favorite perfume delicately on her neck and wrists. Jake Welsh would not be able to resist. She would have full access to Troy. Perhaps Jake would be the icing on the cake.

***

Jake was a nervous wreck by the time he arrived home. He was not accustomed to lying to Arin, and had not even settled on a story yet. When he pulled in and noticed Rae's truck in the driveway, his confidence in his ability to lie convincingly dropped.

It would have been just his luck for Arin and Rae to have planned some special outing with Troy for this evening. He opened the door and slinked inside. He realized that a part of him still fully expected Cooper to tear around the corner to greet him, his paws slipping on the hardwood floors. Instead, Rae came at him with a notebook. He set his lunchbox down and read.

Arin fell down the stairs this afternoon and is banged up, but okay. She needs to rest.

Guilt rained down on Jake in sheets. This whole day had been spent trying to figure out how he could deceive his wife, who at the same time was injured and hurting. He should have been the one here to take care of her, but she had never even called him. She must have sent a message to Rae on the BlackBerry and asked her to come. It stung that she would reach out to someone other than him to be her rescuer. No matter what was going on in their lives, Jake still longed to be her protector; the constant one in her life that she could always reach out to and count on. That was how it used to be with Arin and Jake.

"Where is she?" he mouthed. He did not have the patience tonight to have a conversation with a notebook. Rae pointed to the living room and placed her pointer to her lips, alerting him to be quiet. Jake nodded. He tiptoed into the living room where his wife slept. He stood over her for a long time. Intense love and hurt mingled together and fought for emotional priority in his troubled heart.

Arin slept on her side on the old couch, her reddish hair fanned out behind her. She stirred slightly. Jake knelt beside her and studied her face. She appeared vulnerable and child like, much as she had the first time he had laid eyes on her. Tenderly, he covered her with an old quilt that hung over the rocking chair before he tiptoed out. He grabbed Rae's notebook from the kitchen counter and scribbled a quick note indicating that he was planning on taking Troy out for some dinner and a visit to the arcade to give Arin time to rest. Rae read his lie and nodded with a smile. She obviously approved. Her beaming smile only added a heaping helping of guilt to the load that was already burying him.

Jake buckled Troy into the truck and headed out. When hit with a barrage of questions, he simply explained that Mommy needed some time to relax since she didn't feel good. Troy fell silent for a moment. Jake hoped that it was the end of the query. They had not even traveled a mile from home when Troy turned and watched Jake intently.

"We are going to see Ms. Allie, aren't we Daddy?"

"Who?" Jake stalled. Of course he knew exactly who Troy was talking about. He was simply stalling and racking his brain trying to figure out how Troy could have possibly known.

"Ms. Allie, Jacob's friend. She's the one that Mommy doesn't like," Troy explained. "If Mommy had been nicer to Ms. Allie, maybe she wouldn't have gotten hurt."

Jake gripped the wheel and remained silent.

***

"I'm going over there," Taylor insisted. She wiggled into some maternity jeans and ran a brush through her silky auburn hair.

"These?" Ben asked, holding up a pair of sneakers.

Taylor nodded and held out her foot, thankful for a husband who was willing to help put her shoes on. She was only six months pregnant, but she found bending over long enough to put on shoes not only painful but nauseating. Ben had become quite the expert at selecting the right pair of shoes for her outfit, although at times his choices still made her cringe. She was ready to run out the door when he stopped her.

"Let's pray."

Again, they clasped hands and prayed on behalf of Arin, Jake, and Troy, who weighed heavily on their hearts tonight.

***

"Good night, Emily."

"Night, Mary," Emily called over her shoulder. Although she had only worked a half shift tonight, her feet ached, and she was starving. She couldn't wait to get home. Her mouth began to water as she imagined the leftover General Tso's chicken waiting for her in the fridge. As she settled into her sedan, something caught her eye. There sat Arin Welsh's file. Why hadn't she remembered that when she was there earlier? She could just kick herself sometimes for being such a ditz. Then again, she reasoned, this wasn't exactly the type of thing that people fell all over themselves to deliver. Perhaps she would check in on Arin later this week and give it to her then. Maybe she would just hang onto it, pray about it.

Tonight.

Emily looked around, certain she had heard a voice. She was parked in the center of the employee lot, which was approximately a quarter full, but there was not another person in sight. A shiver traveled down her spine and she hoped out loud that she wasn't coming down with a case of nosocomephobia, the fear of hospitals. The fear of hospital parking lots would have been more precise, but Emily was fairly certain that no phobia had been dedicated to this particular dread. The sedan purred to life and she shifted into reverse. She reviewed her mental calendar. It would probably be most convenient for her to visit Arin on Wednesday or Friday afternoon. As soon as she got home she would call and make sure Arin didn't have plans. Well, she thought to herself, as soon as the Chinese food was warming in the microwave, anyway.

Tonight. Now.

This time the voice was so loud and clear that Emily found it impossible to explain away. Goosebumps pricked up on her forearms as she drove, her hands white-knuckled on the wheel. She stopped at home long enough to grab a protein bar and let Kira out before herding her into the waiting car. The Akita sat prim and proper on her hairy pink cushion, her head held high and regal, conveying her certainty that she was canine royalty.

"I don't know what in the world we're getting into, old girl," Emily called to her royal highness from the front seat. "Sometimes you just have to do what you're told." Emily glanced in the rearview and was amused by the knowing look in Kira's eyes, communicating to her master that she understood that lesson very well indeed.

***

Arin wandered through the hallways of the confusing office complex. Each hall dead-ended into another long dark corridor lined with closed doors. The closed doors were randomly numbered. Three-fifteen might be next to 610. Arin searched her mind for the number of the room she needed to find, as well as what she could expect to find once she got there. Puzzled, she wandered the dingy hallways, intently scanning each door, desperately hoping that she would recognize the number when she finally laid eyes on it.

She became aware of the fact that someone was behind her. When she paused to check the number on a door to the left, she snuck a peek over her shoulder. A large figure stood about twenty feet behind her, wearing an oversized hooded sweatshirt, its face a shadow in the dim light. Arin breathed in sharply, horrified at the thought that this person had no hands. After a moment she realized that the hands weren't visible simply because they were stuffed into the pockets of the black sweatshirt. The figure continued steadily toward her, and she became conscious of a strangely familiar clicking sound that seemed to grow louder as the stranger approached.

Arin picked up her pace, frantic for some reason. Her eyes shifted wildly as she hurried to scan each door. None of them seemed right. Panic welled within her and gave way to fear. Silently, she begged for an exit sign, for evidence of another person besides her and the dark stranger who was steadily closing in on her. The haunting clicking grew louder by the second. The long hallway finally ended in a T, forcing Arin to make a decision. She froze like a scared rabbit for an instant. There were no signs of life to the right or to the left. Arin broke into a full-fledged run and turned right. The stranger easily kept pace with her. The now manic clicking seemed to be coming from directly behind her.

The air seemed thin and she was exhausted. Although her breathing was now labored and her feet had turned to lead, she continued. Arin kept her eyes on her sneakers, willing them to cooperate.

Abruptly, she smacked a cinder block wall, and it took a few seconds for the horror of the situation to fully sink in. The hallway had unexpectedly dead-ended. Closing her eyes, she braced herself for an attack. Behind her, the sound slowed to a rhythmic *click, click, click.*

Determined that she would not go down without a fight, Arin boldly turned to face her surely soon-to-be attacker. She forced her eyes open and drew a quick breath as she attempted to plaster herself against the wall. The hooded figure stood approximately one foot from her face. The odor was rank and nauseating, its face completely hidden in the shadows of the pitch black hood.

Click, click, click.

Arin was on the verge of begging for her life when the clicking suddenly stopped. She cried out and protectively covered her head and face with her hands, anticipating the first blow. After a long moment, she rustled up the nerve to peek between her fear-stiffened fingers. A mixture of confusion and relief washed over her when she realized that instead of some razor-sharp hunting knife, the pale knotty fingers clutched a silver pen. Just her luck. She was going to be murdered by a Bic, which she was certain would be much more painful than your everyday butcher knife and take five times as long to boot.

Icy appendages grabbed hold of her left hand and forced it open. Arin gasped but did not struggle, allowing the creature to manipulate her hand with its popsicle fingers.

Click.

The tip of the pen touched her trembling palm. Three numbers were meticulously scrawled in black ink before the subzero hand simply released her. The mystifying figure turned and walked away. As it retreated, the horrible odor began to dissipate. Arin finally found her voice and shouted to the retreating hooded apparition.

"What does it mean?"

Just before it made a sharp right up ahead, it hissed an answer, its otherworldly voice reverberating off the dreary walls.

"Ask Jake what it means." It rounded the corner offering no further explanation, though the pen never stopped working.

Click, click, click.

J ake pulled into the office complex and studied the directory through the truck's dirty window. At last he found Dr. McIntyre's suite. The mere sight of her name in print made his heart race and the butterflies in his stomach flutter anew. The well-lit parking lot was essentially deserted, as most of the offices were closed by five, six at the latest. A fresh wave of appreciation for Dr. McIntyre washed over him. It was so considerate of her to make special arrangements to stay late just for them. She must be a very devoted worker, Jake thought. As he admired her dedication to the mental health of children, his mind wandered and he found himself wondering about her social life. Troy murmured something from the seat beside him, interrupting his private thoughts.

"What'd you say, Buddy?"

"Who do you like better—Daddy, Mommy, or Kate?"

The blood drained from Jake's face and his heart sank into his boots. In total shock, his hands were momentarily paralyzed on the wheel and the truck jumped a curb, narrowly missing an electric box before he snapped out of it and managed to regain control.

"Why would you ask that?" he snarled, harshly shifting the truck into park in front of Dr. McIntyre's building. His voice echoed throughout the cab, his venomous tone shocking even himself. Instantly, he regretted his words. Troy's eyes brimmed with tears and his lower lip began to quiver. Jake took a deep breath and tried to smile.

"Sorry Buddy, Daddy should not have been so mean to you. But Troy, I need to know what would make you ask a question like that. You know that Mommy and Daddy love each other very much, and we love you, too. Please tell me. I promise I won't be mad."

"I didn't ask you anything, Daddy."

It was then that Jake began to wonder if he was then one who was losing it.

***

Arin's eyes sprang open and she let out a shrill cry. Quickly and painfully, she sat up and tried to orient herself. The events of the day came rushing back in a welcome torrent. She had fallen down the stairs. Rae was keeping an eye on Troy. She was not, nor had she been, trapped with a Bic wielding sicko in some corridor that reeked of garbage. She must have dozed off, and it was nothing more than a dream; an odd, senseless, yet extremely vivid dream. Although she knew it was ridiculous, Arin tentatively opened her palm and examined it. Of course there was nothing written there. Try as she might, she could not place any relevance on the number that had been scrawled across her palm. Two-sixteen. She grabbed a pen and Post-it from the coffee table and jotted it down before she would forget it altogether. The weirdo in her dream had suggested that she ask Jake what the number meant, and that was what she intended to do.

Arin sighed when she heard the steady knocking on the front door. Tentatively she stood, and her hip painfully objected. She utilized the walls and furniture to maintain her balance as she limped through the kitchen to the foyer. Rae, who of course was oblivious to the rapping on the door, sat in the kitchen flipping through one of Jake's old motorcycle magazines. Arin was pleasantly surprised to see Emily Raines at her doorstep. She was still outfitted in her bright teal scrubs, which complemented her dark hair and deep blue eyes. It would not have surprised her to have been met by the polite but unwelcome Detective Lyons yet again. In comparison, Emily Raines was a godsend.

"Hey," Emily said lamely.

"Hi."

"Something told me that I should check in on you."

"Did you think you would need protection?" Arin asked and gestured to the stately dog who sat obediently by Emily's side.

"She's just along for the ride. Do you mind? I know it is terribly rude to assume that it would be okay to bring her. It's just that she hates to be alone."

Arin grinned and warmly gestured for them both to come in. It struck her that Cooper would have been ecstatic to have a canine visitor. Her heart wrenched as she pictured his sweet face in her mind. The house seemed so quiet and empty without him, especially since Troy was no longer his jovial self. Arin thought of all the times she had fussed at Troy and Cooper during their rambunctious play. Now she would give anything to hear the sounds of Cooper's nails scraping the hardwood or Troy's childish laughter. Emily allowed Arin to lean on her as she limped her way back to the couch in the family room, Kira following directly behind.

***

Troy, having visited the office of Allie McIntyre quite recently, helped guide Jake through the deserted maze of depressing hallways. At last, they came to a suite with Dr. McIntyre's name engraved on a bronze plate. Jake stood dumbly for a few moments, his hand gripping the doorknob. Every instinct within him suddenly screamed for him to turn around, to run home and forget he had ever heard of Allie McIntyre. He had never gone behind Arin's back like this, at least not since Troy had been born. The knob seemed to turn for him and the decision was made. They entered the vacant waiting room and a bell chimed, announcing their arrival. The décor of the place was jovial enough, Jake thought, attempting to assure himself that his strong urge to bolt was unfounded. Two walls were devoted to the celestial beings of the day, the other two of the night. The artwork was actually quite impressive and demonstrated the love that she must surely have for the children to whom she had dedicated her life.

It only took a second for Dr. McIntyre to emerge from her office door. The mere sight of her literally took Jake's breath away. To say that Allie McIntyre was a stunning woman would have been an understatement. She was drop-dead gorgeous. Allie was paying close attention and was pleased with the obvious effect she had on Jake. Her full glossy lips curled into an inviting smile. Troy's small hand squeezed Jake's hard and he stepped closer to his daddy, clutching his leg.

"Mr. Welsh?" She purred.

"Just call me Jake," he answered nervously.

"It's such a pleasure to meet you. Thanks again for coming in. Would it be at all possible for us to speak alone for a few minutes before I meet with Troy?" she asked as she crossed the room, locking the waiting room door. "There are plenty of toys to keep him busy, and no one can get in or out without the alarm sounding." Her intelligent crystal eyes implored Jake, and he lost all sense of reason. He was already following into her office when he turned to Troy, almost as an afterthought.

"Are you okay out here alone for a few minutes, Buddy?"

Troy's face was a mask of confusion. He scanned the room uncertainly and gave a weak shrug.

The Intrusion

"Just knock if you need me," Jake called over his shoulder as he disappeared behind Allie's office door.

***

Troy stood in the center of the waiting room, Jacob by his side. His father's words rang in his ears. Was he going to be okay out here alone? Bewildered, he scanned the room. Almost every seat was occupied. An old lady thumbed through a magazine. A teenage girl dressed in a plaid pleated skirt and a white shirt sat next to her doodling in a spiral notebook. Men in business suits checked their watches and chatted on cell phones. The kids' corner was teeming with boys and girls about his age. Jacob tried to coax him into playing with the other kids in the corner, and Troy followed reluctantly. Something about Jacob had been nagging at him for quite some time, and he got the same suspicious feeling as he was surrounded by these people. There was something strange and disturbing about them. Sometimes when Troy studied Jacob, he felt like he was right on the verge of figuring out what it was. Half-heartedly, he grabbed the same wooden train he had played with yesterday and rolled it back and forth across the rose colored carpet. When he glanced up, he noticed that every eye in the place was on him. The old lady's eyes shifted back to her paper. The teenage girl looked away, flipping a braid over her shoulder.

Suddenly, his chest felt tight and he had difficulty breathing. Focusing his eyes on the carpet, he slowly sucked in the stale office air. It was then that he realized what it was that had been nagging at him about Jacob and the other people in the office.

***

Six hundred miles away, a frail wisp of a woman climbed from her bed to strategically place a bean bag on the windowsill in a vain attempt to seal out the cruel Maine winter. As she hobbled back to her bed, her heart again was convicted.

Pray for her.

For the third time that evening, she knelt by her bed, her bony knees shielded from the harsh wood floors by a thin pillow. She rested her white fluffy head on the mattress and poured her heart out in prayer for the girl she had not laid eyes on in more than thirty years. It seemed that no matter how often she poured her heart out, the love and concern she had for her daughter would fill it back up to capacity. Carefully she picked up the oval picture frame on the table next to her simple bed and clutched it to her tired heart. Tears poured down her withered cheeks.

"Please Lord, please…" she begged, trusting the Spirit within her to interpret the things for which she could not find words. Under her bed, a few inches from her knees, sat a bulky stack of unopened envelopes tied tightly with twine. Having been baptized many times over with tears, the red ink on the outside of the top envelope was smudged and ran. Kathrynne stroked the bundle with her bony hand, her thin skin almost translucent. "Is there still time, Lord? Is it even possible now?"

Chapter Nineteen

E mily unceremoniously kicked off her nursing clogs and settled in on the couch with some microwave popcorn. Kira curled up obediently at her feet. She was quite a welcome house guest. Arin missed having a dog, and the beautiful well-behaved Akita made her wonder if it was too soon to consider searching for another. The image of the blood spattered playroom wall again flashed in her mind, and she nixed the idea for the sake of the dog. Gingerly, she sank onto the couch next to Emily. Just as she was getting as close to comfortable as possible under the circumstances, there was a second knock at the door.

"Having a party? I'll get it," Emily insisted, when she noticed the pained look on Arin's face at the mere thought of making another trip to the front door.

Sitting on the other side of Arin with her own bowl of popcorn, Rae quizzed Arin about all the activity. Arin could only shrug. She was clueless. For years she had been convinced that she had only one friend in the world, and all of the sudden her home was a hub of social activity. When Taylor waddled into the living room, Arin slapped herself on the forehead. She had completely forgotten to call and cancel Troy's appointment after her spill down the stairs.

"I am so sorry, Taylor."

Taylor cut her off, her hand held up to ward off any further apology. "I'm just glad you're alright. Ben and I have been praying for you all day. I was a little concerned when you didn't answer your phone."

"Thanks," Arin answered, actually grateful for the prayers. She didn't remember hearing the phone ring. It must have been during her nap. Taylor settled into the rocker facing the couch, her hands instinctively clasped across her swollen belly.

"What's that noise?"

Arin listened for a moment until she discerned a faint beeping every few seconds. Someone must have left a message while she was asleep. Rae was a wonderful best friend, but a secretary, not so much.

"Voice mail," Arin groaned as she started to get up. Emily pushed her back down.

"I'll handle it. How does the thing work? Just push play?"

"Yeah, thanks." Arin handed her the Post-its and a pen from the coffee table. She was more than a little relieved to avoid the painful journey into the kitchen.

"Stay," Emily firmly instructed Kira, who didn't move a muscle but observed her mistress intently as she left the room, one ear up, one ear down. Arin's thoughts again returned to Cooper. Although they had loved him fiercely, he had not been the most obedient dog on the block. She found Kira's rapt attention to Emily's commands impressive.

Taylor, who had studied American Sign Language a few years back, managed a slightly halting conversation with Rae. Many deaf and hearing impaired people had little patience with novice signers, but Rae was extremely gracious. She appreciated the slightest effort on a hearing person's part to learn her language and communicate with her. It was exciting for Taylor to finally put into practice what she had been taught in a classroom. Rae was so encouraging and excited when it came to communication. Taylor realized how much she had been missing out on by not being able to speak with this gem of a woman.

Arin politely, but not so discreetly, interrupted their conversation to point out that Taylor was wearing two different shoes. She just wanted to mention it in case she was unaware. Conversation in the room halted abruptly and Taylor's face flushed red. Lifting her legs, she strained to see her feet over her immense belly. She rolled her eyes when she saw for herself that she was, in fact, wearing two very different shoes. They were both sandals, but the similarities ended there. As soon as she returned home she was going to relieve Ben of his duty as her wardrobe coordinator. In other words, he was fired. Self-consciously, she grabbed a blanket off the back of the rocker and threw it over her lap, covering her footwear faux pas.

When Emily returned from retrieving the voice mail she was visibly shaken. She made her way across the room and painfully stubbed her toe on the coffee table. Thankfully, she caught herself before a string of curses could escape from her lips, as they still did at times such as this. She recovered and handed Arin an already crumpled and sweaty pink Post-it. The look in Emily's eyes told Arin to mentally prepare before reading. She was unsure how many more blows Arin could take before being down for the count permanently. Arin drew a deep breath and read the note, expecting the very worst, although she was not exactly sure what that might even be. Emily stated the contents of the note aloud for the benefit of the group.

"Hope from Pediatric Psychological Services called to remind you that Troy has a seven o'clock appointment with Dr. McIntyre." Arin read the note herself, and Emily's words rang in her ears. She was certain Rae had said that Jake took Troy out for some dinner and some father-son time at the arcade.

"Not Allie McIntyre," Taylor moaned.

"Afraid so," Arin answered softly. The reality of Hope's message slowly sank in. It cut her to the quick. Never in all their years of marriage had she felt so betrayed by Jake. Not to mention that she was highly concerned for Troy and incensed with Allie McIntyre, all at the same time. The very thought of that woman spending even a moment in the same room with her husband was enough to entice her inner cat to come pouncing out.

"The last time we talked, you said that you weren't comfortable with her," Taylor said, obviously confused. "I thought Troy was going to see me, or someone else. Anyone but Allie McIntyre!"

"She's not comfortable with her," Emily answered for Arin, then looked at her, just to make sure. "You're not, are you?"

Arin sat in silence for a long tense moment. She stared at her hands folded in her lap, feeling slightly nauseous. "She must have gotten to Jake somehow. The last thing I want is that woman poisoning my kid with her fanatical ideas, but do I have anything better to offer him?"

"She's bad news," Emily interjected as she nervously petted Kira's head. It was all starting to make sense. There *was* a reason why she was here tonight. "God wants you to know Him, Arin. And He wants you to teach your son about Him."

"What I really need to do is to get to her office right now." Arin struggled to stand and again Emily forced her down, a little rougher this time. She strongly sensed that Arin needed to stop running from God.

"Arin, what we need to do right now is pray. That is the only thing of any value that we can do."

Taylor fumbled to translate Emily's words for Rae, who nodded enthusiastically in agreement. Emily continued.

"Arin, I haven't been able to get you off of my mind since we talked the other night after Geoffrey's funeral. I regret that I didn't pray with you right then and there, especially after you told me what you saw in your son's room a few nights ago. I can offer no other explanation other than for some reason; an evil spirit has attached itself to your son, to your family. Your battle is purely a spiritual one. You are not going to accomplish anything by going to Allie's office." Emily's eyes traveled up and down Arin's battered body. "Especially considering the shape that you're in," she added, her voice soft and full of compassion.

Arin hung her head and covered her face with her hands. In a matter of seconds, the dam broke and the sobbing began.

"I am going to lose my family," she managed pathetically between heaves. "I don't know what to do. I am going to lose Troy. Maybe I have already lost Jake..." At that point her sobbing reached its crescendo.

Rae, Emily, and Taylor respectfully allowed Arin time and space to weep. Emily and Rae lovingly rubbed her back in an attempt to reassure her, to let her know that they were there and had no intention of leaving her alone. Arin openly wept for the better part of half an hour. Her three friends were all women who had been through their share of trying times. They were not the least bit uncomfortable with her expression of pain. They recognized her need to release her energy, anger, fear, and grief. At last, when she was emotionally spent and had no tears left, Arin lifted her wet, blotchy face.

"I give up," she announced. "I can't keep this up anymore. I understand now that this is a fight I cannot win." She turned to Taylor, her eyes begging for help and hope. "When I was talking with Ben the other day, he told me that I needed to accept Christ as my Savior. He warned me not to put it off." She swallowed hard. "I meant to go home and consider it, check into things on my own. I just thought it would be better to do it privately. But Ben was right. The second I stepped out of your home, being saved from my sins was the last thing on my mind. I have not even given it any serious thought until now. It happened just like Ben predicted. The worries of the world crowded in and I no longer even cared." Arin stopped and took a moment to collect her frenzied thoughts. "I even went to the Divine Connection and had a reading by Sister Amber," she blurted out. Rae just about fell out of her chair when Taylor translated the news for her. That was exactly the sort of spiritual trap she had always feared Arin would fall into someday.

"Don't worry," she wryly assured her faithful friend. "I must not have the right energy or something, because I found the experience to be bizarre, not to mention expensive." Rae's face relaxed and she settled into the rocker again, intently observing her best friend with her bright eyes. Arin clutched a throw pillow protectively in her lap. Her fingers nervously worked a corner where the stitching was becoming unraveled.

"Sister Amber did tell me something that I believe to be true, though." Immediately, there was a tension in the room. All three of the women leaned in, afraid that their friend was being enticed by some new age guru.

"She said that I did not have the power to stop the spirits that had claimed Troy, or something to that effect," Arin said. The room let out a collective sigh of relief. Somehow, that statement was not the advice that they had expected someone with a name like "Sister Amber" from the Divine Connection to give. But they all agreed with Arin that it was the absolute truth.

"Would you do something for me, Taylor?"

"Anything," Taylor answered without skipping a beat.

"Please call Ben and ask him to come over so I can do it right now. Accept Christ, I mean. I know it is getting late, but I don't want to wait anymore. I can't afford to wait another day."

Taylor smiled and relaxed in her chair. She felt as if she had been holding her breath for the last half hour and was finally given permission to breathe again. "Arin, you can receive Christ right here, right now. You don't need Ben or anyone else. It is completely between you and God."

"At church Ben always says that anyone who wants to become a Christian should come to the front and he will pray with them," Arin said, obviously confused regarding the logistics of the process.

"Ben does that so he can be sure that the people who come are sincere and know what they are asking God to do, not just emotional and doing it on a whim. Ben has no more access to the throne of God than you or I, Arin." Taylor continued to interpret the conversation for Rae. Rae halted her steady rocking and sat completely still, her face so full of joyful expectation that she practically glowed.

"Oh," Arin answered. She still seemed a bit hesitant.

"It would be an honor to me if you wanted me to lead you in prayer."

After taking a few seconds to mull it over, Arin nodded urgently. She felt exhilarated, terrified, and eager at the same time. Suddenly, she had become aware of the substantial load of guilt and filth that stubbornly clung to her soul, and she was frantic to rid herself of it. She knew it was foolish to assume that any amount of charity, wishful thinking or good deeds would ever be able to cleanse the filth from her soul. Miraculously, all of the things that she had heard over the years at Downsville Christian Fellowship made perfect sense to her. It was as if a fog had been lifted from her mind; a blindfold had been removed and she had seen the light. She knew without doubt that her soul desperately needed saving, and that Jesus was the only Savior. She was not willing to wait another second.

"I don't have the right words…" Arin was frustrated. Silently, she chided herself for not paying better attention to Ben's sermons. She had probably watched hundreds of people convert to Christ over the last five years. She should certainly know the drill by now. Yet, in her heart she knew that although she was preparing to make a public profession of faith, it was also the start of an extremely intimate relationship with her Maker. She would finally have her Daddy.

Taylor, Emily, and Rae glanced at each other, their eyes shiny with unshed tears. In unison, they stood. Together they scooted the coffee table out of the way and formed a tight semi-circle around Arin, each one kneeling.

"Please pray with me. I don't know what to say."

"I'd love to," Taylor responded sincerely.

"Heavenly Father, we thank you that you have brought each of us here tonight. What a miracle. Thank you for the opportunity to be present as Arin becomes your child, your precious daughter." Taylor opened her eyes and held her hand out to Arin, who clasped it with her own trembling hand. "Do you admit that you have sinned? Simply put, that you have turned away from God and went your own way?"

Tearfully, Arin nodded. Some recent scenes replayed in her mind. She had no issue at all with admitting she was a sinner.

"Do you accept the cross of Christ as payment in full for your sins? Do you know what I mean by that?"

"I think so," Arin stammered. Taylor bit her lip, considering how to proceed. It was vital that Arin comprehend what Christ had done for her.

"It means that your sins, past, present and future, are covered by the blood of Christ. It means that God's wrath and punishment for those sins were poured out on Christ at the cross. By accepting His payment for your sins, Christ has given you a clean slate. When you die, you will be with Christ in heaven. For the rest of your life on earth, you will be a follower of Jesus, and his Holy Spirit will live inside of you."

"Can God forgive anything? I mean, what if I..." her voice trailed off, but Emily knew that Arin was thinking of the child whose life she had made the heart-wrenching decision to terminate. She knew this because of the doubts about her own salvation she had struggled with since her own abortion.

"God will forgive you, Arin. He will." They locked eyes and silently understood each other. Emily knew the abortion was the stumbling block in Arin's way.

"Are you ready to accept Christ as your Savior?" Taylor asked again.

"I am. Yes, please," Arin answered, this time with urgent confidence. Again, they breathed a collective sigh of relief.

"Father," Taylor continued, her hands roughly translating for Rae, who by this time had tears rolling down her face, "Arin has confessed her sins before You, and is requesting that You forgive her and wash her clean. We know that You never lie, and You say in your Word that whoever calls on the name of the Lord will be saved. Thank you for welcoming Arin, your daughter, into your kingdom."

"Amen," Emily answered, also crying now. Her face was lifted heavenward and filled with an expression of utter amazement. She remembered so clearly the time before she had been saved. She had been afraid that her life would become dull after she became a Christian. What a joke. What a lie. In reality, she had never felt so excited and alive.

Time seemed to stand still as the four women wept and prayed in concert. Arin fumbled through her first humble communications with her Maker and Savior. Emily's prayer was full of thanksgiving that she could be a part of such a special conversion. Taylor was simply in awe of God's sovereign plan. Rae's hands moved in a beautifully intimate prayer directed toward the heavens. She was both overwhelmed and overjoyed that God had answered the faithful petitions for Arin's soul that she had made daily in earnest from her oasis for the past five years.

***

In a separate realm, one more substantive than the one the women currently resided in, thousands of silvery warriors were dispatched the exact second that Arin Welsh, daughter of the Living God, was claimed as His own. Though she stumbled through her prayer, it had been heard loud and clear, and her halting requests were regarded with the utmost urgency. *Help my son*, she had begged silently. *Rescue my child, please, Father.* Brand new in the faith, she did not yet trust that her pleas were even worthy of being heard. The One who holds all things together immediately sent a team of mighty soldiers to Troy Welsh's side to do just that; to rescue the son of the King's newborn daughter.

The evil one's claws had sunk deeply into the fabric of the Welsh family. His spiritual stronghold could not be denied; however, with his limited perspective, there was no way he could have anticipated that this very night, Arin Welsh would be reborn as a child of the King. The leagues of the wicked one initially panicked, but they regained their cruel composure and rallied quickly. They were fully intent on salvaging the remaining members of the Welsh family and winning their eternal souls to the dark side. The Holy One's warriors sped to their destination. They were grateful for the prayers of the saints, and hoped they would not cease.

J ake followed the lovely Dr. McIntyre into her office like an obedient puppy enticed by a meaty bone. He found it simply impossible to take his eyes off of her. Physically, the woman was exquisite. Her gait was fluid and confident. She spun around and caught his eye, and was quite pleased to observe that she had achieved the desired effect. She gestured to a worn vintage armchair and he sat. She slid into a more modern red chair beside him. Jake tore his eyes from her and took a moment to study Dr. McIntyre's office. The tone was warm and eclectic. Carefully selected abstract and impressionist paintings adorned the creamy yellow walls. A tall pewter lamp in the corner shed its light directly onto the ceiling. The radiance bounced off the ceiling and softly illuminated the room. Jake discreetly sniffed the air, easily detecting the scent of lilac, his favorite. Arin liked the flower well enough, but had never worn the lilac essence oil he bought her years ago. She had explained that although she liked the fragrance on the bush, she had no desire for her body to smell like a plant. He sniffed again, his nostrils filling with the intoxicating aroma.

Allie crossed her legs, brushing her lean, tan thigh against Jake's knee as she did so. He cleared his throat and attempted to focus on recalling the exact reason he was sitting there in the first place, and to ignore the intense desire her touch had awakened in him.

"Troy is quite a remarkable child, Mr. Welsh. Exceptional, in fact," she started. Her words were like honey dripping from the comb.

"Please, it's Jake, and yes, he is. Troy is a different kind of kid."

"What do you mean by different?" Allie inquired. Seductively, she removed the pen that had been holding her hair in a tight knot, allowing the healthy blonde tresses to tumble down dramatically.

Jake felt his face flush and he concentrated on his boots while he gathered his thoughts. "He senses things. I don't know how to explain it. Lately it seems like he can even see things we can't, as insane as that sounds. Of course, it is possible that he just has an overactive imagination."

"Honestly, I don't think that is the case with your son, Mr. Wel-Jake," Allie caught herself and smiled warmly. "As I attempted to explain to your wife yesterday, I believe it is possible that Troy is a child with significant spiritual awareness. Although quite rare, it is possible that he was born with a natural ability to perceive activities in other realms of consciousness. I was in my thirties when I began to work toward developing this skill. It is both amazing and puzzling that your son has developed it without any effort, training, or stated desire to do so. Do you realize how remarkable that is?"

Jake shrugged. He hadn't given much thought to Troy's recent behavior as a gift until this evening. A thought struck him, bringing with it more than a little paranoia in regard to this so-called gift. "Is it possible that Troy could simply know about things? Things that happened before he was even born? Things that he has never even heard about?" Jake shifted uncomfortably in his chair. Hopefully Dr. McIntyre did not have this gift herself and wouldn't think to ask for specifics.

Allie's face lit up and she nodded enthusiastically. "That is exactly the sort of thing I'm talking about. I am telling you Jake, there is so much we don't know yet. The spirit world is filled with light and knowledge, and we spend most of our lives without ever even attempting to tap into it. Troy's gift could provide us with a real opportunity here. It would be a shame to waste it. Do you realize how many people your son could help?"

Jake held her crystal gaze. His insides started to churn with uncertainty and skepticism. So far, this gift had not exactly manifested itself as sweetness and light. He thought of poor old Cooper, backed in a corner and viciously slashed to death by his formerly innocent four-year-old son. Troy was anything but violent, and Jake had to assume he had done this under the power of some spirit. "What leads you to believe that these spirits are positive, that they don't mean harm?"

Allie leaned back in her chair and eyed Jake curiously, twirling a golden lock between her red-tipped fingers.

"Pardon me for saying so, Jake, but that sounds exactly like something your wife said yesterday," she replied at last. "I'm curious Jake. Do you attend Downsville Christian Fellowship with your family?"

"I've been there."

"I'm sensing from your demeanor that perhaps you may not agree with their narrow-minded view in regard to spiritual things. If I am out in left field on this, I apologize. I just don't take you to be the kind of guy who buys into the whole Jesus thing."

"Look, I have done the whole spiritual thing. My wife and I met in a cult, for heaven's sake. I'm just not sure what to believe. Pastor

Wesley made some really good points in his sermon last Sunday. It got me thinking."

Allie visibly flinched at the mention of the pastor's name. Her disdain for him and his wife couldn't have been more obvious.

"As a matter of fact," Jake continued, "I think Arin has contacted Taylor to start some therapy with Troy."

Allie lurched forward in her chair, placing her hand on Jake's knee. "Taylor Wesley is not a serious therapist, Mr. Welsh." Removing her hand, she leaned back, obviously struggling to regain her former cool composure. "May I be frank with you?" she finally asked through clenched teeth.

Jake nodded, surprised at his ambivalence. He felt torn between defending the Wesley's, who had been good to his family and seemed like nice enough people, and agreeing with Dr. McIntyre, the intelligent and superbly passionate woman sitting dangerously close to him.

"Troy is at stake here, so I am not going to sugar-coat it. Ben and Taylor Wesley are nothing more than religious nut jobs. Taylor uses her degree to push her beliefs onto her clients, which is highly unethical and downright despicable in my book."

"With all due respect," Jake said, slowly and cautiously after a moment of careful consideration. If at all possible, he wanted to avoid offending her, due to his near phobia of social workers. "Isn't that what you are trying to do with Troy, share your spiritual convictions with him?"

Allie inched to the edge of her chair until she was as close to Jake as she could get without actually sitting on his lap. Her intense crystal gaze held his, and she smiled as she slightly tilted her head. She appeared to be searching for the right words, processing his words as well as his body language.

"I can understand why you would feel that way, and here is the difference. My goal is to assist Troy along a path that he obviously has already chosen for himself."

Jake chewed his lip nervously. Her statement made sense and had the ring of truth. Sensing his indecision, Allie continued her line of thought, her tone smooth and persuasive.

"Churches like Downsville Christian Fellowship do nothing to promote people's growth along spiritual lines. Instead, they oppress their followers with a long list of do's and don'ts, and terrify people into submission by preaching hellfire and damnation for anyone who doesn't strictly adhere to their exact brand of religion." She shook her head in disgust, her silky blonde tresses fanning out slightly.

"That sounds an awful lot like the church I grew up in." Jake shuddered, equally disgusted. The last thing in the world he wanted for Troy was for him to be stifled and suffocated in a church the way that he had been.

As soon as the words had left Jake Welsh's mouth, Allie knew her message had hit its mark. She had the deep well of Jake Welsh's despondent childhood and negative religious experiences to draw on. She would start there and build her case, drawing bucket after bucket until he could no longer see any reason why Troy should not travel the path that the gods had for him. She flashed Jake a sympathetic smile and touched his hand lightly. Without a doubt, she would have unrestricted access to Troy Welsh, the innocent child that her spirit guide Sayger had prophesied about.

***

"W-w-w-why don't you breathe?" Troy asked Jacob, the wooden train clutched tightly to his chest as if for protection.

"What would make you ask such a stupid question?" Jacob barked, his deep voice agitated by the inquiry.

"I am the only one here that breathes," Troy said, muffling his voice with his hand. "Don't angels need air? Don't you need it to sing and stuff?"

Jacob stared at him hard, his eyes growing black the way they did when he was angry, which seemed like all the time lately. Troy thought back to that day at the greenhouse. Jacob had smiled and laughed and played then. That day, the day the man had died, Jacob had insisted that since they looked alike they were supposed to be best friends. At the time, Troy had been a little lonely and had readily agreed. Back then, his eyes were never black and mean like they so often were now.

"I don't need air. That's how powerful I am. I don't need anything."

Nervously, Troy turned the train's wooden wheels. Finally, he gathered his courage and decided to ask the question that had been spinning inside his head ever since Cooper had gone to heaven.

"Are you a bad angel, Jacob?"

The question enraged Jacob. He let out an ear splitting shriek, his eyes again turning dark and ugly. The old lady across the room threw her newspaper down and glared at Troy with vacant black holes. The teenage girl's eyes became sunken pits. Even the children instantly ceased their rough play. They all glared at Troy through hate-filled eyes of coal. Terrified, Troy started to cry and stumbled backwards until he was trapped in the corner. He squeezed his wet eyes shut. He couldn't help but wonder if this was how Cooper had felt. He braced himself for an attack. Then it happened.

In a flash, a brilliant light filled the entire room, radiating an otherworldly peace and energy. Even through his tightly squeezed lids, Troy could see the vivid whiteness that filled the room. At the same moment that Troy had gathered the courage to shield his eyes and peer upward into the face of this great being beside him, the vision began to fade. He was fortunate enough to catch an indescribable glimpse of the majestic warrior. Troy wasn't positive, but he thought that the being had flashed him a smile as the vision faded. Troy knew with perfect confidence that this mighty protector was still standing there beside him. He knew that his brief glimpse of this powerful one was a gift. The bad angels in the waiting room now gaped in horror. It only took a moment for every last one of them to disappear. Troy's heart leapt within him. Could it be that he was finally free of Jacob? There was not a shred of doubt in his mind that the invisible great being beside him was a real angel, a good angel. It was the kind of angel that would protect and care for him, instead of throwing tantrums and threatening to kill beloved family members. Could it be that the nightmare was over?

"I will fear no evil, for you are with me," Troy repeated over and over, basking in the safety of divine protection. Jacob had attempted to drown out the message that God had planned for Troy to hear that day. The few simple words that had penetrated his evil cloud had managed to connect with Troy's young heart, where even now it was accomplishing the work it was predestined to do.

***

"So, I think we are on the same page here." Allie glanced at her watch, growing slightly aggravated at the amount of time she had wasted on persuading the father. Jake Welsh had required more convincing than she had anticipated. "Do you think I could have just a few moments alone with Troy to get acquainted? I know it is getting late, but it really won't take long at all."

"Sure," Jake easily consented, deceived by her beauty and spiritual sounding arguments. He felt a little foolish to have defended the Wesley's at all. Dr. McIntyre was right. They were religious nuts. He could not believe that he had almost been sucked in by them.

"What time is it?"

"Seven-thirty," she replied. They both shook their heads. Where had the time gone? Guilt rapped sharply on the door of Jake's heart. He had not once thought to check on Troy the whole time they were chatting.

Dr. McIntyre strode confidently into the waiting room, calling Troy's name sweetly. She stopped walking so abruptly that Jake ran smack into her. Embarrassed, he mumbled an apology and stepped to the side. He was shocked to witness her beautiful face twist into a mask of contempt. Her crystal eyes flashed with anger. Jake followed her eyes to the corner of the room.

Troy stood smiling. No, not smiling, Jake thought, beaming. The very sight of him lifted Jake's spirits. He had not seen a genuinely happy look on his son's face in a long time. Too long.

"Troy?" he asked, his face a question. What wonderful thing could have transpired to produce such a joyous expression?

"Hi, Daddy."

Those words melted his heart like a blow torch. Suddenly, he felt grounded again. A few moments ago, he was caught up in lust and desire for a woman he didn't even know while his son sat alone in a strange room.

"Sorry we were in there so long..." he offered lamely, unsure how to finish the sentence. The realization hit him that Arin would find out where they had been, and it wasn't going to be pretty. He turned to face Dr. McIntyre again. Her sudden change in demeanor confused him greatly. It was as if she would pounce on Troy at anytime. Jake moved to stand between them and assumed a protective stance.

"Look, it's getting late. Would it be possible to reschedule?" he asked, although he had absolutely no intention of doing anything of the sort.

"Don't bother," Allie spat. She turned on her heels and left quite a trail of expletives in her wake. "I can't use him anymore," she screamed, slamming her door. A feral cry erupted from the office. Jake snatched Troy up and hurried from the office.

Chapter Twenty-One

Get up, my precious daughter! Your prayers have been answered!

Kathrynne lifted her gray fuzzy head from the musty quilt covering her bed. Her knees complained fiercely, and both of her feet were completely numb. She had been so deep in conversation with her Father that she hadn't even noticed the toll her position had taken on her failing body until now. She strained to right herself, and was mildly annoyed to find her aching limbs unresponsive.

"A little help?" she asked, glancing upwards, her cinnamon eyes alive and joyful. It was a struggle, but eventually she maneuvered into a standing position. For a few long moments she stood with her hands pressed against the bedspread, uncertain of whether or not her back would go along with the program and straighten. Thankfully, it did in its own good time.

"May I go now, Lord? Please, may I see him before I come to see You?" Immediately, she received the confirmation in her spirit that she had sought so desperately for the past several months. Her bony hands covered with tissue-thin skin suddenly became quick and nimble as she packed a few meager belongings. The very thought of holding him was even now drawing her old heart southward.

***

Kira yelped urgently, regretfully interrupting the women's prayer time. Emily muttered an apology and rose to let the old girl out. Each of their faces was lined with the salty resin of tears. Rae and Arin embraced for an extended hug. Arin whispered words of thanks into Rae's deaf ears. She was certain that her hug communicated the message clearly enough, but somehow her gratitude seemed more real when she spoke the words, even if they did fall on the deaf ears of her best friend. Fresh tears sprang into Arin's eyes and overflowed as she thought of the times she had entered The Silver Fox during lunch and had come upon Rae praying at the oasis. Praying for her. All of these years, Rae had never once given up praying for Arin's soul, despite Arin's many assurances that she was wasting her time.

As a baby, Troy had always been soothed by the sights of the birds and plants and the sounds of the hundreds of fountains flowing simultaneously. Arin recalled one particularly nerve-racking morning with Troy when nothing she tried succeeded in calming him. Finally his cries seemed to cut right through her, and she had bundled him up and headed to the greenhouse where Rae had said she was always welcome. Unlike most babies, Troy had not been lulled into sleepy contentment by the hum of the engine. In fact, it often seemed to have the opposite effect on him. Arin often wondered if her son simply longed for his brother, with whom he had shared her womb for all those months. She could still picture him as a plump six-month-old, sprawled out on a thick downy blanket on the floor of the gazebo, his tiny fists clenching and unclenching as if he were attempting to brawl even in his slumber. As he'd slept, Arin had picked up Rae's journal and immersed herself into the secret life of this woman with whom she had become so intrigued. Entry after entry contained Rae's pleadings with her God to be near her friend Arin, to strengthen her. She begged for opportunities to show her his love, and thanked Him for bringing Arin into her life at a time when she was dealing with loneliness and despair herself. In her mind's eye, Arin could see Rae's tears as they struck the pages of her journal, smudging the inky blue prayers.

By Troy's first birthday, his demeanor changed dramatically. He no longer cried for hours on end for no apparent reason, or squirmed when Arin would attempt to comfort him. Instead, he readily accepted and reciprocated her affection. Overwhelmed with gratitude, Arin realized that she had been carried through by the faithful prayers of her friend. Rae had never ceased petitioning God for her or her family. Now she understood that as she had read the prayers of her friend that day, a seed had been planted in her hard heart. It had taken much tilling over these last four years, but the seed had finally taken root and pushed its way to the surface.

"Help."

Arin broke from the embrace and snapped back to the present. She giggled at the sight of Taylor struggling to get up, her clashing footwear displayed for all to see.

"Thanks a lot," Taylor spat, feigning disgust. She attempted to keep her composure as she rolled from side to side trying to gain enough momentum to get up off of the floor.

"Are you sure you're not having triplets or something?" Emily asked as she re-entered the living room, Kira at her side. "You should be able to get up without help for another month and a half," she teased as she helped Taylor to her feet.

"I am not having triplets."

"Whatever you say. You know that sometimes they don't show up on the sonogram...," Emily teased.

Rae, who had followed the conversation fairly well through read lip-reading, had missed out on the sarcasm. Incredulous, she signed to Arin "She's having triplets! And we were praying for you!" Arin relayed Rae's message, and the four of them roared with much needed comic relief.

***

The cab of the truck was filled with comfortable silence as Jake and Troy made their way home. Several times Jake had opened his mouth intent on begging Troy to not tell his mom where they had been, but he couldn't make himself do it. He could not ask his son to lie. As the truck neared their home, a knot formed in the pit of his stomach. His mouth went dry and his palms were slick on the wheel with sweat.

As Jake pulled into the driveway, two vehicles he didn't recognize were pulling out. He caught a glimpse of a dark haired woman and a dog in one of the cars. He was certain he had never seen her before. *Great*, he thought. *What on earth was going on here tonight, a Tupperware party or something?*

Gently, Jake unbuckled Troy, who had given into his exhaustion halfway home. He cradled his son's limp body, clutching him tightly to himself. Troy felt so huge in his arms. It seemed like yesterday when he was able to carry his baby boy in one arm and a few grocery bags in the other. Troy was a full load now, no doubt about that.

Arin opened the door for them. Jake steeled himself against the warranted accusations that he knew were coming. He found it impossible to read her expression, which only added to his sense of impending marital doom.

"I'm going to lay him down," he mouthed to Arin. She kissed Troy's sleeping face lightly. Sniffing, she turned and hobbled into the living room. Troy awoke for a moment as Jake was snuggling him in bed nice and tight, just the way he liked it.

"I love you, Buddy."

"Love you too, Daddy." Troy yawned. "Guess what?"

"What?"

"Grandma's coming." With that he rolled over, hugged his car-shaped pillow and slipped into a peaceful sleep.

I doubt that, Jake thought as he tip-toed down the steep wooden stairs. He envisioned his mother lowering herself enough to contact him to try and make things right. It just wasn't going to happen.

***

"Can I get you anything?"

Arin smiled weakly, shaking her head.

"How are you feeling now? Rae told me you fell. What happened?"

"I slipped on some of Troy's cars that were left on the step."

"Troy never leaves his toys on the stairs. He knows better."

Arin nodded in agreement. There were a few moments of silence. Arin wrung her hands and Jake studied the ceiling. He decided to just get it over with.

"I took Troy to see Dr. McIntyre this evening."

"I know."

Jake was taken aback. Her words knocked the momentum right out of him. He had been fully prepared to make a complete confession and beg her forgiveness. He had emotionally steeled himself against the verbal assault that he so richly deserved. Instead, Arin sat serenely on the couch, already knowing what he had done.

"Are you on painkillers or something?"

"I wish!" Arin chuckled lightly, rubbing her sore hip.

"She didn't see Troy. In the end it just didn't work out. You were right about her." Expectantly, he sat waiting for the lecture, the scolding words, but Arin offered none. Drawing closer, he gingerly slipped his strong arm around her bruised neck, lightly kissing her.

"Something happened tonight, Jake." Arin started, asking God for the right words to describe to him what she herself had not fully grasped yet. She decided to keep it simple. "I became a Christian tonight."

Jake pulled back, arms crossed and eyes skeptical. Apparently, the tender moment had passed. "What? They finally talked you into joining that church or something?"

"No. It has nothing to do with church membership. I always thought it did, but I never really got it until tonight. I accepted Christ's forgiveness and turned my life over to Him."

"You don't think that is something we should have decided together?"

Jake pulled further away from his wife, his face a shadow of contempt.

"No," Arin softly countered. It is not something that can be done as a couple. It's a choice I wish I had made years ago. Jake, please, just consider learning more. Just open your heart a little and He will do the rest."

"I can't believe this, Arin. Don't you remember the cult? We did the whole Jesus thing, and I thought we were in agreement that it turned out to be nothing but a huge lie."

"This is different." Arin struggled with her words. She felt ill-equipped to explain what Christ had done for her.

"Sure it is." Jake bristled. "That was exactly what they taught us to tell our parents and friends, remember?" He stood, looking down at his wife, who had apparently stepped over the line to join the religious nut-jobs, leaving him on the other side with the spiritually unaffiliated.

"I guess you're sleeping down here," he said coldly as he rose from the couch.

"Yeah, the stairs and I aren't exactly getting along today." Arin tried a little humor to break the tension, but Jake did not even so much as fake a smile as he strode past her.

"Jake?"

"What?"

"Two-sixteen. Does the number mean anything to you?"

"What? No!" Jake answered sharply. "What would make you ask that? Is it some new religious thing? Are you going to get it tattooed on your forehead or something?" Jakes sarcasm cut her to the quick. Arin simply waved him off. She did not trust her voice to explain her strange dream. Being as he already thought she had gone a little nutty, now probably wasn't the greatest time to bring up clicky-pen-guy. Jake disappeared through the doorway and Arin settled into the comfy couch for the night. Although it would have been easy to deny it, Arin admitted to herself that she had seen it; the flicker of panic and recognition that had registered on Jake's face at the mention of the number two-sixteen.

***

Allie seethed with rage. Her pulse pounded in her ears as her blood rushed through her veins. Her chest rose and fell rapidly, each breath ending with an animalistic grunt. How could this have happened? Her spirit guide Sayger had promised to deliver him that evening, assuring her that a wise and dependable spirit had the boy under control. She slipped into Hope's cramped office and slammed the door. Expletives flew as she searched for the key to the file cabinet. Loudly, she cursed Hope for remembering to lock up. At last she retrieved the key from under a box of tissues. She unlocked the drawer and swiftly pulled Troy Welsh's file. It took her only a moment to memorize the address. Carefully, she returned the file back to its proper place with the rest of the W's, relocked the cabinet, and replaced the key. She grabbed her coat and sprinted from the office and down the dingy corridor to the elevator.

The sleek Mercedes obeyed Allie's every command as she sped toward the Welsh house. She pushed the car to its limit, the engine whining at full throttle. As she approached the old brick farmhouse, she downshifted and slowed to a crawl. Her genius mind worked overtime. In her fury, she had concentrated on following Troy, but she had no plan and wasn't even certain if the boy's spiritual gifts could be salvaged. Sayger certainly thought it was a lost cause. The Welsh's porch lights blazed, and Allie noticed three cars pulling out of the driveway as a truck was pulling in. She jerked the Mercedes to the shoulder of the road, cut the lights, and watched. The third car to pull out was a blue Saturn sedan. As the car slowly passed, Allie strained her neck to get a look at the driver. With recognition came a new wave of rage. Taylor Wesley. She should have guessed that she and her holier-than-thou husband had something to do with this. Allie screamed blasphemies into the night air and punched her dashboard.

Blinded by her wrath, she didn't even bother to check for approaching traffic as she turned the wheel all the way to the right and punched it. Only one thing mattered to her now—pursuing Taylor Wesley and making sure she paid. There was now no doubt that the boy had been spiritually ruined. Any hopes she had of unlocking his supernatural potential had gone down the tubes with the sight of this woman. From their very first meeting several years ago at a local mental health fundraiser, Allie had despised Ben and Taylor Wesley. They had been forced to share a dinner table, and even after Allie extensively described her disdain for all organized religion, Taylor still had the nerve to invite Allie to their church. Allie knew for a fact that Downsville Christian Fellowship was full of small-minded bigots and religious freaks, and that the Wesley's surely wanted her money more than her company. She considered that to be true of all churches.

The Mercedes easily caught up with the Saturn. Allie flashed on her high beams and rode Taylor's bumper closely. When the Saturn sped up, Allie stayed right with her, craning her neck as she screamed obscenities through her driver's side window. The sight of Taylor sticking her arm out of her window and gesturing her to go around nearly made her hysterical. *Not a chance*, Allie thought. She was having entirely too much fun playing with the little church mouse. Taylor continued at a sensible pace, despite being bullied by the Mercedes.

Suddenly, Allie recalled something she had heard a month or so ago at some mandatory health department meeting. Taylor and Ben were expecting their first child. For a few moments, her foot left the gas pedal. Heavy conviction settled onto her spirit. Deep down, in the pit of her haunted soul, a remnant of the person Allie had once been protested weakly. *Don't do this. She is carrying a child. This woman has never done you any harm.* Sayger, the malevolent spirit who had laid to claim to Allie McIntyre long ago, extinguished the objection immediately, as if snuffing out a struggling flame with his gnarled fingertips. Her conscience freshly seared, Allie gripped the wheel firmly and pursued Taylor with renewed vigor.

***

"Lord, please help me. Please protect me. Please protect the baby," Taylor repeated the same words over and over. The blinding starbursts reflecting in her rearview mirror caused white spots that disrupted her vision. "If I could just make it home. Please, Lord, just get us home safely." Taylor slowed to turn onto her street. Only a few miles now. They could make it. They had to make it. The car behind her lightly tapped the Saturn's bumper and pursued her onto the deserted country road.

The Intrusion

The white spots from the insane driver's headlights made it even more difficult to navigate on the narrow road. In an effort to keep panic at bay, she continued to pray loudly, calling on the God of the universe to guard her and her unborn child from harm. Suddenly, the lights behind her disappeared. Taylor blinked rapidly, checking and re-checking the rearview in disbelief. Just as she was uttering a heartfelt prayer of thanks, the car reappeared, this time right next to her. Taylor let out a scream. The bridge up ahead was wide enough to allow only one car through at a time, and the crazed driver next to her seemed determined to be the one to pass. Cradling her swollen belly protectively with one hand, Taylor slammed on the brakes and turned the wheel sharply to the right. The Saturn left the road, lurching and bouncing through the darkness until it finally stopped.

A cloud of dust obscured Taylor's view out the windshield. It took a long time for the particles to settle and for Taylor's legs to return from jelly to flesh and blood again. There was no sign of the car. Apparently, the demented driver had gleefully headed off to torment another victim. Taylor swung the driver's side door open and heaved her swollen body out to get her bearings. She waddled to the front of the car to survey the damage. What she observed caused a shiver to travel down her spine and her heart to lurch into her throat. The Saturn had stopped within mere inches of a thirty foot drop that would have landed her right into the river.

Her hands clutching her chest, Taylor glanced down the steep embankment to the swiftly flowing water. It was not likely that she or the baby would have survived the fall, or escaped the wreckage if they had. Tears of fear mixed with awe and gratitude flowed down her lightly freckled face, which was already lined with the previous tears of the evening. It was then that she glanced at the hood. In the dust, she saw the perfect outline of what looked like two hands, only they were at least four times the size of even a large man's hand. Taylor clumsily dropped to her knees and raised her trembling hands to the heavens, overcome with emotion. Her heavenly Father loved her so deeply that he had dispatched his angels to save her and her precious baby. This was a night that would be with her forever, strengthening her faith in her God. Indeed, what the dark one means for harm, God uses for His good.

***

170

Chapter Twenty-One

Emily coaxed a small fire to life and curled up on the floor next to Kira. Mentally exhausted and exhilarated at the same time, she praised God that she was able to be there when Arin accepted Him. Lost in the dancing of the flames, her mind wandered through the past and rested on Geoffrey. She recalled the first few months they had worked together, and how just a glance thrown her way had the power to stop her heart. She replayed their disastrous affair followed by a farce of a marriage. And finally, she allowed her mind to consider the child that could have been.

Back then, she had been far from God. His will for her life had been the furthest thing from her mind. Viewing the past through the bittersweet knowledge of hindsight, Emily was able to appreciate how God had used even her outright rebellion to bring not only her but others to Him. Geoffrey had been a wicked man, but could she really believe that his heart had been stained any blacker than hers had been? Emily trusted that if even he had just sincerely cried out to God, he would not have been refused. She prayed that he had done so before his death. Although she certainly had no human love for the man, the thought of him spending eternity without Christ was too painful. Her heart was comforted by the loving touch of her Father and the knowledge that His justice is perfect.

Sighing deeply, Emily rolled onto her back and caressed Kira's soft fur. As grateful as she was for her ever-present canine friend, Emily admitted to herself that she was lonely, sometimes desperately so. She no longer craved the white-hot excitement and danger that a man like Geoffrey offered. If she wanted that, she could surely have her pick of any of the doctors at the hospital. Emily had made the decision to trust that the Lord already had someone special for her. She had resolved to wait on his timing. Admittedly, waiting was not exactly her forte. Perhaps she suffered from macrophobia, the fear of long waits. She did go out of her way to avoid the motor vehicle bureau, after all.

Arin's medical file rested on the edge of the brick fireplace. Emily eyed it, indecisive. She had started the fire, intent on burning the thing, thinking perhaps it had not been coincidence she'd forgotten it multiple times. She decided to let the fire die out without consuming the file. Perhaps the timing had not been right.

Bright and early the next morning, Kathrynne headed out, closing the door to her apartment without locking it. In fact, she considered leaving the door wide open. Lord knew she had nothing worth stealing. If someone stole from her, they were in pretty desperate shape indeed, and they were welcome to it. She made her way to the ancient Datsun, praying that the old girl had one more trip in her.

***

Jake left for work without waking Arin, something he never would have done even a week ago. He wondered at how little time it had taken them to grow apart, and the years it had taken them to grow together. He missed the closeness they had shared. With practically no family involvement outside of Cousin Dave, it had always been Jake and Arin against the world. It now seemed more like Jake and Arin against each other.

Rubbing his tired red eyes, Jake wrestled with the number Arin had thrown at him last night. She might as well have tossed a live grenade his way. How could she possibly know? Had Troy's "gift" somehow revealed it to her? Maybe Jesus had told her, Jake thought, his lips twisting into a wry smile. How she could she be so naïve?

Dave was already at the shop when he pulled in. Jake arrived at least five minutes early every day, but somehow Dave always managed to get there first. He shuddered at the thought of Dave finding out about Arin's conversion. When they had left the cult, Dave set them up at his place until they found a fixer upper. He gave Jake a job, and when he proved to be worth his salt, he made him an equal partner. Still, Dave never tired of teasing Jake about his involvement with the cult. It had just been in the last year that he had stopped calling him "Jesus Man." Lately, he had settled into a groove of "Yo Mamma" one-liners and the occasional crude joke that one would expect to be told in a garage. Jake was determined that Dave was not going find out about Arin's newfound religion. Dave would have a field day with it, and Jake just wasn't in the mood.

***

"Mommy, wake up," Troy said softly. Arin stirred. Her hip and neck were stiff and ached.

"Hi, snuggle bunny."

"I am a big boy mommy, not a bunny."

"Hi, big boy snuggle bunny."

Troy rolled his eyes. "I made you coffee," he announced proudly.

Arin sat up slowly and accepted the mug from his hands. In it was lukewarm water with coffee grounds floating around. It's the thought that counts, she decided. Troy watched her intently, so she took a small sip, using her teeth to filter out the grounds.

"Mmmmm, good coffee. Thanks, Buddy."

Troy jumped up on the couch and cuddled up to his mommy, glad that she liked his coffee. Arin swallowed hard. It seemed like a long time since Troy had shown her emotion of any sort. Suddenly he seemed like his old self, interactive and affectionate. *Thank you, Lord*, she prayed.

"How'd it go last night?" she asked nonchalantly.

"I don't have to go back, do I?"

"No way."

"Bad angels like that place."

Arin put her hands on his shoulders and looked into his eyes. "What do you mean?"

"Bad angels like Jacob. They all like Allie and wanted me to like her too. I was really scared until the real angel came and stood by me. Now Jacob can't ever bother me again."

"Jacob is gone?"

Troy nodded, flashing his priceless grin. Arin hugged him tightly, overcome with gratefulness to God. This was no coincidence. Pastor Wesley had been right. Arin had been trying to fight a spiritual battle without any gear. It almost took the ruin of her son before she humbled herself and admitted that she needed the Lord. It may have been at that very second that He sent an angel to guard her son. Wow.

Arin told Troy all about how she loved Jesus now and wanted to live a different life and be a better mommy.

"You love Jesus like Aunt Rae?"

Chapter Twenty-Two

"Yep."

"I want to love Jesus too. Jacob hates Him," Troy said solemnly.

"I bet he does."

Arin had the privilege and joy of leading her son in prayer to receive Christ as the savior of his soul. Although her own knowledge was quite limited, she was careful to make sure that Troy understood what he was saying and doing. After questioning him, Arin was convinced that he knew better than she did. A fresh batch of tears flowed. She must have cried more in the last three days than she had her entire life.

"Want me to make you breakfast mommy?"

"How about we go out to breakfast to celebrate?" Arin suggested, her mouth still gritty with coffee grinds. With that, Troy leapt off the couch and did victory laps around the coffee table. The boy loved Waffle House with a passion.

***

The road ahead of the ancient orange Datsun was dusted with a powdery snow; fair weather conditions as far as most Maine residents were concerned. Kathrynne gripped the wheel with her bony arthritic fingers, praying that the bald tires and slipping transmission would not fail her.

Long hours on the road without a functioning radio gave her mind plenty of time to wander. She knew she had no right to see her daughter, or her grandson for that matter. Regret gnawed at her insides painfully, along with the cancer that ravished her body a little more each day. She had wasted her life. It had slipped by like sand through her fingers. The fact that God had reached down and touched her miserable heart almost one year ago humbled and amazed her. She had nothing to offer back to Him other than the remaining days of her life, which the doctors at the free clinic had assured her would be few.

Kathrynne thought back to that day, as she often did. The day she had really started to live was the day she was told she soon would die. The pain in her abdomen had finally driven her to the free clinic downtown. It had been well over a decade since she had willingly submitted to an examination by a doctor. Several times some good Samaritan had noticed her on the street and called an ambulance before hurrying on his way. It had not been an uncommon occurrence for her to wake up in the ER, some bored nursing student chained to a desk by her bed on suicide watch.

Dirty and desperate, Kathrynne had allowed Dr. Jeb Wilson to examine her. Despite the shape she was in, and the lack of monetary reward he would receive, Dr. Wilson, or Dr. Jebby as she affectionately referred to him now, had treated her with compassion and dignity. He'd looked her in the eye, asking questions regarding her alcohol and drug use, sexual history, and other personal areas with respect. She could not remember the last time someone had maintained eye contact with her.

Unlike the slew of emergency room doctors she'd had the displeasure of meeting over the years, Dr. Jebby took his time evaluating Kathrynne. It was as if he'd known that she would probably never willingly step into another doctor's office again, and he'd better give her the works while he had her in a gown. She'd begrudgingly allowed him to draw some blood, impressed that he'd done it himself instead of shoving the job off on some underling. She'd promised to return in a few days. He had prescribed a powerful painkiller, and he had enough experience with addicts to know that she would abuse it, but he also knew that she was in a great deal of pain and needed it.

It had been Dr. Jebby's kindness, not anticipation for her test results, which led Kathrynne back to the free clinic several days later. Her soul had been starved for human contact and compassion. Although she had looked forward to seeing him since the moment she had stepped out of the clinic, her pride forced her to glower at him, arms crossed in an angry pose when she returned. Tenderly, he had delivered the dismal diagnosis. He'd rolled his stool closer and shocked her by gently grasping her hand in his. In that moment, he'd presented the gospel, claiming that the God of the universe was interested in her soul. Although it had seemed too good to be true, Kathrynne had bowed her head to the God she had been running from and rebelling against her entire life. The transaction had been immediate. Just minutes after she'd learned she would soon die, her heart had been flooded with light and her real life had begun. In time, God had even healed her from the addiction that had controlled her for far too long.

Most Christians would have considered their job done at that point, patted themselves on the back, and gone about their business. Not Dr. Jebby, the dear soul Kathrynne had come to love as a son. His wife's family owned a small apartment complex and they'd set her up in a first floor unit. Leanne, known to Kathrynne as Mrs. Jebby, made sure that her refrigerator was stocked; she had a blanket and sheets for her bed, and even gave her the old orange Datsun, for what it was worth.

Kathrynne had never been one to accept charity, but at this point, she was too sickly to protest.

It took a long time for her to grasp why on earth this kind affluent doctor and his lovely wife gave a rip about an old homeless alcoholic whose body was ravaged by years of self-abuse. One evening, while she knelt and poured her heart out to God, He whispered the answer to her heart. What was done for her was done out of the depth of her heavenly Father's love. Dr. and Mrs. Jebby were just the earthly vessels, used by Him to lavish His perfect love upon her. She was certain that there was not a person on earth as undeserving as she was, or as grateful.

The old Datsun puttered along with Kathrynne at the wheel singing old hymns, horribly out of tune. To God, they were beautiful. Two silvery beings pushed the orange dinosaur along, ensuring it would make it to its destination without incident.

Arin dropped a Styrofoam container heavy with artery-clogging Waffle House home fries on the desk. Rae's eyes grew wide. She licked her lips and took off for the back room to retrieve the ketchup. Troy walked backwards in front of her, signing the news that he was a friend of Jesus. Rae was overjoyed and scooped him up, hugging him forcefully. Troy breathed in deeply. He loved the smell of Aunt Rae. Mommy called it white tea and ginger.

Arin and Troy sat in Rae's tiny office watching as she ravaged the ketchup-smothered home fries. Arin openly admitted to being more than a little jealous that Rae could eat like a lumberjack and never gain an ounce. She told Rae about her little preacher, who had asked the purple-haired waitress with a lip ring if she loved Jesus. Arin left a generous tip and hoped that the light in Troy's innocent face had stirred something within the sad looking purple-tressed teen.

Rae and Arin became absorbed in conversation. They understood the intricate details of each other's lives as only best friends can, and there was so much to share. Troy wandered from the office, heading for the oasis.

"Hello, Norton."

Norton let out a loud whistle, "Whatcha doin, Cutie?"

"Oh Norton, you're so silly," Troy giggled. He treated each of the birds to a walnut from the bucket Rae kept stocked in the gazebo. He climbed into a chair facing the place where the man had died and thought back to that day. Out of the corner of his eye he thought he spied Jacob near the Pathos, sneering at him. Fear surged through his small body. Immediately, he recited the scripture from Psalm 23. He would fear no evil.

The next day was Saturday, and true to Welsh family tradition, Jake and Troy watched cartoons until noon and slurped sugary milk from the bowls. Arin caught up on her housework, as much as her still aching hip and neck would allow, and returned a few phone calls. Dawn, from DeafMed, thought she had fallen off the face of the planet. Arin busted out her calendar and, for the next half hour, they bickered good-naturedly over her schedule. Arin found herself relating to Dawn on a more personal level than before. She knew that Dawn's son Bryan, who was just a little older than Troy, was undergoing extensive treatment for Leukemia.

Arin listened for a long time as the pain and fear poured from Dawn's aching heart. Although she tried, Arin could not imagine being in her place, watching her child suffer day in and day out, while at the same time working to pay the bills and do all of the things that life requires. Dawn, a single mother, was overwhelmed. Though she had a sick kid, her life could not come to a screeching halt. The laundry continued to pile up, the dirty dishes mounted, the car broke down. Arin's heart went out to Dawn.

"I think my church has a support group for parents. Maybe you and I should check it out."

"That sounds good, but I'm not really a religious person."

"That is not a problem," Arin promised.

After a long, emotional conversation, they made plans to get together and hung up. It occurred to Arin that in the past, she would have been too consumed with her own life to consider what Dawn might have been going through. Now it seemed natural to ask others about their struggles. Even though she did not know all the answers, she knew the one who did. In the short time since she came to Christ, others were at the forefront of her mind. She had always thought Christians did kind things to earn their way to heaven. Now she knew that caring for others was non-negotiable. It was done through you, not by you.

Although Arin's attitude and outlook on most things had done a one-eighty, Jake, on the other hand, stood his ground stubbornly. He accused Arin of tricking Troy into believing her way. It was obvious that he fiercely resented his son's conversion.

"Mommy, Daddy says we can go to the park now. Are you coming with us?"

"Yeah, but you're not going anywhere in your pajamas. Get dressed, lazybones."

Troy pointed to the picture of the Incredible Hulk on his pajamas. He roared and flexed his muscles. Arin patted his bottom and sent him upstairs to get dressed, yelling after him to please choose something that matched.

"What park are we going to?" Arin asked.

"Baker, I guess." Jake's voice was cold and distant.

"Jake, why are you so angry with me?"

"I'm fine. Get off your 'I love Jesus' high horse, okay?"

His words hurt, and a bitter reply was loaded on her tongue. She literally had to cover her mouth to prevent it from escaping. He went upstairs to change and Arin stuck her tongue out, enjoying a juvenile moment. She was about to resort to a few choice words to give vent to her anger when she was distracted by a knock on the door. She glanced out the window and noticed a rusty orange clunker in her driveway.

"You try," Mary said, flinging a chart at Emily. "I am getting nowhere with this one and I'm off in fifteen minutes."

"Gee, thanks." Sighing, Emily flipped through the chart as she headed to exam room B. Twenty-four year old female, twenty-two weeks pregnant. She scanned the most recent blood work and amnio results. Everything appeared to be in order. Her stomach lurched when she saw the familiar initials on the last physician's order: GR.

She sent up a short but efficient prayer and entered the small exam room.

"Hi, Susan. I'm Emily." Susan had the look of a frightened animal caught in a trap.

"Can you tell me what brings you in today?"

Over an hour later, Emily bolted from the room like lightning. It had been nearly impossible to maintain her composure as she interviewed poor Susan Walters.

"I need a minute," she called to her supervisor, breezing by before she could ask any questions. Emily started on one of her power walks around the hospital grounds and attempted to process what Susan had told her. She knew that Geoffrey had changed in the last few years and had become consumed by greed, but she never imagined what a monster he had truly become.

Of course, he was no dummy. She had to give him that. Susan Walters was the perfect victim. She was poor, single, and she'd provided no religious information in the slot on the form. She'd told Emily that Dr. Geoffrey had seen her several months ago at the free clinic downtown. Right away, red flags were waving. First of all, never in his entire career would he let a patient address him by his first name. Secondly, Geoffrey would never ever, under any circumstances give his precious time and skills without getting something in return. It just didn't fit until Susan continued her story.

Susan had been well into her first trimester when she'd shown up at the free clinic. Geoffrey had ordered extensive labs and an amnio, not something most free clinics offer to women with low risk pregnancies. Due to funding and staff limitations, the bare bones approach was usually all the struggling clinics could offer. Tears had filled Susan's eyes when she explained to Emily that her baby had Down syndrome. Dr. Geoffrey had assured her that the only responsible option was a therapeutic abortion.

Checking the chart again, Emily's blood began to boil. The amnio had come back negative for any fetal abnormalities. But Geoffrey had taken this young woman under his wicked wing, offering her a thousand dollars cash for every month she would wait to abort.

He'd explained that although the inferior fetus would just be an emotional and financial drain on her and the system, if she would just allow it to develop further it would be invaluable to science. He had even referred her to a counselor friend of his who knew the challenges of raising a Down's kid. Susan had described Allie McIntyre to a tee. Emily snorted and tossed her hair, her power walk more like a power run now. It did not surprise her that Allie was in on this, but lying about having a child with special needs seemed low, even for her. As a nurse, Emily had worked with the parents of many special needs kids, and she had noticed a common denominator. The parents considered their children a blessing, not a curse.

Susan had collected several thousand dollars from Geoffrey, but was beginning to have second thoughts. Since his suicide, she'd felt lost and unsure. Dr. Geoffrey had constantly reminded her to stay detached from the "fetus," but she had found that impossible to do as her belly stretched and jerked with every kick. Breathless, Emily fished her cell phone from the pocket of her scrubs and dialed Taylor's number.

***

"May I help you?" Arin leaned on the doorframe waiting for the sickly waif of a woman to answer.

"Ma'am?" Arin asked a few moments later when she still hadn't responded. "Are you okay?" Her fuzzy gray head lifted and their identical cinnamon eyes locked.

"Arin…"

Recognition was followed by a wave of emotion. Years of heartache and yearning had morphed into fury and hatred. Caught off guard, she almost extended a hand to her, almost.

Chapter Twenty-Four

"What are you doing here?"

"I wanted to see you before-"

"Well, you've seen me." Arin slammed the door and turned on her heels. So much for the love of God flowing through her.

"Anyone but her, Lord," she prayed aloud.

Troy pounded down the stairs and over to the window as the junky orange car slowly pulled out.

"Was that Grandma?"

"No," Arin lied. The question hit her like a jolt of lightning. "What makes you think that was your Grandma?" Troy had never even met the woman. The one old photo that Arin had was carefully hidden and she certainly didn't talk about her.

"I had a dream about her and she was driving a silly orange car like that one."

Arin was already carrying the cooler out to the car when Jake arrived back downstairs, determined to enjoy a family picnic for Troy's sake. A scrap of paper had fluttered to the ground when Arin opened the front door. She'd fumbled with the cooler, snatched it, and shoved it in her pocket before Jake could notice.

***

Taylor sat at Susan Walters' bedside and listened, the very thing she did best. Susan, not exactly the church-going type, peppered her story with language that would make a sailor blush. Taylor listened without judging, sensing the hurt and fear behind Susan's foul words. Susan, a waitress at a local bar, and Taylor, a pastor's wife and therapist, could scarcely have led lives more different. The fact that they were roughly in the same stage of pregnancy acted as a sort of bonding agent, common ground for them to stand on.

"You guys want some ginger ale or something?" Emily poked her head in and asked.

"Please," they both nodded.

"She's nice," Susan said. "So are you. Thanks for talking to me," she added shyly. Despite the tattoos and rough language, Taylor detected a child-like innocence in her. Before long, instead of considering when to abort her fetus, Susan was wondering what to name her baby.

***

The Intrusion

Arin sat on a bench watching Troy and Jake play tag. She fished the scrap of paper from her pocket and read it quickly before balling it up and tossing it in a nearby garbage can. Mommy Dearest wanted a chance to talk and was staying at a cheap hotel in town. Too bad, Arin thought. It felt good to be the one doing the rejecting.

After the service on Sunday, Arin and Rae sat on the picnic table near the church playground while Troy played. Arin's sharp jerky signs annunciated her anger. What right did her mother have to just show up out of the blue? What sort of reception did she expect? Rae selected her words carefully and asked the Spirit for guidance, not wanting to rub salt into her friends gaping wound. Deciding to let God speak for her, she gently advised Arin to read Luke 15:11-31, the parable of the prodigal son. She hoped that God would reveal to her that His mercy was for prodigal mothers as well.

***

"I am fine, Dr. Jebby," Kathrynne assured her unofficially adopted son. "The old Datsun made it all the way without a problem. That's a miracle, huh?" she joked. In reality, she had no idea how much truth there was to her statement.

"You know you shouldn't be traveling, Kathrynne. You're not well."

"So I should wait to see my grandson after I am dead?"

Jeb Wilson sighed. Kathrynne was a tough old bird. God had laid it on his heart to witness to her and then make sure her last days were comfortable. Watching her transformation had been an absolute blessing for him and Leanne.

"I don't know why I bother," he teased. "You did bring your medication with you, right?"

Kathrynne winced. "The weather here is really nice. Much milder than up home."

"So that's a no?"

"I would rather have a few good days instead of a bunch of days wishing I was already six feet under, okay?"

"I just care about you," Jeb answered softly, amazed at the love he had in his heart for Kathrynne Gruber.

"I know you do, honey, though I'll never know why."

"Me neither."

Kathrynne smiled as she hung up the phone. "He's a good boy," she proudly proclaimed to the abnormally large cockroach making its way across the dirty carpet. "And she's a good girl. Quite a beauty, too. Must get her looks from her father." The cockroach stopped and appeared to be studying her. She decided to name him Eugene. He just looked like a Eugene to her.

"Good night, Eugene. Sweet dreams." Eugene waved his antennae her way and continued his quest to the other side of the room.

***

"I really appreciate this," Arin said. "And I don't mind paying. I know you need to make a living too."

"Don't be silly. It is my pleasure to talk to the little man." Taylor ruffled Troy's hair, secretly hoping that if she had a boy, he would turn out to be just like him. "Troy, do you want to come with me to my office?"

"Sure. Is that okay, Mom?"

"Go for it." She replied. "I'll be right here."

Ben Wesley stumbled into the kitchen in his normal pre-coffee stupor. He nearly dropped the pot when someone greeted him from behind.

"Hi, Ben."

He turned, suddenly aware of his Snoopy pajama pants and Woodstock t-shirt. What could he say? He was a Peanuts fanatic. "Hi, Arin..." He looked around for Taylor, confused.

"Taylor is meeting with Troy this morning."

"Oh," he poured his coffee and sipped, perking instantly. He sat across the table from Arin. He had been meaning to talk to her anyway, and this seemed like a golden opportunity.

"I've been thinking a lot about our last visit and wondering how things were going for you."

Arin filled him in on the latest. At the mention of Allie McIntyre's name, he nearly spat out his coffee.

"She is the last person on earth I would ask for advice, Arin. Just take my word on that, okay?"

Arin agreed wholeheartedly and Ben's shoulders sagged with relief. Arin went on to tell him about her first meeting with Dr. Raines, and the loss of the twin she had named Jacob.

Chapter Twenty-Five

"I am so sorry," he said softly. "That explains a lot."

"What do you mean?" She could use some explanations right now. She sure had enough questions.

"Perhaps the demon appeared as a child to Troy in order to gain his acceptance and friendship. The fact that he was identical to Troy and used the name you had given to the son you lost leads me to believe that he wanted to drive you further from God using guilt. Satan is not all knowing by any stretch. Only God knows all. I think it is safe to assume that Dr. Raines was used by an evil one, and it would have been there the day he took your son from you."

"So Jacob appeared to be Troy's twin to mock me and throw the past up in my face?"

"It makes sense to me. Scripture tells us that Satan can appear as an angel of light. I imagine if he can do that, he can appear to be pretty much anything to anyone. I know how badly it frightened you, but it was a gift from God that you were able to see Jacob that night."

Arin nodded in agreement. "I know for sure that what I encountered that night was pure evil. If God had not allowed me to see him for myself, I might have believed Dr. McIntyre's lies about him being a companion or some sort of wise teacher."

"Exactly, the fact that you and Troy have come to the Lord is proof that all things work together for the good of those who love Him. What Satan meant for evil, God has used for good."

"You can break into a sermon at any time, can't you?" Arin teased.

Ben threw up his hands, "It's what I do." For the next forty-five minutes they chatted and laughed easily. He found it difficult to believe that this was the same woman who had sat across from him last week and scoffed. Truly, nothing is impossible with God, he thought.

Troy zoomed into the kitchen, "Mommy, Ms. Taylor says it's your turn." He turned to Ben and smiled. "I like Woodstock, too." Ben grinned and held out his hand for Troy to high five.

***

"You've got a great kid."

"He's incredible," Arin agreed.

"I'm really impressed with the way he's handling everything he's been through. The one thing he did express some anxiety over was your mother. Apparently, she visited recently? He is very concerned about her."

"He has no business being concerned about my mother," Arin blurted, instantly defensive. "She's a stranger to us. Why would he be bothered about her?"

"He mentioned that he had a dream she was sick."

Arin drummed her fingers on the dinosaur desk. One look at the woman was enough to know that she was not well. She felt something within her break, a chink in her anger allowing hurt and fear to escape. "She didn't want me, Taylor. What do you expect me to do?"

Taylor leaned forward. "She wants you now," she said gently.

Arin closed her eyes and breathed deeply. "I am just so angry at her."

"I am going to say something that may be hard to hear, but just think about it, okay?"

Arin steeled herself. "Shoot."

"Think about the things in your life that are most precious to you. Troy, Jake, even your friendship with Rae. Would you have met Jake if you'd had a stable mother and father to support you? Would you have learned sign language? Perhaps you would not have come to the Lord."

"So I should write her a thank you card?" Arin snapped. Instantly, she regretted her words. Taylor was only trying to help, and for free. She felt like a total jerk. "I'm sorry. I didn't mean it to come out like that."

"I know, don't worry about it."

Taylor sensed that Arin needed time to think things through. Nothing she could offer would be helpful until the Holy Spirit had softened her heart. She let Arin know that she and Ben would be in prayer for her family, including her mother. Arin went to collect Troy, who was sitting at the kitchen table across from Ben, playing a highly competitive game of Go Fish.

"Ben's nice, and kinda funny." Troy exclaimed on the way home. "I never knew that grown-ups wore Snoopy pajamas. Maybe we should get Daddy some."

"I think we should," Arin agreed.

A rin and Jake lay in bed talking late into the night. Arin's tears quickly melted his icy heart, and for now, their differences were shoved aside. He held her and listened as she vented her anger and fears about her mother.

"If only Troy did not want to see her so badly, I could forget she ever showed up."

"Could you really?"

Arin thought a moment before deciding that no, she probably couldn't. Finally she made the decision to see her mother tomorrow, hear her out, and be done with it. After a few moments of comfortable silence, Arin bravely started the conversation she had been longing to have with Jake for the past five years. It was time.

"I need to tell you something," she blurted. Half of her was afraid she would lose her nerve and the other half terrified she wouldn't. "Remember when you went away on business before Troy was born?"

Jake's heart sank, sure he was about to be confronted with his own adulterous secret. "Yeah," he squeaked.

Instead of confronting him about his one night stand, she shocked him with her own hidden truth. Arin told Jake that during her pregnancy she had been carrying twins. She revealed that after collapsing she had been talked into a 'therapeutic abortion' by the same doctor who had hung himself at the Silver Fox. The doctor had convinced her that the only way to save one of the children was to abort the other, and out of sheer panic at the thought of losing both babies, she had consented. Confused, Jake asked her to repeat her story twice until he got it.

"Why didn't you tell me?"

"I should have. I am so sorry, Jake. Please forgive me."

He pulled her close and they wept together. They both wanted nothing more than to have another child, and grieved for what could have been. The pieces fell together in Jake's mind. Now he understood what had caused Arin to fall into a deep depression the few months before Troy was born. A fresh wave of guilt washed over him. While he was being unfaithful in room two-sixteen, Arin had been going through hell at home. Ready to confess, he opened his mouth, but the words stubbornly refused to come. What was the point? He might feel better, he thought, but at what cost to her?

***

Confession is good for the soul, Arin thought as she lay awake in the wee morning hours, Jake snoring softly beside her. She felt like a heavy load had been removed from her chest, and for the first time, she knew that she was forgiven—by God, by Jake, and by the little one she would see in heaven. She studied Jake as he slept, knowing instinctively that he was holding onto secrets of his own, wondering if he would ever find peace and forgiveness. She prayed he would.

***

The ugly orange Datsun fit right in with the other junkers in the parking lot of the scummy hotel. Arin sat in the Explorer for a long time staring at the door, her emotions cycling from anger to fear to longing. Hands shaking and heart pounding, she made her way to the door and rapped firmly. She stood there for several minutes. When she put her ear to the door, she heard nothing. A shifty looking guy exited the next room and eyeballed her. He grinned and lit a cigarette.

Knocking hard enough to make her knuckles ache, Arin grew increasingly uncomfortable under the gaze of the creep next door. When he took a step in her direction, she nervously tried the doorknob. It turned and she stepped inside, shutting the door behind her. It took a few moments for her eyes to adjust in the darkness. At first Arin saw no one in the sparse room. Then she detected movement. Her mother's paper thin body lay under the covers, her hand twitching. Flipping on the light, she rushed to her bedside. Kathrynne's face was gaunt, her eyes sunken. Unsure of what to do, Arin rushed to the bedside and slapped her face, trying to rouse her. It worked in the movies, but in reality, not so much. She bolted from the room as if it were on fire. After a frantic search of the Explorer, she found her cell phone. It would have made perfect sense to call 911. Instead, she dialed Emily, ferociously praying that she would answer.

Twenty minutes later, Emily's silver Accord pulled into the parking lot. She flew out of the car and ran toward Arin, who waved wildly from the doorway of the grungy hotel room.

"What medical problems does she have?" Emily asked, grabbing her stethoscope and yanking the covers back.

"I-I-I don't know," Arin stammered.

Emily listened for a few moments. Her patient stirred and moaned.

"She needs to be in the hospital," Emily stated.

"No hospital, please," Arin and Emily jumped when the wisp of a woman spoke.

"Can I see him?" she rasped, eyes focused on Arin. "Please."

***

"You understand that grandma is sick, right?" Arin asked Troy as they stood outside the hotel room. She did not want her son scarred by image of the emaciated woman lying in the room near death. It felt strange to address her as "Grandma."

"I know, Mommy. In my dream she was sick, but she still wanted to see me," Troy insisted. He had been chomping at the bit to get in the room for nearly a half hour. Jake stood several feet away, uncertain of what he should be doing. Emily emerged from the room, talking on her cell.

"Can I go now?" Troy asked impatiently. Arin nodded and he disappeared inside the room.

Emily snapped her phone shut and gave Arin a quick hug. "I tried the number next to the phone. It belongs to her doctor in Maine. He says he talked to her recently and she seemed to be doing okay, but the cancer is so far advanced that he doesn't expect her to recover this time. He is amazed that she's made it this far."

Arin's eyes filled and quickly overflowed. "I should have let her in."

"Don't do that, Arin. You know you can't change the past. Go be with her now."

Troy was perched on the bed next to Kathrynne, stroking her withered hand with his plump fingers and chattering away about his toy cars and dinosaurs. Although her face was gaunt and sallow, her eyes danced as they drank him in. After standing in the doorway listening in for a long moment, Arin sat on the other side of the bed and gently took her mother's hand in hers.

"I'm so sorry," Kathrynne gasped weakly, her eyes begging Arin for forgiveness.

"Me too," Arin replied quickly. The miracle of forgiveness had already begun to take place in her heart.

"I'm glad you are not mad at Grandma anymore, Mommy. She's nice."

Kathrynne was overwhelmed by his simple words. How she wished she had come earlier. She felt her life slipping away and knew it would not be long before she was done with this world. She was grateful that her last moments would be spent with her daughter and grandson. Troy continued telling her about his life in great detail. His voice was like the music of angels to her dying ears. When he told her that he and Mommy had become friends of Jesus, her heart leapt joyfully. God had heard her prayers. She felt the odd sensation of her soul starting to detach from her body, and she urgently turned to Arin and struggled to speak.

"Please read…" Using her last ounce of strength, she motioned to the floor with her bony pointer finger.

At Arin's feet was a thick bundle of envelopes tied together with twine, red pen scrawled across the front. Deeply ashamed of herself, she picked them up and hugged them to her chest.

"I will, Mom. I'm so sorry."

Kathrynne relaxed and breathed her last breath, a peaceful smile on her withered face.

"T hat's her. That's Dr. Smith." Susan was positive as soon as she looked at the picture. "I'll never forget those eyes."

"No, that's Dr. Allie McIntyre," Emily corrected.

A string of curses escaped Susan's lips. "Sorry. I just can't believe they were lying to me that whole time." Susan was still trying to grasp the truth. Her baby was perfectly normal as far as the amnio and sonograms were concerned. Dr. Smith was actually Dr. McIntyre. "Let me guess. She doesn't have a special needs child either, right?"

Emily shuddered at the thought of Allie mothering any child, special needs or not. "No, she has no children. I don't think she has a motherly bone in her body."

"You should have heard her, Emily. She went on and on about how hard her life was with her daughter, and how if she could do it again, she would have done the right thing and aborted. She even cried, for Pete's sake!" Susan paced around Emily's kitchen island as she ranted.

"Calm down. You're going to go into labor." She poured Susan a glass of orange juice and rustled up a multi-vitamin from her cabinet. It wasn't a prenatal, but it was better than nothing. Susan sat obediently, taking the vitamin and gulping the juice.

"You've been real nice to me." Susan said. Her tone was more accusatory than thankful. "What's in it for you?"

"Can't I just be a nice person?"

"No one is that nice."

Emily sighed, unsure of how to explain her desire to help. "I had an abortion several years ago. It was the worse decision of my life. I don't want you to go down the same road."

"Oh," Susan said, feeling like a total heel for doubting Emily's motives.

"Plus, as you know, I was married to Geoffrey, and for some reason I feel somewhat responsible for his actions."

"I can't believe that someone as nice as you was married to that dirt bag."

Emily laughed. "When I met him, I was not exactly the person I am now. When God got a hold of me, everything changed."

Normally, that was the sort of comment that would trigger a nasty reaction in Susan. She thought for a moment about all of her so-called friends who had abandoned her when she stopped drinking and drugging. She compared them to Emily and Taylor. The former were selfish losers, the latter giving strangers. She preferred the latter any day, thank you very much.

"Who knows? Maybe one day God will decide to get a hold of me."

"He would love to," Emily said, her blue eyes sparkling.

***

"Thanks for calling. We are going to try to move a few things on our schedules so we can be there." Jeb wrote down the address before hanging up. "What do you think, Hon. Can we make it?"

Leanne sat at the kitchen table with both of their schedule books. It looked impossible. "Let's just decide that we are going and make it happen." She knew Jeb. If he started to review his jam-packed schedule for the next few days, he would be overwhelmed.

"Okay, I'll call the office and let them know."

***

Arin was amazed at the size of the crowd that gathered around her mother's grave to hear to Ben's short but poignant sermon. She had fully expected the turnout to be pitiful given the fact that her mother knew essentially no one in Maryland. But car after car pulled into the circular drive of the cemetery, most of them occupied by members of Downsville Christian Fellowship. They had never met Kathrynne Gruber, but they wanted to show love and support to her daughter. By the time Ben started speaking, there was a respectable crowd by any standards.

Ben's words were direct and succinct. He read from the one and only letter that Arin had opened so far, dated just twenty days before her mother's death. Kathrynne knew she had squandered her life, and sought to live for God with every precious second she had left. She had fervently prayed for her daughter and grandson, asking God to do a miracle and reconcile them before she went home. God came through, as He always does. The deathbed reconciliation of a mother and daughter was enough to inspire a good cry. Several people in the crowd sniffed, and tissues were passed around.

After the simple service, everyone was invited to attend a casual lunch at the park adjoining the cemetery. Rae, Emily, and Taylor had been hard at work during the service setting everything up. Because Kathrynne Gruber had been a Christian, they'd decided on a celebratory theme, they even had a banner made up reading "Welcome Home Kathrynne!" Rae knew that the funeral and gravesite, simple as they were, had strapped Jake and Arin financially. She insisted on handling the meal. She banded together with Emily and Taylor, and they had done a bang-up job. Most people decided to stay and walked over from the cemetery. The March afternoon was sunny and mild. After the long, cold stretch, the day seemed practically tropical.

The mood was more similar to a family reunion than a funeral. People quickly separated and formed pockets of conversation. Laughter and hugging ran rampant throughout the group. Jake and Dave, who knew no one, fell into a conversation with Ben, who happened to know quite a bit about motorcycles. For years he had dreamed of riding, although Taylor was less than thrilled with the idea. Dave had always dreamt about D&J's automotive technology becoming more specialized in motorcycles. An avid rider himself, he almost had Jake talked into getting a bike, which would have taken some getting used to for Arin.

Dave was prone to taunt and ice out anyone who expressed their faith in any way; however, Ben's knowledge of motorcycles and his understanding of their intricate mechanical parts seemed to earn Dave's respect. He was somehow able to overlook the fact that Ben was a preacher by trade and they managed to hold a lively conversation. Jake watched in amazement. He had never seen Dave have an intelligent discussion without the use of four-letter words.

After lunch only a few people straggled off. Most returned to their conversations or initiated new ones. Arin finally had the pleasure of meeting Jeb and Leanne Wilson, the lovely couple who helped her mother survive since her diagnosis. The night of her mother's death, she had talked with Jeb at length, thirsty for an idea of what her mother's life had been like. Jeb gladly poured details of Kathrynne's last year, which made Arin proud. Her mother was anything but the monster her wounded heart had painted her to be. She was flawed, yes, unfortunate, absolutely, but not sinister in any way. Jeb described in great detail his first and second encounters with Kathrynne and the overwhelming call on his heart to help her in any way he could. He had not experienced more clear instructions from God before or since.

Jeb recounted Kathrynne's conversion; it was not like anything he had ever seen. Minutes after he delivered the news that she was dying, he felt an open door to share the gospel. That was why he volunteered precious time he really did not have to the free clinic. What were they going to do, fire him? They were so grateful to have an actual MD around that they looked the other way when the occasional patient griped about his proselytizing.

According to Jeb, Kathrynne had responded to the gospel with enthusiasm and thankfulness. Her soul had been ripe, and he merely jiggled the branch, shaking the fruit free.

"She started praying for you and Troy almost immediately," Jeb told Arin. Leanne nodded in agreement next to him.

"She prayed for you guys all the time," she added.

"I can't believe how stubborn I was to never open one of her letters," Arin groaned.

"Don't be hard on yourself, Arin." Jeb urged. He thought for a moment. "You were saved just a little while ago, right?"

"Several days ago, actually,"

"Think about it. What would you have thought about your mother's letters before you became a Christian yourself?"

"I would never have been open to hearing about God from her," Arin admitted.

"I know you are young in the faith and you are grieving for your mom, but try to keep something in mind, okay?" Jeb's demeanor was kind and gentle. Arin shook her head and he continued. "God is always on time. Never early. Never late. Your mom showed up at your doorstep only a day or so after you were saved. You showed up at hers a few moments before she died. The last thing she heard before going to be with the Lord forever was that her prayers on earth had been answered. If that is not God's perfect timing, I don't know what is."

As he spoke, Arin looked around the pavilion at the crowd gathered. Rae was busy making sure everyone had enough to eat and starting the clean up. Emily and Taylor huddled close to a rough looking young pregnant girl at a far table. Jake, Dave, and Ben talked motorcycles in the other corner of the pavilion. Dawn from DeafMed sat with Betty and Ed Webber. Ed had greeted her at the picnic after the funeral and insisted she join them for lunch. Dawn's son Bryan had paired off with Troy the second they had arrived, and they'd been playing ever since.

Though he was weak and pale from chemotherapy, Bryan was able to enjoy being outside playing trucks in the sandbox with Troy. Bryan pointed at whatever truck he wanted, and Troy ran to grab it so he could rest. As Dawn watched her son interacting like any other kid, tears slid down her cheeks. That had been her prayer just the night before when Bryan had been so sick. *Lord, if you are even there, just let him be a kid.* Watching Bryan and Troy play was an answer to her prayer. Ed Webber had invited her to attend Downsville Christian Fellowship about nine times now. She might just do that this Sunday. What could it hurt?

"I agree," Arin finally replied to Jeb. "If my mother had come even a week earlier, I probably would not have tracked her down. It would have been a wasted trip." She sighed. So many things were running around in her head. "What can I do to bring my husband to the Lord?"

"Live it, Arin. Live it in front of him every day. Show him the peace that Christ has brought to your life."

***

The mild March afternoon was a gift from the Almighty. Children who had spent too many winter days indoors giggled and played in the sunshine. It pleased their parents so much to see them rolling around in the grass having fun. They pushed the mountain of laundry and other undone chores from their minds. Each person honed in on enjoying the very speck of life that was in front of them, the exact thing that Kathrynne Gruber would have wanted them to do.

The jovial gathering was completely unaware of the battle going on in the unseen realm. The pavilion shone bright as the sun with hundreds of mighty warriors encircling the Lord's precious ones. A smaller circle of silvery soldiers was assigned to the one named Dave, who the Lord had plans for. The evil one who had laid claim to him years ago was forced to flee. Orders were given for Dave to be protected until his soul made its journey home.

The mightiest of the angels knelt beside a pale sickly child, peering into his eyes. The angel knew the Lord's heart was broken over this dear one's misery. He knew there was a purpose to his suffering that would be revealed soon enough with not just temporal, but eternal ramifications. Gently, he stroked the boy's white cheek with a huge

"Are you sure this thing's going to make it?" Susan asked, her face a mask of concern.

"Follow Jeb and Leanne. You have a cell and so do they. If anything goes wrong, just call." Emily calmly explained. Susan was nervous about the move and Emily didn't blame her. The orange beast didn't look like it would make it out of the parking lot, much less to Maine. The Wilsons had promised not to leave her stranded on the roadside. Emily and Susan both knew they were trustworthy.

As far as Emily was concerned, the more distance between Susan and her drug dealing ex-boyfriend and assorted colorful cohorts, the better. When she had heard Jeb Wilson talk about the housing ministry he and his in-laws ran, a light bulb had gone on in her head. She had sensed disaster for Susan if she'd stayed around, and wanted more than anything for her to succeed. Jeb and Leanne had jumped at the opportunity to help the young mother, which was all the confirmation Emily needed.

In no time at all, Susan's meager belongings were loaded into the Wilsons' SUV and they were ready to make the trek back to Maine. After tearful goodbyes, everyone agreed to keep in touch, and they were off. The Datsun miraculously pulled out and loudly followed the SUV. It would make the 600-mile trip home in the same way it had arrived-on a wing and a prayer.

***

Allie McIntyre stood in her doorway, not comprehending what the officer was telling her.

"Why would you need me to come to the station?"

"Ma'am, you are under arrest." Detective Lyons repeated himself, this time with more conviction. He nodded to the female officer and they prepared to take her into custody.

"You can't do this," Allie screamed as they came toward her. "Get off of me. You can't do this to me!" By this time, her neighbors stood on their porches, clustering together and pointing. Allie put up one heck of a struggle, kicking wildly against Detective Lyons as he restrained her long enough for the other officer to cuff her. When she bit his hand, he maced her. He silently admitted to himself that he enjoyed it much more than he should have. Allie McIntyre might have been a beautiful woman by the world's standards, but to Detective Lyons, she was downright hideous.

Emily Raines watched from her car. She had expected to feel triumphant, and was surprised at the pity she felt for the angry woman flailing as she fought the officers tooth and nail. Finally, they were able to subdue her enough to cuff her. Allie remained uncooperative, and she forced them to drag her to the squad car, an officer on each side. When they passed Emily's car, Allie looked up and their eyes locked. Pure hatred beamed from Allie's crystal eyes.

"This is your fault," Allie screamed, her voice hoarse from her prior protests. The neighbors were shocked at the string of obscenities Allie released. Covering their children's ears, they scampered back inside.

Emily pulled away, sadly shaking her head. She thanked God for bringing Susan into her path before her baby had become fetal parts to be farmed out. She couldn't help but wonder how many babies had been sacrificed on the altar of Geoffrey and Allie's greed. Arin's file lay on the passenger seat, and Emily toyed with the idea of introducing it to her heavy-duty shredder and forgetting she ever saw it. By the time she pulled into her driveway, she decided to put it away for now, praying that Susan's statement was enough to put Allie away for a long time.

∗∗∗

Arin curled up on the couch with a blanket and a steaming cup of tea. Using a beautiful antique pewter knife, she ceremoniously opened the next letter from her mother. The thought of reading them one after the other was tempting, but she promised herself that she would savor them, enjoying them one at a time. Kathrynne had been a gifted writer. Arin studied each word, her mother's personality and flair for the dramatic came through loud and clear.

She read the precious letter several times before gently folding it and returning it to the envelope. Something fell out and fluttered to the floor. Arin picked the small square up and turned it. Words could never express the joy she felt when it registered in her heart that this was a family portrait. Her family's portrait. Most people take such things for granted, but Arin had never seen a picture of her parents together, and did not even have one picture of herself as a baby. This small photograph meant the world to her.

Her father had been a handsome man. His eyes were intelligent and bright. His hair was dark and thin, his hairline slightly receding, which only made him look more fatherly to Arin. She studied the way he held his baby daughter, maybe six months old at the time, and came to the conclusion that he must have loved her very much. Her mother looked strong and beautiful, nothing like the shell of a woman she had been at the end of her life. The three of them appeared to be so happy, oblivious of the disaster to come.

For the first time, Arin felt real pity for her mother. The smiling woman in the picture had no clue that her husband would soon be taken from her, that she would be consumed by her addiction. Searching her heart, Arin found not a single bit of lingering anger or resentment toward her mother or father. As she gazed at the image taken so long ago, she realized that for the first time she felt genuine love for them, knowing deep in her heart that in their flawed way, they had loved her.

Placing the picture on a shelf next to her favorite one of Troy, Arin stood back and smiled for a moment, a prayer of thanksgiving on her lips. It was as if a chapter of her life was drawing to a close. She felt a new freedom within her soul. As she let go of the past, she felt a huge chunk of her heart released from the burden of anger and resentment. Feeling light and a bit giddy, she snuck into the playroom and pounced on unsuspecting Troy, who squealed in delight.

The day of Troy's fifth birthday party could not have been more beautiful. The early June sun was hot, but not unbearably so. Troy had requested a campout for his birthday and Jake agreed enthusiastically. He dug around in the basement for hours, dusting off the camping gear he had not used since Troy was born. Their backyard was peppered with tents in every shape and size. The camouflage pup tent Troy and Bryan would share had the primo level spot under an ancient cigar tree. Balloons announced to all that the birthday boy would be sleeping there.

Although Arin had begged everyone on the extensive guest list to bring a covered dish instead of a gift, the mountain of brightly wrapped boxes on the table grew with each new arrival.

"Just a little something," Emily said, winking at Troy. Feigning anger, Arin snatched the gift and rolled her eyes, adding it to the stack of presents she had playfully dubbed "Mount Troy."

"Bryan's here!" Troy announced, and took off to greet his new best friend.

"Those two really get along well, huh?" Emily remarked, watching as Troy helped Bryan with his overnight bag and toys. "Looks like he is getting his hair back. I pray for that kid every day."

"Me too," Arin said.

Dawn grabbed a pan from her passenger seat and headed their way, her smile radiant.

"What are you so happy about? I thought you hated camping." Arin teased.

"We're finished with our last round of chemo and Bryan is feeling great. And by osmosis, I feel great, too."

"You look great," Emily said, meaning it. She was not prone to empty flattery.

Dawn pulled a large box wrapped in dinosaur paper from her bag. Arin shot her a withering glance. "It is from Bryan. What do you want me to do? Tell him he can't get his best friend a birthday present?

What kind of mother do you think I am?" Triumphantly, Dawn balanced her present on top of "Mt. Troy."

The partygoers sat in a semi circle facing the action, catching up on what was going on in each other's lives. Troy and Bryan were preparing menacingly stretched water grenades and placing them gently into buckets, secretively discussing their attack plans. Taylor and Rae sat on the picnic table and chatted. Rae held the beautiful three-month-old Lilly in her lap, easily signing with her free hand. Jake and Ben walked circles around Dave's new Harley, nodding appreciation and approval.

"Nice bike," Emily said.

Dawn and Arin clucked, "I'm sure he wouldn't mind giving you a ride."

Arin nodded in agreement and whistled. Emily punched her in the arm and ordered her to shut up. It was a well-known fact in their growing circle of friends that Dave had a thing for Emily. He was even willing to forgive the fact that she was a Christian, although Emily was not willing to overlook the fact that he was not. She had been down that road once, and once was more than enough.

"He has potential," Emily said, watching him closely from behind her dark shades. She had to admit that he was easy on the eyes.

"It certainly would be easier if both parties had the same spiritual beliefs," Arin said, her voice low and distant.

"He still isn't open to the gospel at all?" Emily asked.

"Nope, not even a little. At dinner when Troy and I pray, you would think we were circus freaks by the looks he gives us."

"Geoffrey would leave the room if I even bowed my head. A few choice words were usually exchanged," Emily sighed. She knew what her friend was going through and made a mental note to be more persistent in praying for Jake.

Dawn stood up to refill her drink, which was only one-quarter empty. Although she had been attending Downsville Christian Fellowship for several months now and was quite active with the singles group, Arin sensed that she was there more for the social aspect than the spiritual one. She seemed uncomfortable with the spiritual aspects and usually would quickly change the subject. They were just thrilled to have her there, for whatever reason.

"She'll come around, as well," Emily said, nodding in Dawn's direction. "I think she is in a real questioning phase right now. She has been through so much in the past two years."

Arin nodded. Dawn's story was heartbreaking. A month after Bryan's cancer was diagnosed, her creep of an ex-husband took off with his mail lady, leaving Dawn to clean up the mess. Adding insult to injury, the new couple was expecting a baby any day now. And even though they were less than thirty minutes away, his father rarely made an effort to see Bryan. It didn't help Dawn's attitude that the ex and his new wife were very active in their church.

Dawn had survived the last two years on shear adrenaline, doing an awesome job of nurturing Bryan through incredibly rough times. Now that he was medically out of the woods, her hurt and anger were just beginning to surface. Trust was not something she was ready to dole out right now—to God or to men. Arin, Taylor, Emily, and Rae had decided several months ago that they were going to pray daily for Dawn and Bryan. They also made it a point to include her in things and call her regularly. She seemed to be flourishing, and even blooming, under their shower of love and friendship.

***

"She's a beauty," Ben said, fighting against the spirit of envy as he circled the shining motorcycle for the hundredth time.

"Yes, she sure is." Dave agreed, although his attention was fixed on Emily Raines, who sat next to Arin, laughing and talking as women do. Glancing over his shoulder to make sure no one else was in earshot, he added, "Why is it such a big deal to you Christians that you only date other Christians? That's kind of snobby, don't you think?"

Ben took a moment to reply. He had been praying for an opening with this rough character ever since they'd first met, and this was the first time he had spoken about anything other than motorcycles. Ben didn't want to blow it. "The Bible warns against being married to someone who does not share your spiritual beliefs, or being 'unequally yoked'."

The look on Dave's face was all Ben needed to know that he was not speaking his language. He decided to regroup.

"It is just difficult to have a relationship with someone when they do not share the same core beliefs."

Dave shook his head, understanding his point minus the churchy words. As much as he found Emily attractive, the cold religiosity with which he was raised ensured that he would keep God at arm's length.

Despite being hit with a few renegade water grenades, the day had been just about perfect. Arin tucked Troy and Bryan into their tent, assuring them that there would be no shame in changing their minds and opting to sleep in nice warm beds. They assured her that never in a hundred-million-billion years would they think of leaving their tent for the boring indoors. Smiling, Arin made her way to her comfy bedroom. She had a feeling that in a few hours they would wander in.

***

The nondescript Honda slowed to a near stop at the Welsh house, and the heavily tinted driver's side window electronically lowered. An exotic-looking woman with dark eyes examined the old farmhouse, and the cars and tents parked in the grass. She smiled wistfully. The Welsh's must be having a party. Good for them. She was glad that they enjoyed excitement, because she planned on making their lives real exciting in the very near future. She passed the house and sped off, glancing at the farmhouse obsessively in her rear view.

Jacob sat next to her in his true and vile-beyond-description form. Since the woman lacked the capacity to see him, he had not bothered to take on any special form that would make him more palatable to her. However, that in no way implied that he was not in control. He stretched his scaly face across his pointed yellow teeth in an evil smile. He had such plans. He could hardly wait.

Need help? Reach out.

Abortion Recovery InterNational (ARIN)
www.abortionrecovery.org
1-866-4-MY-RECOVERY (1-866-469-7326)
info@abortionrecovery.org

In Our Midst Ministries
A Safe Place Abortion Recovery Center
http://www.InOurMidst.com
http://www.ASafePlaceARC.com
1-970-663-9596
staff@inourmidst.com

SafeHaven Ministries, Inc
www.postabortionpain.com
1-217-370-6562

SaveOne
info@saveone.org
PO Box 95043
N Little Rock, AR 72190
501-681-8979

Silent No More Awareness Campaign
www.SilentNoMoreAwareness.org
mail@SilentNoMoreAwareness.org
1-800-707-6635

DEMCO

LaVergne, TN USA
19 January 2011
213150LV00006B/97/P